"The author deftly simulates a complicated woman's diary, creating a document that feels entirely authentic. . . . The author includes interesting political and historical details in the entries, shedding light on a woman with a front seat to American history." —*Kirkus Reviews*

"This imagined diary of Mary Pinchot Meyer, socialite and lover of JFK, simmers with intrigue and sensuality, painting in vivid colors both the magnificence and dark underbelly of Camelot." —*Newsweek*

"Mary Pinchot Meyer, JFK's lover, kept a secret diary that vanished after she was murdered in Georgetown in 1964. In this intriguing novel, Paul Wolfe creatively conjures up the life story she might have written."
—Meryl Gordon, bestselling author of *Bunny Mellon, The Life of an American Style Legend,* and *Mrs. Astor Regrets*

The Lost Diary of M

The Lost Diary of M

A NOVEL

Paul Wolfe

HARPER

NEW YORK · LONDON · TORONTO · SYDNEY

HARPER

For Jordan and Cameron.
And for Mary.
So outspoken in life. So unspoken in death.

The Lost Diary of M

If you are reading this, I am dead.

James Jesus will have seen to it. He will have planned it meticulously, smoking and plotting in the Office of Lies. James Jesus Angleton. Cold man and cold warrior. CIA chief of counterintelligence. Godfather to my sons, as ironic fate would have it. He will have seen to my death, with his dusty drapes drawn against the distant memory of sun, and the death-encrusted orchids growing in his cold basement.

He will have silenced a woman who wouldn't be silenced.

So now this diary will speak for me, a transaction of secrets amassed. Secrets are such a burden, sentencing you to carry undigested truths. They don't go away. They don't return to nothing as thoughts do, simply disappearing and letting you move on into the future.

To Anne Truitt, my dear friend, I hope it's you who find this book, hidden in my painting studio, locked in the mahogany box Kenneth Noland gave me. A woman's voice stops, but a diary is articulate forever. And they would so love to find it.

You will find the facts, Anne, in defiance of Cord Meyer and James Jesus Angleton and the entire claptrap and apparatus of the CIA, about what I did in the White House to push the cause of peace.

And how I became witness to the secret history of the assassination.

What an incalculably strange journey it's been from Grey Towers. From my girlhood castle, from my black Arabian stallion, from my golden sisters Tony and Rosamond, we naked girls in the sun of Pennsylvania, with the candles and waterfalls and French lessons. To these stoned and cobblestoned nights in Georgetown. Perhaps I'm with Jack now, if I am no longer here, Anne. Perhaps we are making love again amid the draperies of American history. Perhaps he need no longer promise he will divorce Jackie after his second term and marry me. Perhaps we have melted into infinity where energy just returns to energy. I remember that day at Joe Alsop's, watching his smile dissolve, that indestructible Irish smile as famous on the face of this earth as the face of Mickey Mouse.

We're together in death just as we were in the White

House—what irony! Dispatched to heaven by Central Intelligence. We were once two royal lovers in the Lincoln Bedroom. Today, we are two of the unsolved murdered by the secret forces that run the nation.

How will James Jesus Angleton arrange my death?

A standard-issue hit, no doubt. Company routine. Is there an order pad on his desk for these things, these rub-outs, with carbon copies, *Retain this copy for your records*? Or maybe it's not written down at all, these things, the way mobsters don't write things down, their deadly decisions carried out in an oral tradition dating back to preliterate Sicily. Except James Jesus and every crew-cut killer in his employ went to Yale.

In plain fact, it will be boring, my hit. My . . . assassination. It is strangely freeing to talk about a time when you as you will no longer exist. There will be no one living who will be me. The hit will be boringly predictable, a return to routine, fresh off their success in Dallas. Assassins will be assembled at the usual day rate. My behavior will be tracked to the smallest detail. When does she buy Tampax on Wisconsin Avenue? When does she slurp strawberry shakes at Packer's on M Street? When does she walk the towpath by the Potomac and gaze out at the gray waters of the Chesapeake and Ohio Canal? It's that towpath. I walk it every day at noon. It will not be hard for those big strong men to find me. It will have to be a public place, as delineated in the

guidelines of Central Intelligence. Every recruit receives
a handbook when they learn the assassin's craft. The
liar's protocol. The art of the snoop. The business of other
people's business. James Jesus Angleton received his
training manual in Italy, recruited to the Eternal City to
spy on Mussolini.

So it will have to be in a public place. Someplace not
overly trafficked, because a hit site can't be crawling with
witnesses, but public enough for some random criminal
act to befall me. Because random criminal acts tend to
befall luscious blondes who live a little too freely, don't
they? And of course a stooge will be set up to take the
fall. There is always a stooge, an Oswald, each time there
is a James Jesus Angleton. On the other hand, maybe I
will conveniently commit suicide. I once heard James
Jesus himself say "Anyone can commit a murder, but it
takes a real pro to commit a suicide."

And so my jottings. A secret record, and a record of
secrets, written on the walls of history with invisible
ink. Who will stumble on these words in the years to
come and just keep walking? I remember moving into
the old white clapboard house in Virginia, when I began
steaming off the wallpaper, and there were names, names
of soldiers, scrawled upon the walls, revealed like cave
paintings by the simple act of peeling off wallpaper.
The house was a hospital in the Civil War, and wounded
soldiers, bleeding, dying, had written their names with

lead bullets on my walls of history. The world will little note nor long remember. Anybody. But the soldiers' unremembered names scrawled on my wall flash in my memory. Ezekiel Cook. George Wesley Clayton. Aurelius F. Cone. Braxton Bragg.

And here I scrawl, not with lead bullets but with blood, upon the walls of the twentieth century, the unremembered Book of Mary.

·

1964

JANUARY 2

I write on the creamy paper of a French journal.
Papier de luxe. Jack gave it to me, and I assume Jackie
gave it to him. So I am, in a sense, writing Jackie's diary
for her, spun from the scrawl of my own life. So whose
story is this? Amos Pinchot's headstrong daughter,
sunbathing in the stone beauty of Grey Towers? Quentin
and Mark's sexy mama? Kenneth Noland's color field
protégé? The love of President John F. Kennedy's
life?

I am my voice, let us say.

I am not the accident that time and place gave
birth to.

So as Jack said, let the word go forth from this
time and place. Let it shake the ivy-covered lies of
Georgetown. Let it smash the halls of Congress and
shatter the glass walls of Central Intelligence.

This is more dynamite than diary.

JANUARY 4

Shadows have begun to follow me, Anne. I need you
to know that. Now that charming brother-in-law Ben
Bradlee has sent Jim across the world to run *Newsweek*,
and you and your husband walk among cherry blossoms
in Tokyo. Just as the forces close in. I can feel them. My
energy body senses them. I'm not insane. There are *beep
beep beep*s on my phone. They sound like warnings from
alien intelligence. I come home and things have been
rearranged. My things. They occupy places different
from the places I gave them. They have not been
replaced. They have been re-placed. I'm not crazy. And
threats have started. They come through the wives of
Company men, the cold men with their cigarettes and
highballs and affairs, with their red faces and little
coughs, they are warning me through the mouths of
their wives. I talk about Jack too much. I know too
much about what he did in the White House. They
know we worked for peace as they readied the world for
war. While they assembled megatons and contemplated
nuclear death in the millions, I pushed Jack toward
peace. It threatened their power forever. And I know
what they did to stop him.

JANUARY 8

It is a dance at the beginning of time. It unspools here in
my memory, here in my little house in Georgetown. It is
the Choate Winter Festivity Dance of 1936. Bill Attwood
was my date but Jack was there. I have no idea why

Jack was there. He had already graduated, but he came back to Choate that night, came back without a date, for reasons undisclosed. I imagine it was the only time in Jack's life he went somewhere alone, no brother, no crony, no entourage, no flunky, no woman accompanying him. Why he returned to Choate that night, why I met him, who arranges this infinity of details that determines who you will meet and who will change your life forever, remains the untold story behind every story.

I was sixteen. And Jack came at me with vehemence, cutting in as I danced with Bill Attwood, tried to dance with Bill Attwood, voracious. I remember his fingers sweating on the bare flesh of my shoulders when we finally danced. And all those teeth, grinning. He said—I think this is what he said—"At last I know what love is."

You are reprehensible, I told him. I am with Bill Attwood. Surely there is another fine girl in this vast party. Surely amid all these beauties in chiffon dresses and swept-up hair, their eyelids shining with Vaseline. Surely in this enormous hall there is the perfect girl for you. But it's not me. And that just emboldened him; defeat held no sway with Jack Kennedy, though he was skinny and just nineteen. He grinned big teeth and forced his presence into my eyes. "Mary, Mary, quite contrary," he said. Silly Boston accent all over his words.

I thought him shamefully superficial that first night. But who knew back in 1936 that soon we would all be tested, and that a great war would engulf the world and devour our lives? For the moment, at the Winter

Festivity Dance, I concluded that girls were simply
sport for Jack Kennedy, and touching me just another
form of touch football. How much later would I learn of
the innumerable agonies that infiltrated his body, the
sickness in his cells and the wounds of war, the pain of
unsustainable demands that Daddy Kennedy left on the
souls of his sons? And I would grow intimate with this
man for whom intimacy was impossible; that was
the paradox of loving Jack Kennedy. I think he knew
he would be president one day. I don't think he knew he
would die young. And take such terrible secrets with him.

1961

MAY 1

It is a burnt ocher swatch of parchment. My name is etched in florid calligraphy. I have been invited to the White House for Jack's birthday, here in the early days of his presidency, this spring that floods our hearts with the promise of a young land. Who made the decision to invite me to the White House, Jack or Jackie? I shouldn't think it was Jackie, as Jack has been seeking entree into my pants since the days of Choate. He has carried on his campaign of conquest like an extended political campaign, pursued doggedly and alone, without the aid of Bobby at his side. The campaign has traveled from the gravel paths of Vassar, where I walked in bobby sox and saddle shoes, to the cobblestoned streets of colonial Georgetown, with the red doors and shutters, and I have traversed a campaign of refusal with a tenacity matching his own. A woman can be obstinate, until she isn't.

When we were neighbors on N Street, back when Jack and Jackie lived in the town house next to Cord and me, Jack stood on the sidewalk one night throwing pebbles up at my window. I pulled aside the curtains and there he was, throwing tiny pebbles at my glass, beckoning frantically for me to come down and join him. Cord was in the next room, Jackie was God knows where, and a US senator was throwing pebbles, a knight gone berserk at a fairy-tale window. I shook my head at the ludicrous irresponsibility, at the fever dream of need raging inside him, leaving him oblivious to stature and position. He looked up and raised his hands in prayer, as if to say should I choose to stay in my bedroom and remain hidden behind bricks and vines, should I refuse him, he would have no choice but to promptly die.

What chemical cocktail turns men into clowns of biology? What is it, testosterone crashing through the neurotransmitters, that imprints the image of a woman so vividly on men's souls? "A rag, a bone, a hank of hair and the fool called her his lady fair." It was a poem I read at Vassar. And there was the fool down on M Street, throwing pebbles. And here was I, who? No model for Max Factor Iridescent Magic. Hardly even rigorous in matters of shaving beneath my arms. Spidery lines have crept into the skin beside my eyes. The fingers that might glide across his body are chubby, not slim and long as my sister Tony's. And the fool calls me his lady fair! And what exactly was the goal of pebbles on the windowpane? Sliding into the alleyway between our houses like fourteen-year-olds, so he could push down my panties and insert a senatorial finger inside me?

No, I shouldn't think it's Jackie's idea to invite me to the White House. On the other hand, that stiff parchment and lavish calligraphy, they are Jackie's touch. My Vassar sister, bringing breeding and style to Mamie Eisenhower's mousy White House. Pablo Casals will be playing cello.

MAY 5

I first took LSD in 1958 when I was out west finalizing my divorce from Cord. One break to freedom engenders the next. In a medical room in Palo Altó, in the company of a poet named Allen Ginsberg, I swallowed 300 micrograms of lysergic acid diethylamide.

The tablets were engraved with the word SANDOZ, an ominous name seemingly descended from outer space. California was already redolent of a separate planet, a place that was no place exactly, where America stopped abruptly prior to a leap into the Pacific Ocean. All that strange, cactusy sunshine.

Allen Ginsberg was chanting on the floor when I arrived, balding and bearded with stringy hair that hung down like spaghetti around his glasses. Me, an ex-wife of the CIA, inaugurated into her new life of freedom by the trance-inducing syllables of some Indian language. I sported a short blond bob, khaki capri pants, and little white tennis sneakers, as exotic a creature to Allen no doubt as he was to me. I apologized for unfamiliarity with his poetry. He took my hands in his, so warmly, and in a resonant monotone said: "Congratulations on the courage to push the world's tawdry boundaries and partake in William Blake's angelic consciousness." I had no idea what that meant. I imagined it was how a rabbi might speak, though I had never heard one.

Then we swallowed our Sandoz tablets, lying on opposite sides of the medical room, giddy with the promise of LSD igniting our nervous systems. The psychologist played music: operatic, German, bombastic. Allen identified it as *Tristan und Isolde* and waved his hands slowly in a mock conducting of the orchestra as the acid circulated in our brains, as I began to float— that's not precisely how I felt, but it would be impossible to describe it more accurately. I was light-headed in the sense that my cells began to illuminate with light. I let the music enter me and wondered how a man could construct something so lovely, and then a moment came when it wasn't music anymore, it was something else, more a visual pattern etched on the air, or onto the air of my mind, I wasn't sure where it was taking place.

The potted fern on the ceiling had been a lonely splash of botany in a dead room, but the leaves became intensely vivid, luminous, the leaves pulsed and breathed and I realized they had always pulsed and breathed, it was only I who hadn't noticed. "This is how Van Gogh saw flowers," I shouted, though I couldn't quite remember who Van Gogh was. Allen Ginsberg repeated the name Van Gogh with a Dutch accent; it sounded like a clearing of phlegm from the throat, and I repeated the American pronunciation back at him, which sounded like "van Go!" and he repeated the Dutch phlegm-clearing back again and I began to laugh uncontrollably. Laughter overcame me. I wasn't really laughing so much as I became laughter. I would have been locked up had I been anywhere else, and I realized that being out of your mind simply meant not being in your mind. Allen smiled radiantly, and I concluded he was on intimate terms with this altered reality, or real reality, and said to him: "Please don't go anywhere."

These are all the words of memory, woefully inadequate to surround and convey the places where words cannot go. As best as I recollect it, it was the sensation of tumbling, of spinning toward some central point of light, terrifying as that might sound, yet I wasn't terrified. I was spinning toward light as if everything in the world was made of this light and everything else suddenly felt so silly. The idea of being married to Cord or not being married to Cord seemed absurdly trivial. A joke.

Will I remember this when the trip is over? I wondered, and suddenly I was wondering who "I" was, really, and then I wondered if I would forget and simply return back to the illusion you inherit by virtue of being human. Maybe that is what past lives are about. That you don't remember the life you lived when it is over and you simply return back to the illusion. Like a tumultuous dream that stays with you when you wake, yet you can't even remotely begin to describe it.

Lying on that bed in Palo Alto, with Allen Ginsberg stretched out across the room, making the motions of chanting though at that point no sound was actually emerging, I realized there was nowhere to go. There was nothing to do. Everything was fresh and new, and I wished my ghost sister Rosamond could have been there to share it with me, my sister who left this earth so early, yet marked her days with such beauty.

MAY 12

The White House banquet looms. As the Divorcée of Georgetown, I will be plus one. Minus one in marriage means plus one at parties. The card says it: I will be "plus one" with William Walton, my official escort, my presidentially approved escort, and Jack and Jackie are terribly fond of him. They have even mounted one of his romantic paintings on their wall. William is a reassuring presence to wayward girls waylaid to official events. When do I smile? Who lights my cigarette? When do I walk over to the royal couple, plant a kiss on Jackie's cheek, and wish the president a happy birthday? When do I hobnob with the overfed and abundantly jeweled beneath history's chandeliers, and how much do I rein in my big mouth, my big Pinchot mouth? Mine is a family of troublemakers stretching back into the last century.

It is fortunate that Kenny O'Donnell has placed me on the arm of William Walton. Who is more comforting to a woman than a man who has no interest in conquering them?

MAY 18

I am a debutante. I was a debutante. I came out in 1938,
a fairy queen of the WASP ascendancy. That's what
my Washington columnist friend Joe Alsop calls it: the
WASP ascendancy. I think it more a WASP descendancy,
the whole alcohol-swilling, guilt-ridden Anglo-Saxon
tribe who run this town and this cold war. Once I was a
fairy queen. Now I am a mother, a pacifist and a painter,
an explorer on the frontiers of consciousness, and a
divorced homebody with no husband and a yen for men.
I debuted, and now my debut is behind me. I retain little
enthusiasm for froufrou and no penchant for dress-up.

So I have nothing to wear to the White House.

In this matter I veer sharply from my Vassar sister,
so penetratingly gorgeous on the arm of the president.
For her, the sheer act of being a woman is an art form,
sheathed in fascinating fabrics, all memory of blood and
fluids forgotten, while I consider a minute devoted to
fashion a moment of my life never again to be recovered.
Long ago I decided to apply art to the canvas rather than
to my closet, and I live with the consequences.

I have nothing to wear to the White House!

I own exactly six pairs of capri pedal pushers, four
pairs of Bermuda shorts, eleven pairs of trousers (tweed,
cotton, khaki), a dozen white tops, nine sweaters, two
small black dresses—nothing worthy of a presidential
ball. Luckily my college roommate, Cicely d'Autremont
Angleton (the woman who vowed her life to James
Jesus Angleton!), and I both classify as size 4. I will ask

to borrow her shining gold gown covered by a copper-embroidered tunic, and I will encounter Jack for the first time as president of the United States. I will remember to treat him as a historic personage rather than the skinny lothario from Choate. I will not embarrass him, I will not criticize him, I might even let him cop a feel when we are both alone off near the restrooms. In deference to history. Or our history.

MAY 23

I am planting beautiful blue salvias in my yard. I am painting in the garage behind sister Tony and Ben Bradlee's house. I am depleting the supplies of bourbon at the Alsops', the Grahams', the Wisners', and the Coopers' on a regular basis. It is a spring of renewal.

I remember I was also planting blue salvias the day an envelope arrived. It was two weeks past my odyssey in California. It was three weeks past my divorce. It was thirty-eight years past my incarnation into the life of Mary, released finally from domination and degradation at the hands of a CIA husband. Womanhood untrammeled, planting flowers.

The envelope was marked in a strange handwriting of blocky print. It was from Allen Ginsberg. He had written a poem about LSD, about the shattering of ourselves we had undergone together. Two people who really had no business being together in the same room at the same time, who had arrived in a medical room in California from opposite ends of the universe and then returned back to their lives, reconfigured.

At the top of the page he had written: "To the Super Shiksa of Lysergica, from Allen Ginsberg." The poem begins:

> *I am on the last millionth infinite tentacle of*
> *the spiderweb, a worrier*
> *lost, separated, a worm, a thought, a self . . .*
> *I allen Ginsberg a separate consciousness*
> *I who want to be God . . .*

MAY 30

The banquet was a triumph. Jack successfully turned forty-four, and those who live for the glamour of power and the power of glamour celebrated the historic event in tumultuous style. Jack's brother Teddy emerged from the Rose Garden at one point, his hair a mess, his pants torn completely up the back. He had no idea of the cause. Jack's friend Red McIntyre fell backward into the birthday cake while demonstrating the Twist for Jackie. Lorraine Cooper announced that her senator husband's sense of humor was simply too dry and poured a bottle of Dom Perignon over his head. Jack chased my sister Tony into the ladies' room—this according to Constantina de la Salle, who was in the stall at the time—and was rudely rebuffed, which I find totally amusing. The president of the United States seems to have a penchant for the women of my family. And we seem to possess an equal and opposite streak of resistance.

We all sang "Happy Birthday," that corniest song ever conceived by man, and then "Hail, Hail, the Gang's All Here." Only the Irish could conceive a happy song so devastatingly morose. Then Jack's eyes locked with mine. I moved instinctively to turn away, then looked back, and he was grinning, grinning as he had at Choate when I was sixteen and he said that at last he knew what love was. He seemed to have forgotten about my sister Tony, or simply decided he had chosen the wrong sister back in the ladies' room, because we sat looking at each other, smiling, as Jackie stared in the other direction, her own aristocratic smile frozen as if for history. I suddenly felt Jack was my son, I felt he was my husband, I felt he was my friend. The heat of bourbon flamed in my head and places far lower, and I longed to grip him and fall beneath him. I took this chaos of thoughts with me as I rode home in the limo with Ben and Tony. "Now that's a birthday!" said Ben, looking away oddly through the car window, his bow tie all askew over the collar of his tuxedo shirt and one stud missing. Tony was silent.

JUNE 2

Kenny O'Donnell called from the White House to say Jack wanted to speak to me. I held the phone, and there was the president of the United States, speaking through my pink Princess phone, saying I looked beautiful in gold. I said it was just a costume from Cicely Angleton.

Why rave about me when Jackie was resplendent in
a ruby-red velvet-and-silk gown by Cassini and white
gloves extending up her arms? He told me we shouldn't
talk about husbands and wives with each other, or he
would ask me how an SOB like Cord Meyer could have
landed someone like me. He said he wanted to see me. He
wanted to meet me privately.

I am familiar with the urgency of men calling you,
needing you, craving you, but hitherto I have never been
ordered to sex by the commander in chief of the Western
world. A newsreel of American history flashed through
my brain. I pictured children in years to come reading
about me in textbooks—Mary fucking the president,
right alongside the Louisiana Purchase and the Spanish-
American War.

My heart pounded. I told Jack I needed to think about
it; he said some things don't require thought. I had to
admit that was true, I was a free woman, and my long
campaign of resistance ended there and then on the
Princess phone. Life happens like that.

JUNE 4
The call from Jack has settled into my being, as all
things that change the nature of your cells do, and I am
reminded of the day I told Cord to leave. The day I said
the marriage was over. Every loss pulls the great chain
of loss along with it, and the specter of my disappearance
from his life invoked, first, the loss of his eye in war, and
then the death of his twin brother. And then perhaps

back to the primal loss of all, being born into this world of oxygen in the first place. He erupted in tears, and all I could think was: Why do we only miss what we can't have when we can't have it, but do nothing to keep it when we can?

"Why are you crying?" I asked him. "Why are you surprised I want you to leave? You're never here anyway. You never see the boys—they are your sons on official documents only, their entire upbringing has been my job. And you never talk to me anymore, you don't tell me what you do because you can't tell me what you do, but not being allowed to hear something doesn't make it any easier not to hear it."

The torrents came, the dams had burst. "You're always angry," I continued. "You're always angry. And if I worked in the house of lies every single day with James Jesus Angleton instead of writing the prose your gifts once held out as your destiny, I would be angry too."

I paused, and Cord raised his hand as if to slap me, as if to slap down the eruption of bitter truths my words had summoned forth, but he stopped himself. He checked himself. Whatever was left of the man he might once have been stopped him. He finally said: "I can't protect you if you're not my wife." It was an ominous retort.

"What the fuck does that mean?" I screamed back at him. "Are you threatening me?"

"No, I'm not threatening you," he said. "I'm protecting you."

"I don't need your protection!"

"Yes, you do."

"Who's following me?" I screamed. He stared at me. "I see them at the drugstore. They're looking over their newspapers at me, they're peeking awkwardly through their peripheral vision at me when I drink a milkshake. I see shadows when I walk down the street, there are figures on the towpath where I walk every day, even when there should be no one at the canal but me. Who's following me?" I shook him. "You know, don't you?"

"I don't know."

"I don't believe you. Do you actually have goons from Central Intelligence following me?"

I shook him, and he lifted my hands from his body and said, "Married to me, you have the full faith and power of the United States government protecting you. Without me, you're just a cunt with loose lips and even looser habits."

I slapped him. I knew he was speaking of my refusal to be a Company wife, beautiful and dutiful. I knew he was speaking of the Spaniard, the owner of the little hotel on Mallorca that Bebe Highsmith and I escaped to last summer. But I slapped him anyway, blinded by that WASP venom, the bile of his ancestors spewing out onto a woman he once loved. He grabbed my arms. I shouted at him to let go, but he held them, and I flashed upon Grey Towers when I was five years old, when my cousin Remus would pin me to the floor. I'd scream for him to let me free, but he would just lie on me, holding me down and smiling that crazy smile, and I could smell his stinky breath and thought maybe he would hold me down

forever and I would never be a free-moving person again.
Now I knew I could not be married to Cord a moment
longer.

"I don't care about your secrets," I said. "The secrets
are killing you, they're devouring your soul, they're
eating the vital organs of your body. You were always a
human being, a humanist being. We spent our fucking
honeymoon at the United Nations charter conference. It
was you who wanted to build a just world, and now you're
just half human. You're just an employee of secrets, and
secrets are cancer. Don't you know that?"

"Mary."

"Don't say my name!" I yelled. "Don't say my name! I
can't stand it when you say my name."

"Mary, secrets are what protect us. When Quentin
and Mark are playing in the field and don't have a care
in the world and the sun shines on them, it's because of
secrets. It's because of James's secrets and mine, and you
don't want to know anything about them. But secrets are
all that stand between America and a force worse than
anything you can imagine."

"Yes, the Communists have made you angry. The
Communists have made you ignore your children. The
Communists have made you a rotten husband who treats
his wife like shit when we once stood together at the
founding of the United Nations."

He went quiet and walked off to his study. There he sat
for an hour. With what spirits he communed during that
hour, and who exactly he spoke to in his mind—because

whenever we are quiet, we are speaking to somebody in our mind—I have no idea. All I know is that when he came out again, he said he didn't want to leave, and I told him it was already decided and he would be leaving.

JUNE 8
It is a week since we spoke. Jack has entered my life without my even entering his bedroom. Now we may not be able to get together till July. How can twenty years pass by with barely a flicker of a thought of him, and yet three weeks now seem like eternity?

JUNE 9
I had lunch at Rive Gauche with Lorraine Cooper and Evangeline Bruce. I feel style- and marriage-challenged around these two queens of Georgetown, both famously married to important men, an ambassador and a senator, both annually victorious on everyone's best-dressed list. While I'm just Mary.

Evangeline commanded the restaurant's attention with her crown of brunette hair and multipatterned stockings that accentuated legs that needed no accentuation. The limbs upon which Evangeline Bruce stands begin at ground level and seem to proceed somewhere up into the stratosphere. We were just beginning our gin and tonics when Lorraine Cooper burst into the restaurant— Lorraine doesn't enter, she bursts in. She had a swirly blue-and-pink parasol resting on her shoulder.

"It's not raining," I said.

"What does rain have to do with parasols?" She closed the parasol adeptly with gloved hands.

Vangie Bruce smiled at Lorraine as if she were a prized work of sculpture. What did I think she'd seen, she asked me, when she arrived at the Harrimans' pool on Sunday?

"What did you see?" I felt robotic for answering this artificially induced question, but I also felt the warmth of belonging, as if I finally belonged to the tribe of women who eat lunch and chatter, women who stride beside commanding men on the world stage and then compare notes over Parliaments and highballs.

"I saw Lorraine here standing on a rubber raft in the middle of Pamela Harriman's pool, holding a parasol in one hand and a cigarette and cocktail in the other."

"It was a pool party!" yelled Lorraine, removing her pink hat with its overlarge pink bow atop and veil and depositing it carefully into the hands of the eager young waiter who had sprinted over to retrieve it. "What's a pool party without a parasol?"

JUNE 11

Jack is back from a summit with Khrushchev, and according to news reports, it did not go well. Khrushchev is something of a bully, but soon Jack and I will have our own summit. I will be a far more sympathetic comrade.

JUNE 12

Georgetown spring. The covert men, the overt men, the senators, ambassadors, spies, and scribblers, with their overeducated and under-attended-to wives, the whole Georgetown "family," was gathered at the Wisners' for Polly Wisner's birthday. Polly is a devoted Central Intelligence wife and a quintessential Georgetown hostess. Here at the headquarters of the Cold War, in these early days of Jack's presidency, birthdays are a good excuse to test the limits of the human liver and to acquire political intelligence. You don't breathe air in Georgetown so much as inhale information.

I gave Polly a music box from Prague, one of the more exquisite from my collection: a chirping bird flutters up when you open the cover. She listened for a moment to the tiny tinkling melody, kissed me, and told me the box would sit beside her bed forever. Polly is not beautiful, but she is the model of refinement, refinement in a chemical sense, as if her essence has been distilled repeatedly until what remains is clean, is tremblingly delicate.

In the living room, James Jesus Angleton was situated strategically in the corner, staring through owlish glasses and a penumbra of cigarette smoke. He must smoke five packs a day. He is ghostly, angular, and otherworldly, looking like someone who has spent years searching in fetid underground caves for moles and Russian spies, emerging into the light only to attend Georgetown dinner parties.

Dean Acheson and Allen Dulles faced each other in club chairs, holding forth on the recent Bay of Pigs fiasco, the issue du jour in Washington. Acheson was crusty and irritated. "It doesn't take Price Waterhouse to discover that fifteen hundred Cubans aren't as good as twenty-five thousand Cubans," he said.

Dulles removed the pipe from his mouth, the stem glistening disgustingly in the chandelier light, and shook his head solemnly, oblivious to Lorraine Cooper and me sitting languorously just a few feet away, sipping martinis and staring straight at them like observers in a zoo.

"Doesn't he look like the British captain in those war movies?" Lorraine asked, nodding toward Acheson, and I laughed and agreed, though I have never seen any of those war movies. I was concerned with Allen Dulles. I cannot get near the director of the CIA without a shudder. It takes a day for me to recover from simply being in his atmosphere, the obscene electricity of his vibrations. Though that has never stopped numerous women in Washington from opening their mouths to his mustached, pipe-tobacco-polluted lips and their legs to the central intelligence of his cock. Poor Clover Dulles. Or maybe lucky Clover Dulles. Maybe she cherishes abandonment's freedom.

"Stylish shoes," said Lorraine, nodding toward the velvet bedroom slippers Dulles wore on a Saturday night due to gout. Were his swollen, throbbing feet retribution for a life too privileged? Or perhaps medical science will discover one day that deceit is a toxin that turns to uric acid in your veins and corrodes your circulatory system. Joe Alsop came padding by, nodding toward Dulles with a smile and then turning to Lorraine and me and whispering conspiratorially, "He cares more about learning secrets at these parties than dispensing them. Fuck him!"

I got up, and Dulles grabbed my hand. I felt a shudder go through me, I felt his eyes pierce mine and reach down into my uterus. "I know I hired your ex-hubby, Mary, Mary, but we can still be good friends, right?" His mustache was yellow and rancid. His blue eyes were composed of ice from a dead planet, frozen behind wire-rimmed spectacles. I pulled my hand from his grip and felt the brutal cold of unsafety. There will be no man to provide for my safety, I thought, I am a woman who has meticulously burned every bridge to the protective custody of a man, and now I am on my own. This is the deal I have cut with life. I pulled my hand away and walked off. I was not polite about it.

Passing Joe Alsop, who nodded, amused and impressed by my abruptness with the director of Central Intelligence, I walked into the kitchen, where Rowland Evans and Walter Lippmann were also bloviating on Cuba, as most people are these days. The bearded man in Havana, the uncouth denouncer of all we stand for, seems to have driven half the world crazy. The other half wants to fuck him. Evans insisted that Fidel had to be removed immediately: a cancer only metastasizes if left alone. Lippmann advocated a grander vision for the containment of Communism. Art Buchwald, the funny man, came up to me, smiling, sweating around the mouth, a bit soused, it seemed to me, a bit horny as well, and asked me if I'd seen the new Castro record player. I played along and said I hadn't. "It delivers High Fidelity!" he said. I laughed, giving him a sexy, girlish push on the chest with my hand.

I returned to the living room, still feeling a chill from Allen Dulles. Inexplicably, James Jesus Angleton had emerged from his fog, from his penumbra of smoke and secrets, and was singing "Happy Birthday" to our hostess. He was loud and passionate, gazing at Polly Wisner as if it were for the love of Polly and Polly alone that he had emerged from his cave. Polly smiled politely, a CIA wife ever dutifully restrained. In front of a blue-and-pink cake, he seemed an emaciated ghost. There was little left now of whoever he once was. He spends his days chasing imaginary double agents. Were they hiding now in the birthday cake as he sang? Secret agents of blue sugar reporting back to a devil's-food command post at headquarters in Moscow?

James is a frightened man, and frightened men end up scaring everybody else.

JUNE 16

Cord was a warrior of light. That's how I saw him when I was young, when we were postwar, postcatastrophe, and prerebuilding the world from the shards and pieces of what was. Cord had left Guam one eye poorer following the carnage of a Japanese explosion. They thought he was dead. That's how it seemed. They telegrammed his parents to say he wouldn't be coming home. Then they noticed he had a pulse and carried him to a coral reef and

treated him and sent out another telegram instructing
the family to ignore the first telegram. He returned
home carrying a Bronze Star in place of an eye. We
married shortly thereafter.

Surrendering half his eyesight to the phantasmagoria
of war would seem payment enough, but Cord felt a debt
to world peace he began paying off in astonishing pulses
of energy. I told him that he saw clearer and farther
with a single eye than most with two-eyed vision. He
opposed war as my own family had done for generations:
loudly, bravely, obnoxiously, naively, relentlessly. And I
loved him. We were a husband and wife, dedicated to
the eradication of the germ of death that projects itself
outward into the collective slaughter known as history.

We set out on the road my father had walked, flinty
old Amos Pinchot, who once told Teddy Roosevelt to go
fuck himself. Amos had started the Progressive Party
with the Rough Rider and written its credo: "To destroy
this invisible Government, to dissolve the unholy alliance
between corrupt business and corrupt politics, is the first
task of the statesmanship of the day." I almost memorized
that credo, reading it over and over again on a pamphlet I
kept in my room as a little girl, my way perhaps of being
close to my father. The party's list of demands glowed
in bold red type: The right of women to vote. The eight-
hour workday. Social insurance for the elderly. A national
health service. All things Daddy considered ridiculously
obvious for a civilized society. But third parties don't win
in America, and when Teddy Roosevelt opened the doors

of the Progressive Party to what Amos called the captains of industry and the profiteers of high finance, my father walked out. Abruptly. Permanently. With profanity. Have I inherited your headstrong bent, Amos?

So we were at it again, still walking toward peace, Cord replacing Daddy beside me. We founded the World Federalist Party, in the Pinchot tradition of creating political movements that fail. The premise of the World Federalist Party was simple: What species annihilates itself?

Cord was a hero before he became a cold man. Before he brought into our life, and the life of our sons, a mentor and man who lived not on the solid ground of earth but in a strange terrain of mirrors. James Jesus Angleton.

JUNE 23

He is now godfather to my boys. James Angleton. A strange godfather indeed, with a strange name, the name of our savior squatting like a Mexican farm worker between his two Anglo-Saxon names, James and Angleton. Two proper Christian names divided by what he must consider a less Christian name—ironic, of course, since it is the name of Christ himself. But James has spent a lifetime trying to erase the shame of Jesus in his name.

Who bestows the name Jesus on a CIA head of counterintelligence? A Mexican mama. She was a dark-haired girl of seventeen in a Mexican village three miles south of hell, explained James once as he, Cicely, Cord, and I strolled an art gallery in Alexandria, Virginia.

One day—James was so proud to relay this story through his Coke-bottle glasses—a force of nature rode into the Mexican town of that Mexican girl. It was his daddy, OG Angleton, a Rough Rider and a man apparently too tough to put periods between his initials. OG was a high-adventure man, storming the dusty plains of central Mexico with General Pershing in search of Pancho Villa. The Mexican bandit remained free to pillage, but OG Angleton returned home with a beautiful young Mexican bride. Upon the birth of a son, the father bestowed the names James and Angleton on his progeny while the Mexican mama slipped in Jesus. So now we have James Jesus Angleton.

Also a hunter of bandits, but Cold War bandits, bandits with briefcases and Russian accents, James is not the force of nature his papa OG was. In fact, James is unearthly, almost comically skinny. He seems to be disappearing gradually from physical manifestation, as if a belief that only the clandestine is visible has overtaken his body.

And now, because he had been named godfather to my boys, this is a man life continually thrusts at me, a force field of charged particles I can't seem to escape, a godfather I cannot trust, a gift of some sort from Cord to his sons.

JULY 2

It was date night at the White House, the first of July and the first of Jack. (My mordant wit. Cord always insisted

I lacked humor, but his charge ignored his own role
in suppressing it.) Last night was my scheduled night,
my anticipated night, the night to become a member
of Jack's bedchamber. His chamber, not his cabinet.
(Another stab at humor, I fear born of nervousness.) What
evolutionary purpose does nervousness serve, anyway?
Natural selection. Apparently, we who survived are the
anxiety-ridden ones, the ones who remain vigilant, ever
prepared for the surprise onslaught. We the nervous were
selected. Evolution is pathetically irrelevant to a tumble
in a presidential bed, but nervousness inhabited me in the
White House last night, nevertheless.

I arrived at seven sharp, a single woman in a simple
dress, armed with nothing but a white satin clutch,
navigating the paintings and bric-a-brac of history on
her way to a bedroom. Kenny O'Donnell led me upstairs
through a series of hallways to the private residence. Jack
was in a rocking chair in a large formal room outside the
bedroom, a briefing book spread out on his lap, easing
the pain in his back and puffing on a cigar. "Mary, Mary,
quite contrary." He smiled and it all came flooding back
in a romantic flurry, a dance in winter when we were
awfully young. I sat on the couch across from him. Then
I crossed my legs and lit a cigarette. "Can I offer you a
cigar?" he said, still grinning, and I said I would start
with a Marlboro and work my way up to something
bigger. How naturally the language of flirtation arises of
its own accord.

I remained nervous on the stiff, formal settee, admitted

to the historic chamber of the American people simply because I carried with me the paraphernalia of a woman. An impostor with a posterior. Stubbing out a lipstick-smeared Marlboro in a presidential-sealed ashtray, I said that things had certainly changed from that long-ago night at Choate, and he said not everything had changed. I smiled, remembering the pebbles on my windowpane, a senator's desire threatening to break my glass, and I knew my window was about to shatter. Jack came over and sat beside me on the couch. He continued puffing on his cigar—the stench of a cigar is the destiny of the nostrils of the women of my generation—and now his arm was around me. We could smell each other, we could smell the future, I knew it was real, I knew eventually I would be on my back with my legs up, and he would be in me. Back when Cord relinquished his hold on me, I had asked the universe for adventure, and now it seemed the universe had giggled, had overdelivered. Jack moved to kiss me, I closed my eyes and kissed him back. We merged tongues, he squeezed my thigh, and I said I needed to go. "Why would you need to do that?" he asked, unaccustomed to resistance but not surprised that the source was me. I had resisted for so long. I said I'd come back soon, I'd even return the next night if he liked, but this night in the White House I told him I needed to go.

"Mary, didn't you hear my slogan: Let's get this country moving again? You're not being very patriotic."

I kissed him and left. Is that the extent of a woman's power: the power to say no?

JULY 5

This random falling forward of myself. Who I wound
up being. The precise life I am living, with very little
volition on my part. A Pinchot? A Meyer? A Vassar queen?
A mom with a paintbrush? A girl named Mary who could
be said to be Jack's girl, in a very vague, roundabout sort
of way? Or, simply, I am just who everyone else isn't. I
didn't go back to the White House the next night.

JULY 10

Joe Alsop is a queer, undisclosed. One more issue unspoken
beneath the vast, lubricated discourse of Georgetown. Joe
and Susan Mary Alsop's salon is now a weekly destination
for our inebriated crowd, fitting neatly between Sunday
soirées at the Wisners', the occasional blowout bash at
Phil and Katharine Graham's (Phil contributing far more
blowing to the blowout than Katharine), and the more
refined political gatherings at Lorraine and Senator John
Sherman Cooper's manor house.

   The open secret of Joe's sexuality is buried beneath
his harsh exterior. Lorraine Cooper calls him the Grand
Inquisitor of Georgetown. Alsop attendees endure
rigorous rounds of questioning and political debate before
feasting on his legendary turtle soup and his impeccable
wine cellar. On Saturday, Joe floated through the party
in a peacock dressing gown, flaunting a cigarette holder
of pure ivory. Some elephant had to die just so Joe could
smoke cigarettes. I pointed it out. "All in a good cause,"
he replied. "All in a good cause."

The strange composition of Joseph Wright Alsop V. On the one hand he is an effete connoisseur who refuses to eat in a restaurant in Paris if the wine cellar is too close to the Métro. He believes the vibrations of the trains will disturb the sediment in the wine bottles. But at daybreak, the flamboyant sensualist turns into a harsh and belligerent political animal, the anti-Communist columnist. A ruthless promoter of the war in Vietnam. Obsessed with the news, he owns no TV. I don't either. I refuse to yield my family to the forces that prepackage and manage us electronically. But Joe's antielectronics posture is less clear to me; he is a newsman, a columnist syndicated in a hundred newspapers.

I asked Susan Mary if she missed having a TV, and she said of course, she's addicted to Westerns, but Joe is the boss. No, I said, you are the boss. She is an elegant stick of womanhood who modeled for Balenciaga. No, I'm just the little woman, she said, filling my champagne glass, then revealing her truth with a blink of long eyelashes: "There's just no future in being an ordinary person leading an ordinary life, is there, Mary?"

I have never asked her, but apparently she has no trouble with Joe's sexuality. Well, clearly she has no trouble with his sexuality. Poor Joe. The world is not currently ready for pansies, an absurd mistake. I watched as Joe held up a wine bottle, explaining its vintage to Katharine Graham, when suddenly a flash of sadness seized my memory and a deep hole opened up so raw, I excused myself from Susan Mary and went to sit alone

on the Chinese bench in the foyer. I thought of Hoyt
Pennington, my teenage friend who attended Collegiate
when I was at Brearley. He was a painter and a poet,
and could even explain Wallace Stevens to me when he
was fifteen. Hoyt and I used to go to the Art Students
League on Saturday mornings and walk home together
along the East Side, talking, talking, talking. I don't
like to think about it, but at Yale they found him in bed
with a boy one day and some fraternity men carried him
out to the entrance of the Yale campus and tied him to
the gate. Naked. Hoyt was found hanging in his dorm
room the following night. I remember something he told
me one Saturday morning as we trudged up a deserted
Park Avenue: "You know the definition of a faggot? A
homosexual gentleman who just left the room."

JULY 11

Joe Alsop conducted a vigorous interrogation of his guests
on their perspectives on Vietnam. Ho Chi Minh. Agent
Orange. President Diem. He fired questions from his
perch at the head of the table, his beloved dinner table,
and who of power hasn't sat here? Twice in the century,
because this massive slab of mahogany once belonged to
his cousin Theodore Roosevelt, and I have often wondered
if my father Amos ever sat at this table too, when he and
Roosevelt worked together on the Progressive Party.

I faced the shooting gallery of questions armed only
with a fine chardonnay. I don't respond well to rapid-fire
questioning. Perhaps it is a matter of brain chemistry.

Cord always maintained I had a slow-moving sort of mind, but his judgments take their place now in the graveyard of dead memories. Perhaps I am unwilling to think at a pace prescribed by others. My intelligence has a speed limit, and perhaps that is why I'm a painter; painting proceeds slowly, the lines of my shapes drawn so carefully.

But in defiance of the bloodshed that continues to haunt the human race, I swirled the wine and let it envelop my tongue, so buttery and fruity, and wondered how the same world could hold tastes like this and dead children in jungles. The words *Vietcong* and *US advisors* entered rapid-fire into the conversation, but I just smiled and sipped, lacking the finesse for the verbal jujitsu of politics. Debate is really just a verbal sleight of hand, each point and counterpoint a slight bend of the truth, a slight inaccuracy, a slight dishonesty, until the deflections multiply and in the end everybody finds themselves far, far removed from where the truths began. At any rate, verbal dexterity in defense of war is an immoral exercise.

"It's just like dominoes," Joe Alsop said, flapping his hand effeminately in a pantomime of falling dominoes. "When one falls, eventually they all will fall."

"How free of any taint of tentativeness are his opinions!" Phil Graham whispered of our host. I repeated my belief that the more facts you know on any given issue, the more confusing the issue becomes.

"Dien Bien Phu on you too!" said Vangie Bruce,

igniting her cigarette with a solid gold lighter. She commanded our end of the table, unintimidated, six feet of woman, crowned by a sculpture of jet-black hair and tossing off bons mots like bonbons. I sat in sharp contrast to her: husbandless, heightless, the crown on my head but a short blond bob.

But Joe fancies me, and I am a regular at his Saturday dinners, his resident bohemian. I have no penchant for politics. I am one half of no distinguished couple, except for the far less than half portion I occupy of a secret, forbidden relationship, no evidence of which I carry to dinner at Joe and Susan Mary Alsop's.

But once Joe said to me: "Mary, you just don't give a crap. I love that in a woman."

Once he said to me: "Every man here dreams of sleeping with you, and you don't even realize it, so they keep dreaming."

Once he said to me: "Mary, you speak so filthy yet enunciate so elegantly."

Once he said to me: "Mary, you're not a bore. To rid the world of bores, that is my passion. I want you to populate the next Earth."

As he lit my cigarette, I confessed I would be thrilled never again to hear the words *Mekong Delta* and *napalm*. I stopped short of the truth, that I feel the war is simply a massacre of innocents in a jungle, because Joe is too fervent a cold warrior. The Anti-Communist columnist. That is a conversation I am saving for a bed in the White House, the conversation I dream that will put an end to war. I will be a peace whisperer to the president. Until then, I remain the antiwar blonde of Georgetown, sipping bourbon and flirting with fools in the salons that are the secret engines of the Cold War.

JULY 23

The pounding of the president. These are the strange words that unspooled through my mind as Jack came into me for the first time. We had chatted away, both aware that the long-ago promise of a winter dance would soon be kept beneath presidential sheets. He had held my hand—it was a tender moment, actually, as if we were dating, or some proper matchmaking friend had simply suggested we meet and see if we hit it off.

He told me a book would soon be coming out about his election, called *The Making of the President*. I asked if the book was about me. He laughed and started removing his clothes. Once he started, he was in a terrible hurry. We made love very quickly that first time; it had taken us past the age of forty to consummate a desire lodged in our bodies as teenagers, and now it proceeded with the speed of teenagers. Barely enough time for my mind to say those peculiar words: "The pounding of the president." And then it was over.

I felt a raging force in him, as though the universe depended on his coming into me at that moment, and I was willing simply to let him spend himself. We were officially lovers. Or unofficially lovers. But I had a flash. I thought the time would come when we would be together

forever, which made no sense. No woman had ever made
Jack Kennedy say the word *forever*. Yes, he had pledged
a death-do-you-part in a church in Newport, Rhode
Island, but that was in a commitment to a masquerade
marriage to Jacqueline Bouvier, my Vassar sister. I knew
he had learned from Daddy Kennedy that marriage was
a stage set. He had learned from Daddy that women
were compensation for the pain men undergo as they
take charge of the world. So maybe he would never be
willing to dismantle the stage set, and maybe he would
never divorce Jackie. But I thought audaciously that the
relationship might change the world, might influence
world affairs, that I would become Jack's collaborator,
a cheerleader for peace in the White House. As if I was
married to the future but cheating with Jack. And if
anyone ever heard my thoughts, they'd probably put my
head in a guillotine.

AUGUST 1

I am hungry for that truth that sets us free. So it has
been called. I am hungry to return to the truth I
experienced in a medical room in Palo Alto with Allen
Ginsberg. Browsing this morning at the Savile Book
Shop, I came upon an old book called *Light in Distant
Realms* by someone named Roxanne Arcturis. She claims
to derive her secrets by channeling the Akashic records,
"the etheric archive of every thought-form and desire of
every human soul ever incarnated." It seems the thoughts
and experiences of every human being through endless

time are recorded and logged, like some CIA of infinity.
Arcturis writes that a new astrological era will soon
overtake us all. It's called the Aquarian Age.

AUGUST 3

Time has been unkind to our dreams. That is the nature
of dreams, the shelf life stamped upon each fantasy.
The United Nations Charter Conference of 1945 was
our honeymoon, my young marriage to Cord Meyer a
microcosm of the greater union we pledged ourselves to
in San Francisco. We whispered of world peace the way
other newlyweds speak of family homes by the lake and
springer spaniels running free.

Cord was chief aide to the American delegate to the
UN conference, who said Cord had the best mind of any
young man in America. Maybe that was so. I was there
as a reporter for UPI, wandering among delegates from
every corner of the world. African princes in glittering
robes. European prime ministers shell-shocked from
a great war. American Indians, descended from the
genocide that founded our country, celebrating their
survival in feathers and silver and buckskin. Russian
commissars devouring vodka and caviar and begging
me up to their hotel rooms. On a street near the San
Francisco Opera House I ran into Orson Welles—so
handsome, with a voice that seemed to emanate from
some grand place outside his body. Orson told me that
history is a record of the folly of men, and that this
experiment of the United Nations would bring that folly

to an international scale. I scribbled it down while he told me I was an angel in yellow tresses. I know my smile was vast in those days, and thoroughly innocent. He invited me for a drink and I declined, though he possessed an aura of confidence that was palpable, a confidence I can still visualize, a confidence electric in nature that pulled you to stare at him in wonder, and had I not been a newly married woman on a mission in San Francisco, I could have seen falling beneath Orson Welles and having him exhaust himself in me.

And then Jack appeared. An apparition. A spirit. An inevitability tumbling at me from the past. He wasn't a politician yet, he was a journalist, a correspondent for Hearst covering the UN conference. I hadn't seen him since Vassar, and one morning in San Francisco we all collided, all three of us, Cord, Jack, and me, a fated collision in the bedlam of the conference. "Mary, Mary, quite contrary," Jack said with his electric grin, and I watched his words penetrate Cord's spine, watched Cord freeze, Cord who was already showing signs of a depression that would grow deeper and eventually engulf him. He was already disenchanted with the conference, disgusted at the powerlessness of the UN charter to abolish war. Cord looked brutally at Jack with his single good eye and walked off abruptly, leaving me alone on the conference floor with Jack Kennedy, who, if memory serves, never stopped smiling at me.

Later that week, Jack asked Cord for an interview and was rudely rebuffed. Cord may have had the best

mind of any young man in America, but he also had a
mean streak that would grow more vicious as the years
passed. Jack never forgot the rebuff in San Francisco.
Years later, when fate had performed its legendary twist
and the young reporter for Hearst was president of the
United States, Cord went to him hat in hand seeking an
ambassadorship. Jack would not even consent to meet
with him.

Kenny O'Donnell, Jack's minister of everything, once
told me this was the difference between Bobby and Jack.
Bobby would curse you, threaten you, go for your throat;
Jack would always remain strong and silent. He'd never
yell, never threaten, but he would never forget. And one
day he would simply pull the string, and you'd be dead.

AUGUST 6

I spent some girlie time fussing over presidential
appointment number two, rubbing L'Air du Temps
into strategic places. Jack was waiting for me in the
Lincoln Bedroom and told me we had two hours. Jackie's
in Burma. He hugged me and I could hear my heart
beating, like every song about every girl who longed for
a man to take care of her no matter how strong she was.
I wondered if he smelled the perfume and considered me
some sort of floozy, as I'm usually boringly natural and
prefer painting canvases to faces. A canvas lasts forever. A
face has to be scrubbed again and repainted tomorrow.

Jack asked about my boys, and I was surprised. Usually
he's either fucking or running the world; he avoids matters

trivial, inconsequential, or overly feminine, though
he does love gossip. But sometimes he's surprisingly
sensitive, as people who live in continual pain are
sensitive. His father's ghastly voice resounds in his head,
relentlessly urging him on to a toughness that is not his
natural style. I can almost hear that father's voice in my
own ears and share Jack's pain inside my own body.

I have no idea what prompted it, but I blurted out
that we should be married. I don't know where it came
from. He both grinned and winced; he was accustomed
to hostile barbs from reporters, but not the domestic
pleading of women.

"Mary, marriage is an institution for children."

"And where did you learn about the institution, from
your dad? He wasn't a great teacher, Jack."

"Well, the ambassador was a character, I will say that.
I still remember him trying to get into bed with my
sister's friends when I was a teenager, wearing his shiny
silk robe and telling the girls to get ready for an evening
they would remember their entire lives."

Jack laughed, but I said I would try to forget he'd told
me that story.

"Everyone has a father, Mary."

"Yes, but not every father is a pedophile."

Why can't I shut up?

AUGUST 11

Everybody's spying on everybody else. Georgetown is
spook heaven. Lorraine Cooper says half the members of

Christ Church in Georgetown are members of the CIA, while the other half work for the *Washington Post.*

I can always tell CIA at the parties. They are the ones wearing three-piece suits, swilling martinis, and jabbering about third-world countries that annoy them. I can always tell Mossad because they pretend to be Israeli diplomats and are not allowed to drink, so by the end of the evening, they're the only ones still on their feet. I can always tell MI6 because they're British and try so desperately to get into me. I think my creamy skin, blond hair, and fleshy tits send Brits straight into mommy fantasies, but since I have never been particularly impressed by the accent and have my fill of secretiveness simply living in Georgetown, I have no use for British men and dispatch them with a shrug.

And if the cup of subterfuge didn't already runneth over, I hear J. Edgar Hoover is spying on the CIA. He sends his men to Georgetown parties as waiters and bartenders to listen for gossip. Evangeline Bruce turned to me at dinner last night and said in perfect French, "The best pastry chef I ever employed turned out to be an FBI agent."

AUGUST 16

Washington is a steam bath in the summer. We are a hothouse for flowers! I met Vangie at Packer's, and she told me that her hydrangeas are a color wheel of purple, pink, and powder blue. Her gladiola are exploding, yellow like the sun. Her peonies are as pink as a woman's

you-know-what. And her clematis are purple like the cape
of the count of Monte Cristo. I said: Vangie, you're a poet!
"No," she said. "I'm a florist."

SEPTEMBER 3

Every woman either wants to mother him or marry him.
That's the cliché surrounding Jack, as related to me by
Evangeline Bruce, who has no knowledge of our affair.
I gather that is the word for it. *Affair.* What a strange,
outdated word. It makes me think of Vienna. But I have
begun playing both roles in Jack's life, both the wife he
never had, but perhaps someday will, and the mother he
never had. I have turned forty. I have raised three sons,
I know their energy and their stink, and seeing Jack so
pale last night, I slipped into the mode of motherhood.
He suddenly seemed like a young prince in exile, needing
me to rescue him, take him back to his true home.

Khrushchev has issued an ultimatum on Berlin. The
buoyancy that usually raises Jack beyond the grip of
pain is gone. I can feel Berlin reverberating in his frayed
autoimmune system, in his throbbing back wrapped sadly
in a corset, in his ailing stomach and inflamed intestines.
And I decided simply to be there for him. A boy whose
mother was never there for him. He had told me this,
that when he was a young teenager, he lay months in the
infirmary at Choate, alone, racked with illnesses beyond
the reach of doctors. And Mother Rose visited him at
school exactly never.

So I will be there. And I will nurture peace in him,

slowly, slowly, peace being the closest thing we Pinchots have to a family business. We have opposed every war the world has thrown us for a century. I will plant seeds of peace as I watch him soften from the man who led a destroyer into World War II.

"Fuck Berlin," I told Jack, and he smiled. Mary's mouth again. "We can't sacrifice the future of the planet over a shitty city stuck in the ruins of the Third Reich."

This man for whom women are decor, fucking objects fashioned to fill some aching chasm within, appeared to listen. He knows I refuse to be distracted from the heart of the matter, even by matters of the heart. We must not go to war simply to control traffic to West Berlin. I said it again, point-blank.

"Berlin is a burr in my butt" was all he said.

"Then get out."

"I can't."

"Then you don't really want peace."

Pinchots are inconvenient and stubborn and I inherited this gene, but Jack apparently finds it fascinating. I once told him he was full of shit. I did. I shocked myself hearing it burst from my mouth. No woman has ever said that to him, I am quite convinced, and perhaps no man either. But it did not trigger an immediate Secret Service escort out of the White House.

1962

JANUARY 3

We are the lovers who hover ever out of reach, longed for, unattainable. We are the mysteries that never get solved. Jack and Mary. Holdouts. Maybe it's because we're air signs. Or maybe detachment is the secret of attraction. He is beloved because he will never be found. And that is also why he loves me. One great mystery deserves another.

JANUARY 16

The weight of the presidency is starting to age him. The boyish looks remain, the smile that detonates in women's hearts and thrills me, but when I kiss him I encounter wrinkles never noticed before. There is a filigree of lines etched around his eyes, the eyes of cool intelligence through which an entire country sees the future. And in those eyes last night I sensed a shimmering flicker of sadness, hidden beneath droopy eyelids. Why had I

not seen it before? Sometimes I believe depression is the
essential nature of human beings, and life a continual
pursuit of exits. I told him his hair was turning gray,
and he smiled. It was reddish brown when I was a
schoolgirl, before the war turned us all into adults. It
was chestnut when he won the election and still full,
almost too strong to tame, bursting out from the silly
little part on the left. Now it's burnt umber streaked
with gray.

I ran my fingers through it last night, but his back was
in spasm, and waves of pain rippled through his spine as
he moved to pull off his back brace. I told him to leave it
on, I told him to breathe, to just breathe, I just wanted to
hear him breathe and I was happy. He let out a moan and
sank into the gold couch, remarkably shabby for the most
famous house in the world. I removed his trousers and
went down on him. He let out a sigh—he never allows
himself to veer far from control, even in ecstasy. He is
efficient in all things, efficient in stealing momentary
pleasures amid the onslaught of people and problems.
He came quickly, and that was that. With Jack, a woman
must be prepared for "that is that."

MARCH 1
James Jesus Angleton brooded beside me at the Alsops'.
I asked if he'd read any new poetry lately, but he didn't
answer. I told him Allen Ginsberg had sent me a book of
poems called *The Happy Birthday of Death*, written by
his friend Gregory Corso. It was odd going, but Angleton

still didn't respond. Then he asked me if I'd ever been betrayed. You just can't predict James Jesus Angleton. He was in one of his strange moods.

He whispered that he'd been betrayed by the Great Betrayer himself, Kim Philby. We had long known of Philby, of course, knew of the clandestine education James received at the MI6 offices on Ryder Street in London at the foot of this legendary British spymaster. The gangly young intellectual from Yale communed daily with the seasoned, pipe-smoking eminence of British intelligence. Angleton couldn't inhale enough of Philby's sinister wisdom. He used to talk incessantly to Cord and me of Philby, in art galleries, at poetry readings, over dinners, during drunken Georgetown evenings. I learned of Angleton's education in bugging, in plowing through "the take" from bugging, in the hours and monotony and bodily noises; I learned the secrets of codes and agents and networks and interrogation in its nasty and less nasty variations.

How excruciating it must have been for Angleton when the world discovered that the professor of lying had been lying, when Philby defected to Russia, a double agent all along.

"What are you going on about?" Cicely interrupted. "Why are you chewing Mary's ear off?" She knew her husband was in a mood, frozen in a memory of betrayal, and she felt tasked with lightening the load of her peculiar husband on all those assembled.

"It was a Jewish woman," Angleton said quietly.

"A voluptuous Jewess he met in Berlin in the thirties. She ignited his sleepy English hormones. Betrayal is a chemical process. It's lodged in the hormones."

"James, let's go talk to Joe Alsop. He looks like he needs someone to talk at."

Angleton ignored his wife. "It's in the hormones," he went on. "Lodged in the neurochemistry. Someday we'll understand it. So much more powerful than thoughts and decisions, more insidious even than feelings. That's what allowed Kim to be a double agent. The Jewess anchored his hormones in a love of Communism. He didn't care who he lied to, who he betrayed, or who got killed. And the Brits were easily fooled. It was simply unfathomable to MI6 that someone born into the ruling class of the British Empire could be a traitor."

I knew Angleton had filled the empty space where his posh English tutor had resided with an unmitigated species of paranoia, a frenzy for tracking and routing out Soviet double agents, regardless of whether they existed.

"You and all your boys in the white shirts and ties over in Langley are convinced you're doing God's work, aren't you, James?" I said, but he just looked off into the same place he'd been staring all evening.

Then he turned to me and said, "A giant aerospace company once wanted to sell Howard Hughes a few hundred transport planes. Hughes insisted that the entire transaction be discussed only between midnight and dawn, by flashlight, in the Palm Springs municipal garbage dump. Now that's secrecy."

MARCH 23

I stared at a framed portrait of Lincoln as Jack pulled off my bra and sucked on my nipples. The ancient paint accurately captured the places where the pain of the presidency had hollowed Lincoln's face like a ghost. I had no power to undo Jack's hollowing out, so I told him to stop for a second, and I pulled a joint from my purse. Passing it back and forth, we quickly relaxed. My two creamy ladies were still hanging out, exposed. Jack grinned. He said he would be addressing a drug enforcement conference the next week, and even I laughed at the absurdity of it all, the transparency of the cloud of seriousness I carry wherever I go. Then we sat holding hands.

"Well, think about our future a little, when you have nothing else to think about," I said as I fell into his arms, bare breasts touching his suit jacket. It was the first time I'd ever felt vulnerable with him, perhaps a bit of an idiot, but I'm never sorry when I feel idiotic. It means I have taken a chance and gone beyond my usual domination of myself.

"Mary, Mary," he said in response. "You know what the Irish say: Why make one woman unhappy when you can make many women happy?"

I held my breasts up with my hands. "OK, make these women happy."

APRIL 1

Kirkland and Mary Jennings arrived at the Alsops' at the precise moment I reached the door, and it was

a disagreeable comingling. The Jennings comprise a
marriage of darkness and light. Mary is a Vassar sister
of a quality so pure, it feels we actually are sisters. We
breathe an effortless air together, we share a name,
and our sons grew up inseparable. She writes a poetry
of nature so delicate, I have fallen in love with stones.
But her husband, Kirkland Jennings, seethes in bitter
contrast, a bald and bullet-headed Company man so
virulent in his disdain of contrary points of view, so cast
in granite as to the righteousness of his cause, that any
discussion of war and peace with him is pointless. Which
means Kirkland Jennings is no fan of mine.

He is Cord's squash partner. I actually played squash
with Cord a few times, but by and large he refused to
play with me, a woman, though I had been a tennis
champion in my college years. And with the exception
of a different approach to the wrist, my tennis skills
translated very effectively to the squash court. But
Kirkland continues as Cord's squash partner, though
with Cord's voluminous intake of alcohol, relentless
cigarette habit, and only one eye, I find it hard to
imagine him a serious challenge on the court. I am
being cruel, of course. I can feel my nervous system grow
defensive in the face of Kirkland's distaste. He views
me as the tart of the town. Cord has shared drunkenly
and openly his despair and loneliness over our divorce,
now going on three years, and Central Intelligence, in
its wisdom and insight, blames me and me alone for
the rupture. Kirkland's loyalty is unquestionably to the

secret brotherhood and to Cord. Not to mention that once, under rapid-fire questioning at Joe Alsop's dinner table, I expressed skepticism about America's secret operations in Latin America. Channeling Daddy Amos, I said we have given a name to our profits: we call them Democracy. This generated such instant and perilous elevation to Kirkland Jennings's blood pressure that Mary Jennings had to take me aside and urge me never, ever again to speak against the Unites States within his earshot.

So at the door of the Alsops', I felt Kirkland as a profound weight in my solar plexus, a weight that says either he exists or I exist but not both. But I insisted on greeting him cheerfully nevertheless, even pecked him on the cheek, refusing to grant the past dominion over the present. Kirkland nodded imperceptibly, frozen in a manner that nothing in my feminine arsenal could melt. I was a radioactive woman, loved by the poet wife, reviled by the cold-warrior husband. Kirkland removed the ever-present cigarette from his mouth and nodded about a thousandth of an inch, about as much acknowledgment as I could hope for. I had the comical thought that I could probably beat him at squash, but then I would really fear for my safety.

APRIL 2
Insurrection at the Alsops'! After dinner, I made the radical suggestion that the women join the men in the living room for once rather than heading upstairs to

the Nunnery of Gossip. "I'm sick, sick, sick of girl talk," I said to Joe Alsop.

He smiled. "I'm shocked at your contempt for tradition. Men and women together discussing politics violates the fundamental laws of nature, or at least the statutes of Georgetown. But perhaps this once. You rabble-rouser!"

My sister Tony and I joined Ben Bradlee on the couch, while James and Cicely Angleton took seats in club chairs on either side. Cicely said she wanted me to meet her new guru, a man who wears a turban and preaches vegetarianism and abstinence from all intoxicants. I told her that I would wear her clothes, but I would not don her philosophy. I said that for me, steak, liquor, and casual sex were spiritual sacraments. She laughed, and Ben said maybe the women should have adjourned to our customary place upstairs after all. Then he turned to James and suggested that the buildup of US advisors in Vietnam was a quagmire, that we would come to regret ever setting foot in those jungles the French had exited so ingloriously. James Angleton nodded inscrutably, not so much expressing a specific position as allowing any position you wished to be read into his expression.

"Why do we call them advisors?" I burst out suddenly, not considering it a particularly controversial question. "They're not consultants or coaches. They're soldiers, for heaven's sake! Have you noticed this new love for imprecise language and euphemism?"

Tony raised her hand, an admonition for me to end

the conversation. I just love being cut off when I speak, especially by a sister.

Ben turned back to Angleton. "It's guerilla warfare, Jimmy," he said. "How can you expect regular troops to beat guerillas in a jungle?"

Joe Alsop carried over a fine bottle of Bordeaux and refilled my glass, sighing that he feared Jack was growing soft regarding the conflict in Southeast Asia. I joked within the comfort of my own brain that I was responsible for Jack's both getting soft and getting hard, but I said nothing, my relationship with Jack a state secret, withheld even from my own sister, who also harbors a crush on the president. So I am as much a liar as everyone else in this crowd, I have come to admit, and if not an official covert agent—and who exactly are those three unidentified men standing over there and chatting with Kirkland Jennings, looking over every now and then in my direction?—certainly I would say I was a "covert coquette on cobblestones" if Cicely and I were still playing Literation, the game we made up at Josselyn Hall. Having taken a vow of silence regarding my relationship with the president, and exhausted by the continual drone about Vietnam, I asked Joe Alsop if he was still making his duck *à l'orange.*

"Ah yes," he said. "The secret is in the *beurre meunière.*"

I asked if he'd seen the new movie of Tennessee Williams's *Sweet Bird of Youth,* which was playing at the Trans-Lux.

"That fairy!" he replied.

APRIL 8

One loses track of the conversation one conducts with life, the conversation one conducts with life, of course, being life itself.

Somewhere between the sad denouement of the UN Charter Conference of 1945, where Cord and I honeymooned, and the advent of three happy sons in a farmhouse in Virginia, I served for a time as one of the fiction editors at the *Atlantic Monthly*. Fiction editor is a funny title, I thought at the time. A curator of the make-believe.

One day, the editor in chief took me aside and said that I wrote too well. That's what he said. I wrote too well. "Is that actually a problem?" I asked.

He held up a story I had written about a young couple who leave Manhattan on impulse one day to go run a vineyard in Bordeaux. Here is how the story begins:

It is a place born 69 million years ago when the Pyrenees burst upward from the ocean.

It is a place where gray Atlantic waters meet the brown dust and ash-gray gravel.

It is a place where a Chateau St. Georges meets a medieval castle of Issan . . . where the cottages of Pomerol meet the villages of Sauternes, and vinerows stretch through forests and flatlands and slopes all the way to the imagination.

"You Vassar girls are so florid," he said, rubbing the page as if to efface its poetry, to deflower its floweriness.

"Keats and Shelley are gone, sweetheart. America is a work of prose. It's a postwar America, and we need a postwar prose to match it. Unembellished. A just-the-facts sort of writing."

That is what the editor in chief of the *Atlantic* told me. I didn't listen to him then, nor do I listen to him now. Words must equal the mystery I try to encompass, the sentences and phrases must capture the power of the life behind them, or why bother writing at all?

Composing this journal is the only writing I do these days. A diary meant to be read, perhaps, by nobody at all. Which is why I paint, for the benefit of walls and perhaps the admiration of an artist I have just met, Kenneth Noland. So far, no one has told me I am too stylish or too florid on my canvases. But of course, I don't paint in prose.

APRIL 14

I am aware that something leaves my pores and affects men. Something exudes and seizes attention. But I am not Roxanne Childs. To walk beside Roxanne on a sunlit Fifth Avenue last week was to take part in a chemical experiment. The jaws of men lowered in awkward salute to her beauty. She has a new sort of look: her hair hangs down long and straight on both sides as if she has just emerged from the shower, and her lips seem swollen, yet men find it all irresistible, like that pouty French actress. Roxanne walks through it all tall and unconcerned like the model she once was, and our only respite from men's gaze was a detour into Bonwit Teller. Someday scientists will identify this juice, this chemical, this sizzle of electricity, and life will be far less poetic.

So I am not Roxanne Childs. But I have an appeal. Jack said he is growing fond of me. He always underspeaks, and he remains a playboy with a bad back, a lothario with a limp lumbar. Corseted and medicated. The corset is the reason he stands so straight, of course, the nation's leader with perfect posture and a lordly mien, but it's really the corset.

As such, Jack likes it supine, and I give it to him supine. I suppose other girls give it to him supine too—girls are understanding of a man's back pain. In the supine, they afford smiling Jack an endless display of bouncing breasts: the little ones of skinny girls who played field hockey in the Ivy League, the fleshier ones of the more rounded women of my tradition. But those girls don't concern me. Those girls are not mysteries, even my sister Tony, not mysterious at all, so Jack and I have a pact that remains unbreakable. Because we're each of us mysteries to ourselves, as well.

APRIL 22

I survived the Bacchanal on the Rock and lived to tell the tale. On Saturday, Phil and Katharine Graham held their annual "Spring into Spring" soirée in the mansion on Dumbarton Rock. The house oozed sweat and alcohol, and within the bedlam you could feel a palpable hunger for information, as in the crush of men in bars you can

feel the palpable hunger for the juices of a woman. A
sweating Englishman with a perfect pocket square asked
me if I was alone or with someone, and I told him I was
with the president of the United States. Jack roared when
I told him the story last night, but he was more intent on
hearing who got laid and who Phil Graham had pounced
upon. I told him it was too crowded to see much, but I did
walk into an upstairs bathroom at one point and see two
men with their dicks out of their pants and a woman on
her knees between them, going from one to the other. I
apologized politely and went to find a more private place
to pee. Jack exploded, asking who the woman could have
been. I said she was facing away from me, but I'm sure
it wasn't Katharine Graham. It dawned on me that I was
the only person at the party who wasn't either a spy, a
journalist, a journalist pretending to be a spy, or a spy
pretending to be a journalist.

APRIL 25

I ran into Lorraine Cooper as I headed down Thirty-
Fourth Street toward the towpath. She says that she is
becoming a true partner in her husband's senatorial
work, and that even though John is from Kentucky, she's
pushing him into a more emphatic position on civil
rights. "He's more committed to civil rights legislation
now than President Kennedy," she said. I agreed that the
black struggle needs far more of the president's attention.
Then she said that while civil rights are being enacted,
her house needs redecorating, and she has hired Morgan

St. Pierre to re-do the living room, dining room, and kitchen. "You leave it up to John Sherman Cooper and the place will look like Pompeii after a while, with all the paint peeling into ruins. 'Delphinium, John,' I told him. 'Delphinium. Every home should have at least one room that is delphinium blue.'"

APRIL 30

Jackie spun a Milky Way in the White House last night, and I found no flaw in her celestial design. It was a celebration of the power of the human mind, an explosion of jewels and candles and fame's magnetic field as forty-nine Nobel Prize winners were feted and honored by royalty. Royalty both genetic and artistic.

Jackie whispered a vivacious hello to me, kissing the air on either side of my face and sending molecules of Chanel No. Five cascading into my nostrils. She was luminous in a pink silk shantung gown Christian Dior had designed for the event, while I wore a flimsy little silk beige dress that had seemed charming back in my closet, belonging as it did to my great-grandmother, but here in the White House was clearly a horrific fashion faux pas. The young wife of the shah of Iran, Empress Farah, was assigned the seat beside me, and her diamond tiara could have put electricity to shame. Her necklace of Persian emeralds would ravage the economy of many small nations. Mortified by my modest little beige dress, I left the table and circulated in the crowd.

Robert Frost wandered by, ancient and flinty, his

catalog of immortal poems releasing him from any
need for pose or politeness. I told him I had once recited
"Birches" in high school, suspecting it a thoroughly
absurd thing to say as it left my mouth but perhaps not
as bad as gushing that I was a big fan of his poems. He
struggled to hear me and then sighed, "I am so old!"

Tennessee Williams stood puffing on a long cigarette
holder and conversing with Charles Lindbergh, a
flier whom Jack always idolized. My father, Amos,
once worked with Lindbergh in the America First
Committee, they were so dogged trying to keep America
out of war with the Germans. Daddy's isolationism,
of course, was driven by a visceral hatred of war;
Lindbergh's, I believe, by a hatred of Jews. I could only
imagine what Lindbergh and Tennessee Williams had
to talk about.

David Ormsby-Gore, the British ambassador and Jack's
close friend, danced a fox-trot with his exquisite wife,
Sissy, who was bedecked in a gown of pink-and-gold
brocade, a gift from King Saud of Saudi Arabia. Ormsby-
Gore had been instrumental in pushing for a halt to
nuclear proliferation, and I watched him twirl his wife
across the floor, thinking about Jack and me, thinking of
what might have been in my own marriage had it been
a different marriage. When the music stopped, I went up
close and thanked David for his contributions to peace.
He was smiling radiantly; I wasn't sure he understood
who I was, but I was certain it didn't matter.

Ernest Hemingway's widow arrived to represent her

husband and his legendary masculine, stripped-down
prose style, which never really interested me. She went on
to lecture the president on the subject of Cuba for quite
a few minutes, and I heard Jack lament to Dave Powers
that he had not met such a bore in quite a while. Pamela
Harriman passed by in a silk gown of teal and taupe. I
said I wanted to get to know her, but she looked at me,
looked down at me, as if in profound disappointment with
the human race. "In due course, my dear," she said and
turned abruptly to Pierre Salinger, who kissed her hand,
leaving me alone with my flimsy little dress and even
flimsier hopes for a psychedelic future. *You have had sex
on seven continents*, I felt like saying to her. *I'm sure you've
perfected it by now.* But I didn't. I will continue, however;
I have no choice but to continue. In our commitment
to the world's betterment, my family goes on. Though
sometimes we don't. Memories of family tragedy, flashes
of suicides, a dying sister, a father in ruins, suddenly
flooded into the glittering space as memories do, obeying
their own neurological itinerary.

I breathed hard and tried to crush those thoughts,
tried to levitate myself back into present time, into this
dazzling moment at the White House, illuminated with
Nobel Prize winners. Each of them, no doubt, had been
similarly discouraged somewhere in their quest. Each
was being honored because they had persevered, had
chosen the discomfort of what isn't, instead of the comfort
of what is. I am aware that a blonde with Marlboros in

her handbag and a president in her bed is no candidate for a Nobel Prize. But I do have a destiny, no less defined, created by innumerable factors that scientists may figure out in ten thousand years. The circumstances of my birth, an eccentric family lineage, the man I happened to marry, the man I happened to fall in love with, a chemical I happened to swallow, and the cobblestone community I live and drink and paint in. Mine is no less a destiny.

I went back to the table and sat beside Empress Farah, who handed me a glass of champagne. We toasted each other, we toasted the future, we toasted being beautiful women. She was a magnificent specimen, so dark and so young, and when I looked back to the Nobel winners, they seemed awkward in comparison. Genius had diverted the energy that non–Nobel Prize winners normally direct toward perfecting the art of chitchat and promulgating an appearance of unalloyed joy at parties. Seated all together in one section of the ballroom, the winners looked confused as to why they were there, unsure of where exactly to focus their minds. Perhaps they would have been more comfortable back in their laboratories or at their writing desks. But Jack rose at his table and addressed them with a toast: "This is the most extraordinary collection of talent, of human knowledge, that has ever gathered together at the White House, with the possible exception of when Thomas Jefferson dined alone."

MAY 4

I told Jack I was shaken by General Curtis LeMay. The general was holding court at the Alsops' Saturday in his khaki costume of killing, the threads of his uniform practically straining under the weight of so many foolish ribbons. He sat spread-legged on the couch, airing out his crotch—or, as I suggested, making Jack laugh, perhaps his balls are so gargantuan, sitting spread-legged is his only option. Jack loves when I am vulgar; he adores gossip, especially when it pertains to people he loathes, and he cannot stand to be in the same room as Curtis LeMay. LeMay once shouted in the Oval Office that the proper solution to Cuba was "to fry it." Ted Sorensen refers to him as his least favorite human being on earth.

So LeMay sat occupying the space of two people on the Alsop couch with the grande dame Susan Mary Alsop beside him, her back as straight as the Washington Monument, as if the two of them were sharing a booth at El Morocco or some such posh nightspot. One doesn't nab a four-star general every soirée, even in Georgetown, so Curtis LeMay was a four-star coup for Susan Mary. She listened intently, dazzled by the protocols of annihilation. I heard LeMay proclaim that war with Russia is inevitable, that nuclear confrontation is unavoidable; it's simply a matter of scheduling, so why not get it done now, while we still have a missile advantage? Then Joe Alsop walked past. "Hear, hear," he said, and kept going. LeMay was puffing away on a cigar that smelled like a decomposing carcass, but no one in Georgetown dared tell him to put it out, and Jack kept smiling, he himself puffing on a cigar. So there was Susan Mary holding up her martini glass in this peculiar way, her hand twisted oddly around the stem, and she was beaming as if it was just the two of them, she and Doctor Death, and I was getting nauseous.

Jack says LeMay is a cocksucker who once told him we'd be better off with Nikita Khrushchev as secretary of defense than McNamara. I say it isn't the end of the story. LeMay began listing all the cities that will vanish in the conflict, and he sounded as if he were reciting a travel itinerary. A nuclear confrontation would incinerate Washington, New York, Chicago, Detroit, Los Angeles . . . he went on and on. Most of the major cities in Russia would also be decimated, it was all a fait accompli. Nuclear war was already on the way.

Jack says he appointed LeMay head of the US Air Force just to keep him contained. "I'd rather have him pissing out than pissing in."

What quirk of destiny places me, daughter of peace zealots, in living rooms hobnobbing with men who would destroy the world?

"It's you and me against the generals," I tell Jack, my story complete, and he rubs my thigh.

"I'm serious," I tell him.

"So am I," he says.

MAY 8

Robin Nightingale says Phil Graham is after her. She was sipping a strawberry shake at Packer's, and I told her how much I love her ceramics. They look like ancient artifacts dredged from a cave in Zanzibar or extracted from mud at the bottom of the ocean. Strange, bulbous shapes and crusts of dark clay that bespeak an origin impossibly remote. Roxanne Arcturis would suggest the markings of Atlantis, but Robin Nightingale is most assuredly a blonde from our time and place. Who knows where art comes from?

Phil Graham has been after her since he saw her in a bathing suit standing by the Harrimans' pool. "One piece!" she said. "And you know what this means. When Phil's on fire there's no respite, no decelerator pedal, no comprehension of the word *no*. He corners me in the Wisner kitchen Sunday, and I say to him: 'I thought you were married.' 'Only in a metaphysical sense.' 'What the fuck does that mean?' 'It means I'm available romantically.' 'But I'm not!' I answer. I'll probably get a call tonight. If only you could see the number that's calling you before you pick up a phone."

I told Robin I had seen bruises on Katharine's arms and legs. It worries me, but she won't own up to it. "She's protecting him. She worships him. Masochism, right?"

"He's totally Agency, the creep. Operation Mockingbird, they call it."

I told her I was well aware of my ex-husband's pet project.

"He boasted to me the CIA can get a journalist cheaper than a good call girl. A couple of hundred dollars a month!"

I told her Phil Graham had almost come to blows with
the French ambassador one night at his house over Phil's
belief that the United States should never get involved
with the French in Vietnam. The ambassador, kind of a
jerk, as I recall—he kept rubbing my hand, I think his
name was Bonnet—said America was cowardly for not
helping France resist Communism. Phil almost slugged
him in the face. Katharine deliberately knocked over a
tray just to distract them.

Robin laughed and finished her milkshake, making
loud sucking noises with her straw. "I'm not answering
my phone tonight."

MAY 10
Smoky molecules of Acapulco Gold snaked through
the fissures of my brain. Life turned Technicolor, my
senses and nerve endings catapulted to high alert, as I
walked the cobblestone hill again, the hill that leads to
the Potomac and dies down by the towpath. Once they
hauled coal from the Allegheny Mountains through this
sanctuary by the river. Now it's a primeval wilderness
wrapped around a thin canal, a simulacrum of Eden
slicing through Georgetown, through this madhouse of
politics, and I with so little appetite for politics. I am not
so much apolitical as postpolitical. Let's be blunt about
it, life is consciousness, involved in some mysterious
way with flesh. And flesh, in some mysterious way, is
involved with the perpetuation of itself. The scrimmage
of appetite everywhere, wrote some poet. Someone must

lose for someone else to win. Such is the terrain of my
mind when I smoke Acapulco Gold.

I crossed M Street and gazed left to the crossroads,
to the fork of M and Pennsylvania Avenue, where the
Esso station sells cigarettes, and I was put in mind of
crossroads. Once Cord and I linked arms at the crossroads
of an old idea, the World Federalist Party in 1947, the
dream of a world fashioned anew. We were not long
married, and envisioned a honeymoon for the world. It
failed, as all politics fails ultimately, and we just go on.

I walked the towpath, so thin with gravel, toward
Fletcher's Cove. Someone had dropped an engine in the
canal; its rusty haunches jutted from the brown water
like a submarine that had lost its way and no one cared.
How will we move beyond power, I thought, beyond the
imperative to dominate called war, just as this towpath
moved beyond commerce and became purposeless? No
longer coal-bearing, it had become a song to weedy love.
How could we move beyond purpose to love?

It tapped my brain. The only hope for the world is
intelligent women.

MAY 11

The only hope for the world is intelligent women. These
words have taken root in my heart. They speak in the
language with which I compose the earth each day. I
was at Packer's having a strawberry shake when the song
came on. "Chantilly Lace." *Ain't nothing in the world like
a big-eyed girl.* And thus I have a name for the project

of my dreams: Chantilly Lace. The power of women
and the power of chemistry. LSD. Two forces mobilized
against the impulse of domination etched in our neurons.
I think of bloody creatures battling bloody creatures
for dominion, stretching backward through eons of
unrecorded time, stretching forward through secret
corridors in Washington. Who said "All the civilized
nations at war. All the savages at peace"?

Chantilly Lace. Turning men on, but not to propagate
the species. Turning them on neurologically, to preserve
the species. Ushering in a reign of peace in the new
chemical era. I see a psychedelic sisterhood reaching out
to a threatened planet from the precincts of Washington,
DC. Women turning on the Cabinet. Chicks turning on
the Senate. Sisters turning on Central Intelligence.

And I will turn on the president of the United States.

MAY 13

I walked into a blaze of sunshine in Montrose Park to read
Understanding Thermonuclear War. It was penned by a
great fat man squeezed into the poop deck of the military-
industrial complex. The fat man is the lord of megadeath.
He actually coined the term: megadeath, the measure
of human lives incinerated in a nuclear confrontation.
Only a man could concoct such a word. Only a man could
devise the profession of sitting quietly in a room filled with
computers, measuring the dead and the dying. The men of
megadeath will have us in thermonuclear conflict by the
end of the decade if left to their own (nuclear) devices. I

will put *Understanding Thermonuclear War* under Jack's
pillow and remind him that he can't leave the planet in
the hands of cold men and imbeciles.

I continue to think. Taking the men who determine
the destiny of this planet and turning them on to LSD.
Could Chantilly Lace lift their cold fingers from the
buttons of power and, as with some global TV set, change
the neurological channel? Could we alter the course of
evolution? The men who control—yes, they are clearly
all men—control simply because they're men, because
neurochemistry urges them to kill for some delusion of
security. Could we destroy that evolutionary strategy?
Could we stop World War III?

I am thinking: the way to a man's DNA is through a
woman. A crusade to save the planet with the power of
acid and the power of woman. The ladies of Chantilly
Lace: Evangeline Bruce, Anne Truitt, Georgette LeBlanc,
Anne Chamberlain, Cicely Angleton. No, James Angleton
will never take LSD. Maybe Katharine Graham and
Pamela Harriman? Lorraine Cooper? Bebe Highsmith?
We could all band together, the women who control
the men who control the world. If we can turn on and
transform ourselves, we can transform our husbands and
lovers. I have been reading Timothy Leary, a psychologist
at Harvard researching LSD, orchestrating psychedelic
journeys with students, professors, artists, and mental
explorers of every stripe. He will be my contact. He will
be my source.

Megadeath.

MAY 15

Roxanne Arcturis says the Age of Aquarius will begin
when the vernal equinox moves out of the constellation of
Pisces and into the constellation of Aquarius. As we enter
the Aquarian Age, everything will change. The structure
and hierarchy of power that has dominated our history
will be obsolete. The age of masters, experts, and tyrants
will end. In this new age, we will each become our own
guru. I can't escape the sense that if someone found me
reading this book, I would be shot.

MAY 20

Kenny O'Donnell was beside himself. He called to say
Jack was in trouble—it was an emergency, he needed
me immediately. A car was on the way. I had never been
the object of such urgency before. I have never played
a central role solving a crisis, like Bobby or Kenny
O'Donnell or Ted Sorensen or Robert McNamara. I am a
painter and a mother.

So I was tense on the ride down Pennsylvania Avenue
to the White House, a journey I had made so many times.
When I got to the Lincoln Bedroom, Jack was unusually
upset. "Mary, I need you to handle something very
important," he said. Whenever he started with my name,
it indicated concern. "Please go into the next room, and
you'll see what you have to do."

I felt like a playing piece in some board game, a
mystery game, very conscious of my hand turning the
knob, of opening the door and walking into the small

room adjoining the bedroom. I closed the door behind me. The room was not well illuminated. When I looked up, Marilyn Monroe was there. She wore a flesh-colored skintight dress shimmering with rhinestones and was sprawled out in a chair, her hair askew, her lipstick smeared.

"Who the fuck are you?" she asked.

"My name is Mary."

"Well, so is mine . . . sort of. Did the birthday boy send you back here to handle me, to try to make me behave? Does the president himself not have the fucking balls to talk to me and tell me the truth? Is he so ashamed to be seen with me in the White House! I wanna see Bobby!"

I realized Jack wouldn't have chosen me for this situation were it not a genuine crisis, and one he trusted me to solve.

"Bobby's not here," I said, "but we can talk."

"Who are you, his girlfriend for tonight? Or this hour?"

"Look, Marilyn. Can I call you Marilyn?"

"Don't care what you call me. You have very nice skin."

"You think so?"

"Yes, it's so natural. I used to have skin like that, but now it takes me five hours to get ready because I have to be Marilyn Monroe. Tell Jack to get his fucking ass in here now. I'm not going away just because he feels like throwing me into the toilet!"

"Marilyn, he doesn't feel like throwing you into the

toilet. I'm an advisor—I work with Jack, and he's spoken very highly of you. He really cares for you."

"You're an advisor? Jack doesn't take advice from girls. He just fucks them."

"Yes, we speak a lot about peace. I want the Cold War to end—"

"Great. You end the Cold War, and I'm CALLING THE FUCKING NEWSPAPERS TO TELL THEM WHAT THE KENNEDY BROTHERS DID TO ME! I'm not just another blond slut. I'm somebody."

"Of course you're somebody. You're a very talented somebody, but you're somebody just like all of us. Women are special somebodies."

I didn't know where what was coming out of my mouth was coming from, but Jack obviously thought I could defuse the situation. I heard she had sung "Happy Birthday" to him earlier in the evening, but the birthday bash had obviously devolved into a situation. Maybe Marilyn Monroe was more dangerous to him at this moment than Cuba.

"What do you mean, women?"

"Women are special. You know that. We are the nurturers of the world. We are the caretakers of the world. Men run around and build things and then tear things down and fight over them, but women are the ones who are left to take care of things when all is said and done."

"That's right. Fucking and fighting. Even the smart ones. Even the *artistes*! Fucking and fighting. That's a man for you. Especially that man in the White House, over there in the next room."

"Of course, but we don't tell them that because we need to build them up, to make them feel important. Even though we know the truth."

"Make them feel important! That's right, Mary. I really like your hair."

"I don't do much with it. I'm a painter, so I don't have a lot of time to fuss with it. I just keep it short and let it do whatever it wants."

"Painter? That would be fun. By the time I finish painting my face, who's got time for a landscape? I wish I could just let my hair do what it wants. I wasn't always a blonde, you know."

"No?"

"I was a brunette, but then I had to do a shampoo commercial, so they bleached it blond. When I was done, men started going crazy, so I kept it. I am so tired of men going crazy. You know what it means when men go crazy over you?"

"No."

"It means everyone you meet is crazy. So then suddenly I was a blonde, and I invented it."

"Invented what?"

"The whole thing. Marilyn Monroe. I invented the whole fucking thing, and now I'm stuck with it. It's like a prison."

"You're not stuck."

"What?"

"I said you're not stuck. You're a free woman. You can do anything you want."

"Oh, that would be nice. I invented myself and then forgot who I was before I invented myself, so now I do what men tell me to do. Directors, lawyers, doctors, presidents of the United States. They all tell me what to do. You know what my husband Arthur Miller wrote? 'I thought I was marrying a goddess, then one day I discovered I had married a whore.' That's what he wrote. I read it. Can you believe he said that? He's an asshole too."

"No, I can't believe it. It's a terrible thing to write, and it must have really hurt."

"They want me to be Marilyn, and I want to be me, but there's no me to be, so they win."

"Marilyn, listen to me. You don't want to go crazy. You don't want to be hysterical. You don't want to cause trouble. That's what men want you to do. They want you to be ditzy. They want you to be a crazy blonde. But that's not what you are. We're women. We're not just projections of men's fantasies."

"I really like you, Mary. You know, all the men in the world want to be with me, but no one man. Isn't that pathetic?"

"I like you too, Marilyn."

"Can we be friends?"

"Of course. We're going to be good friends. What you need to do now is go home, get out of this dress—"

"This stupid dress."

"This stupid dress, and take a bath and let Jack run the country. I'll tell him what a brave woman you are, and he can be your friend too, but you need someone who will love you. That's what you deserve. Jack's got no time for you. He doesn't even have time for his own wife. You deserve better."

"I deserve better."

"Say it again. I deserve better."

"I deserve better."

"Do you want to stay at my house tonight, and then we can figure out getting you home? I'll show you some of my paintings, we'll take a nice bath, get some sleep . . ."

"I love paintings. I'd love to see your paintings."

"OK, we're going to go through that door, say good night to Jack, and then go to my house."

I held Marilyn by the hand and walked into the Lincoln Bedroom. Jack was in the rocking chair, looking tense.

"Good night, Jack," I said. "We're going to my house, and I'm going to show Marilyn my paintings."

"Yes, Mr. President, I've got to look at some paintings. Good night."

We walked out slowly, leaving Jack rocking. Kenny O'Donnell whisked us out of the White House and into a car.

MAY 21

She wore my pajamas and woke up late in the morning. I had a cup of coffee ready for her. "This is the first night I can remember not going to sleep with a Nembutal," she said. "This is such a beautiful little house."

Kenny had called to say that Jack now regarded me as a miracle worker, and a car would be picking Marilyn up at one to take her to the airport. I told him all was good, in fact I was enjoying it, and Kenny reiterated what an important service I had done for Jack.

Marilyn washed off her makeup, and I gave her some capri pants and a sweater to wear on the plane. I put her shimmering Happy Birthday dress in a Gold's Department Store shopping bag. She said she felt relieved of the burden of being Marilyn Monroe. I said that in this house she was not Marilyn Monroe, she was just Marilyn, and I was Mary. She said she didn't remember what it was like just dressing any way you felt and not caring how your hair looked.

She saw a copy of *Meditations* by Marcus Aurelius on my desk. "I love that book!" she said. "Do you know I had a copy on the set once, and Billy Wilder told me to put it away and not to be seen carrying it. It would ruin my image!"

I shook my head.

Everything went wrong after *The Misfits*, she said. She started overdosing on prescription drugs, and they sent her to the Payne Whitney clinic. She thought it would be a rest cure, but it was more like being sent to prison for a crime she hadn't committed. "I was locked in a cement block cell," she said. "Cement. I had forced baths, no privacy, bars on all the windows, insane patients running around. I remembered a movie I had once done where I smashed a chair against the window in the door to break it, so I did it for real at Payne Whitney, just trying to get their attention. But the more I tried to get out, the crazier they thought I was and the more I needed to be there. I'd still be locked up in hell if my ex-husband Joe DiMaggio hadn't stormed the place and threatened to destroy it brick by brick unless they let me out. Then he left. Just like a man."

What a tragically sensitive soul. I thought of the sad transaction of fame, this illusion of intimacy with someone you've never met. How in the orgy of scandal, divorce, and crack-ups, meaning is restored to the lives of the unfamous, to the lives rendered meaningless by the fame of others. In the crucifixion of the star comes the resurrection of the fan.

I hugged Marilyn when they arrived to bring her back to Hollywood. "I love you, Mary" was the last thing Marilyn Monroe said to me, and I kissed the lips so many had dreamed of kissing.

MAY 28

I had lunch at Le Bistro with Lorraine and Kay Graham. Ever a fashion innovator, Lorraine appeared with an odd but striking scarf around her neck. "A unique scarf," I said. "You didn't buy that in Georgetown, I dare say."

"It's not a scarf," she said. "It's one of John's ties. It looks better on me than him, don't you think? Besides, he's got millions of them."

Kay seemed quiet. She is never the life of the party, but now I noticed that her neck was covered up just like Lorraine's, without a necktie, and there were bruises on her arms.

"Kay, spill the beans," Lorraine said, noticing the bruises. "We're friends here." But Kay was not forthcoming.

"About what?"

"How are you and Phil getting along?"

"We're great. The same. We're OK."

"So what's that on your arm?"

"What on my arm? Oh, I fell."

"You mean in love?" Lorraine continued, but Kay had sealed the door to her marriage and was not about to open it with a Lorraine witticism. "All right, Katharine, but you know we're here for you, and I don't give a hoot in hell how smart or magnetic or magnificent Phil is. He's just another news guy to me, and you're my friend."

"Just finish your drink," Kay said.

Lorraine turned on a dime toward me. "Mary, I know you're into this spiritual thing."

I felt called upon to answer seriously. "Well, there is consciousness, and it's involved in some way with the body . . ."

"No, don't get crazy on me. I haven't had enough to drink. I have a question about heaven."

"I don't think it's about religion," I said. "Someone had an experience of the truth and tried to formalize and concretize and contain it, so they created religion."

"There you go again, Mary. My question is this: When we die and go to heaven, who'll be waiting for us, our husbands or our lovers?"

She had lifted Kay out of her mood, and even distracted me momentarily from my mission for world peace. "Oh, I hope to God it isn't our husbands," she went on.

JUNE 3

I called Harvard University and asked for Dr. Timothy Leary. How odd it sounded, uttering his name. To the operator it was just another extension on the Harvard network, one more wire snaking mysteriously from her office to the Center for Personality Research on Divinity Avenue. Divinity Avenue! She collected her salary, went for coffee breaks, hung her coat in some tiny academic closet, and had no idea that her switchboard was now linked to a new dimension in human consciousness.

The telephone rang as telephones do, with that long pause between rings that is no more than a second but seems much longer, and he answered. "Dr. Timothy Leary," he announced in slow, smooth tones. Such a sexy voice. What is it with these Irishmen?

I told him I was from Washington, DC, and that our conversation required the utmost discretion. He simply said "Fire away," a phrase I found peculiar. Was I hearing a normal voice, another tone among the human community of voices, or was that voice in fact speaking on behalf of a brain transmogrified by lysergic acid diethylamide? I wondered if Dr. Leary experienced himself as everyone else does, as a thing walking around with a history and a set of attributes. Or by now was he a disembodied soul, strolling through time and space as a human representative from infinity?

I told him I was no stranger to LSD. I had taken a 300-microgram dose in California with Allen Ginsberg.

"Ah," he said. "I saw the best minds of my generation destroyed by madness!"

"Excuse me?"

"That's from *Howl*. Allen Ginsberg is a friend of mine."

Anyway, I told him, it had been quite a profound experience for me, and I wanted to learn how to run my own LSD sessions. The people I intended to turn on were extremely powerful people in Washington, DC—so powerful, in fact, that their identities could not be disclosed nor their psyches entrusted to strangers. I wanted Dr. Leary to train me in conducting safe LSD sessions, which he found rather amusing.

"Who are these people you wish to turn on?" he asked, and I reiterated that my friends in Washington were extremely powerful, and I simply could not divulge their names. He grew quiet for a moment and then spoke softly, almost hypnotically. LSD is a revolutionary substance, he said. It causes a quantum shift in the human nervous system. He regarded LSD more as a sacrament than a drug, something that must be approached with awe and a degree of wisdom. He suggested that he and his team come to Washington to run the sessions themselves, and I told him that was out of the question. We arranged to meet in Boston in two weeks, when he returned from Mexico.

JUNE 6

Jack had to get the fucking over quickly last night. When I arrived, I told him I had a crucial matter to discuss, but sex took precedence. It was as if he couldn't open himself to the wisdom of a woman without first establishing his manhood within her. When it was over, I told him that the universe had placed him in a historic position.

"Mary, why are you using the word *universe*? Are you some kind of physicist? I'm not bright enough to discuss the universe." He smiled. "I'm just a politician from the wards in Boston." I told him to cut the bullshit. We are on the precipice of mutually assured destruction, I said, taking the phrase from the book *Understanding Thermonuclear War*. He grew quiet. I said a historic opportunity for world peace had emerged: the convergence of his presidency with the emergence of LSD, a drug that transforms consciousness. I knew it was the first mention of psychedelic drugs in the White House in American history.

JUNE 14

I flew to Boston Thursday to meet Timothy Leary. I boarded the Eastern Air Lines shuttle, convinced my humble Pinchot trust fund was being harnessed to a noble project. Amos and Ruth, Granddaddy Haynes and

Aunt Cornelia—all my forebears on the barricades—
would approve.

We met at a seafood restaurant by Boston Harbor.
Timothy is a long, thin Irishman with a mellifluous
voice, a handsome and curious character who gives the
impression he's in on a joke you're not. Was this man a
performer or a professor? We ordered lobster and a bottle
of Dom Perignon to celebrate our psychedelic future. Tim
is a connoisseur of all manner of substances, the finer
alcohols not excluded.

Retaining a perpetual smile—again, does he know
something you don't?—he told me he was uncomfortable
with my idea. He does not approve of people running
LSD sessions without the proper consciousness or
experience. He's conducted hundreds of sessions himself
and is acutely aware that the nervous system is vastly
complex. Just inches from transcendence lies madness.
The Tibetans had created a handbook, he said, for
people on their journey when the soul departs the body,
The Tibetan Book of the Dead. It tracks the stages of
consciousness that are said to occur during the forty-nine
days after death. Tim has created a psychedelic version of
this book for those embarking on the LSD journey, and
he recommends it as a guardrail against mental chaos. If
I insist on ignoring his warnings and decide to go ahead
and lead my own LSD sessions, he recommends I use the
book as a guide.

I found Timothy equally adept at cracking lobsters
and coining aphorisms. "When the ego dies, the soul

must be ready," he said, a bon mot to which I clinked my champagne flute against his. A foghorn moaned outside.

He likens LSD to a fish swimming in water. The fish doesn't know he's in water. He has no experience of anything outside the water, so to the fish, it's not water, it's just reality. When you take the fish out of water and then drop him back in, the water is exactly the same, but his relationship to the water is transformed forever. Now he knows he is in water, and that water is just a part of a bigger world, and he can never unknow it.

"Everyone's walking around in a fish tank called their mind. Your mind is the water you swim in. You think it's reality. In the psychedelic experience, you go out of your mind and come back, just like the fish, and you'll never be attached to your reality the same way again. You need to go out of your mind and come to your senses."

Again, a maxim I repeat. *You need to go out of your mind and come to your senses.* Timothy Leary is a phrasemaker and showman. His neurological ruminations bear the patina of performance, a monologue honed through repetition. But his nuggets bear repeating with my psychedelic wives in Washington.

I asked if I could count on him to supply the LSD for my sessions. He could arrange it, he said, but I had to document each session meticulously and share the results with him.

"Let's change the world," I said.

His eyes twinkled. "That's a wonderful thing to do with it! But they kill people who try it, you know."

I didn't know if he was joking or warning me, because he never stopped smiling.

"I have friends in high places," I said.

"I have friends in very high places," he replied.

We cracked up.

Chantilly Lace and a pretty face.

JUNE 20

Who am I to change the neurology of the men who lead the free world? I'm just a blonde with a Marlboro, a woman against the grain of every grain there is—in short, a Pinchot. A family that has been shooting off its mouth for more than a century.

I descend from a Pinchot who escaped from France, I am told, after he failed in the battle to free Napoleon. I descend from Granddaddy Haynes, who, family lore has it, died fighting to free slaves on the underground railroad. I descend from Daddy Amos, who raged against war in every form, a fatal strain of pacifism from which he never recovered. My mother, Ruth, fought for the women's right to vote. The Nineteenth Amendment to the Constitution, granting women the vote, was signed the year I was born. And I descend from Aunt Cornelia, who was unstoppable on the picket lines, fighting for miners and demanding civilized wages for workers everywhere. We have all been writers and loudmouths for justice, the women in my family, and I keep on my desk, beside my Russian music box, an essay Aunt Cornelia published in the *Nation* early in the century. "My

feminism," she writes there, "tells me that a woman can
bear children, charm her lovers, boss a business, swim the
English Channel, stand at Armageddon and battle for the
Lord—all in a day's work!"

The olive branch doesn't fall far from the tree. I
feel Aunt Cornelia's blood in my veins, leading me to a
battlefield at the precise junction of nuclear annihilation
and transformational pharmaceuticals. I have to believe
that chemical weapons and chemical salvation have
converged at a specific moment in time—the moment
Roxanne Arcturis calls the Aquarian Age.

JUNE 26

Black Orpheus is all the rage. It is de rigueur now for
every woman in Georgetown to see the movie, and
conversations are not so much whether you have seen it
as how many times. Bebe Highsmith and I watched it
Saturday night at the Trans-Lux, and I was stunned. I
thought I had witnessed a dream forged from pure color.
Painting had merged with film had merged with poetry.
The Brazilians have created the true music of the body,
and I wish I were a dancer. I wish Brazilian samba genes
could inhabit this body, my Pinchot Anglo-Saxon body as
white as paper, that they could melt my flesh, dissolve my
thoughts and agitation. There is a frenzy now over the
bossa nova, and I can understand why.

Bebe Highsmith is half Brazilian, granddaughter of
the president of Brazil. She loves the pulse of it all, the
music and spirit of Carnival, though she has never come

even remotely close to the slums and favelas of Rio, where Orpheus and Eurydice reenact their mythological drama.

Last night at Tony's house, Ben Bradlee asked Joe Alsop if he'd seen the film. Expectedly, Joe scrunched up his nose. "I don't believe in romanticizing the poor. A slum isn't a poem. It's a slum." But sociology was beside the point, I thought; perhaps it is always beside the point. It's clear that a celluloid vision of black people dancing the samba through a carnival of myth was simply beyond the life-crushing grasp of Joe's WASP nature, far more at home as it is with war. I felt like a Brazilian.

JULY 8

Jackie is in Europe. Ruth Selwyn says the First Lady has begun an affair with Aristotle Onassis and likens the relationship to a gorilla mating with a virgin. But— urged on as we all were at Vassar to nurture fierce passions beneath a cloak of sublime femininity—Jackie is no virgin.

Meanwhile I have been spending hours at the White House, preparing Jack for an excursion into psychedelia. I read him T. S. Eliot: "We shall not cease from exploration / And the end of all our exploring / Will be to arrive where we started / And know the place for the first time."

I told him we will only be taking a moderate dose, but LSD removes the filters from our consciousness, and Jack says we need filters, especially the Irish. I tell him to forgo the bullshit, and he laughs—again, no woman speaks to him as I do, but he seems to enjoy it. When the filters disappear, I tell him, there's an opportunity to reprogram ourselves. I show him my copy of Tim Leary's psychedelic version of *The Tibetan Book of the Dead.* I open to a random section and read aloud: "You suddenly wake up from the delusion of being a separate form and you hook up to the cosmic dance. Consciousness slides along the wave matrices, silently at the speed of light."

"Who is this writer?" Jack asks.

"Dr. Timothy Leary, a Harvard psychologist," I say. "He is a friend of mine. He is the chief exponent and explorer of LSD."

"So, Mary, you're trusting our entire sanity and our minds and the future and welfare of the American people to some drug and some Irishman from Boston jabbering about the cosmic dance?"

"Exactly."

JULY 12

Sometimes I think colors are just sounds my eyes are hearing. We are pushed endlessly into our thoughts, and thoughts are bound up with some mechanism of survival. They move inevitably toward fear and worry. How can I just paint? How can I just be with color, empty?

JULY 14

How strange that evolution commands a man to come in order to perpetuate the species, thus assuring that he does, while a woman's orgasm is quite incidental to the imperatives of evolution. The species can go forth and multiply quite well, thank you, without a woman's ever being brought to the moaning stage, and perhaps that is why our pleasure is of no concern to men.

I am having dinner with C tonight at Rive Gauche and hoping for an exception. I am the available woman of Georgetown, and a woman doesn't live by Jack Kennedy alone. Not yet. C stared at me all evening at the Grahams', lunging over to light my cigarettes— aren't men helpful?—wrapping his hand around mine just a fraction longer than it takes to ignite tobacco. The eternal message was communicated. Communication received. It is a telegram of a charge, much finer than the banality of chitchat, more ethereal even than Cicely's new poem, which she read aloud in iambic pentameter to the great approval and fervent applause of her smiling counterintelligence husband James.

I will wear L'interdit again tonight when I meet C. Who said "A woman who doesn't wear perfume has no future"? Probably some adman in the pay of Chanel. And I will eat lightly. Yes, very lightly. You don't want a cow decomposing in your stomach just inches from where a man will enter. Charlotte informs me that C is on the experienced side—at least it occurred to her that way, especially in matters of tongue—and that his wife has long incorporated his fun as a component of her misery. Tonight it will be *viva la vulva*. In honor of Bastille Day?

JULY 18

Can my life be reduced to pure color? There are a
billion sentimental paintings in this world, mounted on
a billion walls, but I am not adding to the collection. I
am working in the color field. I leave my feelings at the
door when I paint. Which means I skip the middleman
of representation. Instead of mountains and sea and
sky meeting at the horizon of my canvas, each simply
an excuse for color, I go to the colors directly. There are
no edges to my painting. In color field theory, edges
are simply the places where the color field ends. This
morning I worked on a circle and built it from four
shades of red, each red slightly different. As my teacher
Kenneth Noland says, color doesn't fill in form. Color is
the form itself. What you see is what you see.

AUGUST 1

Born in time, time melts you. This is the descent of the
decent. This is the beating of events that take you down,
drop by drop.

First went Amos, my father of revolutionary wisdom,
a man who was equal to his times. That is my highest
praise. He was a man equal to his times, and I watched
him disintegrate after the death of Rosamond, my ghost
sister. In the end, this man who built political parties
across the nation and resisted war—even the war against
the Third Reich, adopting as his mantra that dangerous
thought America First—descended, wrecked and reeking.

The descent of the decent for the friends of my girlhood, ushered gradually into varying lands of dissolution and madness. Victoria Palmquist from Vassar, in a hospital now in Corning, New York. Jeannine Toover from Philadelphia, gone by her own hands. I never knew what was in her hands. Carla Swain Garrison, queen of my debutante days, days of champagne glasses and swirling entrances onto ballroom floors, became fat and then angry as Kertin Tarlow's wife, and then one day she too was taken, by pills. Gone, so many of my wayward girls who once carried their future like corsages upon their breasts.

But no one descended as far and fast as Cord, the golden husband. Perhaps it is a saving grace that he didn't go the way of death and decay as so many have in my life. Or maybe it wasn't. I pity him now, a vulture for covert culture. Instead of poetry and lyrical prose—the honed, concise phrase he mastered as a schoolboy—he is spreading the tentacles of Central Intelligence everywhere, planting spies the way I plant flowers. The Congress for Cultural Freedom: a CIA front. Radio Free Europe: a CIA front. The National Council of Churches: a CIA front. The American Newspaper Guild: a CIA front. The Iowa Writers' Workshop: a CIA front. The *Paris Review*: a CIA front. All because of Cord Meyer. He began by infiltrating my life, then spread his tentacles to the vast culture around him until culture itself became suspect.

AUGUST 5

I went to the Harriman pool party on Sunday. At Averell's invitation—I'm sure it wasn't Pamela's idea. I expected to find Lorraine floating nonchalantly in the chlorinated water, parasol in one hand, cocktail in the other. But she and Vangie were stretched out luxuriously on lounge chairs when I arrived, smoking cigarettes. They waved me over.

"We're discussing the origin of husbands," said Vangie.

"You mean, anthropologically?"

"Don't start, Mary," said Lorraine, blowing smoke in the direction of Averell and her husband, Ambassador Bruce, both standing waist-high in the pool, two powerful men time had placed in pear-shaped bodies covered in gray hair. "No, how did you meet your husband? That's the question."

"I'll pass on that," I said. "Just as I passed on my husband!"

"Touché!" said Vangie. "My turn. I was living in London, and David had been appointed ambassador to Britain. Well, he needed a secretary, so friends set up an interview for me. 'I take it you speak French?' he asks me." Vangie imitated the ambassador's proper accent. "'Well,' I say, 'not as well as I would like'—he nods, ready to say 'Next'—'But I do broadcast to occupied France twice a week!' He's a bit stunned, so he says, 'Well, I suppose many young women speak French, but what is really needed is someone who speaks languages from Central and Eastern Europe.' 'Would Hungarian do?' I ask, all big-eyed and naive. So then he says, 'Well, the fact is, we must be looking ahead to a possible occupation of Japan,' and I say, 'Oh, I grew up there, and my Japanese governess spoke nothing but Japanese with us.' Now he's perplexed, a bit afraid, so he says, 'Scandinavian language?' 'I'm afraid my Swedish is a bit rusty,' I say, 'but I can easily brush up.' He hires me, then and there. Oh yes, he also asks me out to dinner."

"He could never have resisted you," Lorraine says.

"We've been together every minute since," says Vangie. "Except of course when we go to sleep."

AUGUST 8

Jack was pensive last night. He is talking more these days and fucking less, as my own chronic detachment wanes and my need for him grows. "I underestimated Castro," he said. Everything comes back to Cuba. "I never got his appeal. I mean, he's a thug with a beard. Then at the Bay of Pigs they handed me my ass. Castro was supposed to be knocked off while the troops were landing, but that didn't exactly work out, like most of the promises over at CIA. A thousand Cubans are taken prisoner on the beach, Stevenson's at the UN lying about it, and then he finds out we've kept him in the dark all along, and Adlai's ass is in an uproar. Then Bobby goes nuts about this whole mess Castro has put us in, so he throws everything against this son of a bitch. Operation Mongoose, except we're the goose. They try to kill the bastard, poison him, they try to create pandemonium, foment chaos, sabotage his authority. Nothing can stop this guy. All because of a piece of land you could spit at from the Fontainebleau. I can't let a thug ranting under a palm tree lead us to nuclear war. It's time to normalize relations. But I can't tell anyone. I can't tell the Joint Chiefs—they're not on my side. The CIA has gone off the deep end about Cuba. They've let these Cuban gangsters in Florida mesmerize them about Castro. They all thrive on the Cold War, they never forget the Bay of Pigs, my calling off the air support, they'll never forgive me for firing Allen Dulles. I need to crush the CIA, Mary. A bunch of half-crazed Yalies running rogue in this country. I've got to smash them into a million pieces."

I nodded and listened, maybe half listened, the way an old married couple half listens. My body ages, I accumulate wrinkles and secrets. I live in the in-between. Between the presidency and Central Intelligence. Between a lover and an ex-husband. Between war and peace. Everywhere and nowhere.

AUGUST 12

Jack and I had dinner in the White House with Dave Powers. He serves as clown in Jack's Irish mafia. If it is Kenny O'Donnell's job to handle every aspect of Jack's life, it is Dave Powers's to keep him amused. Over roast chicken and mashed potatoes, Dave all but spit his food out all over the fine White House china, chewing, gabbing, guffawing, and keeping the president in stitches. I will attempt to repeat a joke.

A man and woman meet at a bar and go back to the man's house. Walking into his bedroom, she discovers the entire wall covered with stuffed bunnies: big bunnies on the bottom shelf, medium-sized bunnies in the middle, and little ones at the top. This man is so sensitive! she thinks, and proceeds to make passionate love to him. When it's over, she smiles and asks, "How was it for you?" The man replies: "Help yourself to anything on the middle shelf."

Jack cracked up, Dave Powers cracked up, I think I smiled. Perhaps it's a man thing. Or else I am a terrible joke person. But I was thrilled to see Jack laughing and happy, which is only the first part of Dave Powers's job. The second part of the job is disappearing discreetly, so he left when the meal was over, leaving Jack and me alone. We wandered into the bedroom, supervised by Abraham Lincoln, and I undid Jack's tie. Such an unnecessary item, ties, yet so sexy to undo. I threw the necktie on the floor with a sweeping gesture, the same floor where Abraham Lincoln and Franklin Roosevelt once walked, and began to undo his buttons. "I understand the Emancipation Proclamation better now," I said. Maybe I'm a joke person after all.

AUGUST 21

"Everybody's doing a brand-new dance, now . . . come on, baby, do the loco-motion."

I was in my bra and panties. Tim was bare-chested with a necktie wrapped around his head, Indian-style.

We were doing the loco-motion at the Ritz-Carlton, overlooking Boston Commons, trying to avoid smashing into tables and lamps. The song had come up on the clock radio in perfect synchronicity with the magic mushroom moment. Tim had placed magic mushrooms in our tea, we had drunk the foul brew slowly, and the occasion called out for a brand-new dance.

"The Aztec word for these is God's flesh." Tim had pulled his bits of mushroom from a plastic bag and placed them carefully in our teacups. "The scientific word for them is psilocybin. It unleashes the neurotransmitter in the brain known as serotonin."

It had begun with a return to Boston to replenish psychedelic supplies. My vision for a Washington wives' LSD club was burning in me, but I didn't want to go anywhere near Harvard. Tim has become a figure of controversy there, ignoring my urgings of discretion, discretion being the better part of Valium and every other drug, I joked to him, but he is even more foolhardy than I am. I told him to meet me in room 717, my usual room at the Ritz-Carlton. The mushrooms were a surprise.

He has journeyed far beyond the province of clinical psychologist. He is a revolutionary now, a propagandist for chemical evolution, a shaman of ecstasy, abandoning the fleeting designations society places on experts: professor, psychologist, doctor. As I waited for the mushrooms to hit, wondering what form of power was about to explode in my brain from these bits of plant material, Tim read from a document he had written, a formal, oratorical document he called "The Declaration of Evolution": "'The history of the white, menopausal, mendacious men now ruling the Planet Earth is a history of repeated violation of the harmonious laws of nature, all having the direct object of establishing a tyranny of the materialistic aging over the gentle, the peace-loving, the young, the colored.'"

As Tim railed against the mendacious men who rule the planet, I poured us a fine cabernet from the Ritz-Carlton cellar. I have spent my life in the confines of this contradiction. At Grey Towers, my turreted family home, the plight of workers and miners was debated daily within the walls of a castle. Forgoing comfort does not answer injustice. Those moldering in shacks in West Virginia or falling in the rice paddies of Vietnam, far, far from the gardens of Boston Commons, would not be helped by the forswearing of cabernet.

"'These old, white rulers have maintained a continuous war against other species of life, enslaving and destroying at whim fowl, fish, animals, and spreading a lethal carpet of concrete and metal over the soft body of Earth.'"

It was a slow-motion explosion. Light began to emanate from Tim. I saw light streaming through the window from Boston Commons, wrap its waves around my chocolate-colored overnight bag, around the tweed club chair, around the king-size bed all pillowed up and stiffly made up by hotel staff.

"'For profit they have polluted the air, the rivers, the seas. In their impotence they have glorified murder, violence, and unnatural sex in their mass media.'"

I felt euphoric. I lay down on the Persian carpet and studied the ceiling. This was how life was supposed to feel, I thought, the repressions of Cord and the cold men a tragic error, life's destruction masquerading as its protection.

"'In their fear they have instituted great armies of secret police to spy upon the privacy of the pacific.'"

"Yes, they have," I said. "Timothy, stop reading. It's becoming just words."

"'In their greed they sponsor the consumption of deadly tars and sugars and employ cruel and unusual punishment of the possession of life-giving alkaloids and acids.'"

I laughed. "What's wrong with sugar? It's so sweet. So sweet. So sweet." I kept repeating the words, my thoughts spinning outward like a radio program I had no interest in listening to.

"'They hate beauty. They hate sex. They hate life.'"

"The caterpillar cannot understand the butterfly!"

At my own brief declaration of deep truth, Tim put down the paper, and his serious face shifted to a large grin.

"How beautiful everything is," I said, and he agreed.

"Reality is just social fabrication," he said. "You could

be anybody or anything. You could be me and I could
be you."

I pulled off my capri pants and blouse, untied his tie,
and wrapped it around his head, unbuttoned his shirt and
flung it across the room. Then I turned on the clock radio
and the loco-motion began.

AUGUST 28

He has a radiance that seems independent of his body.
When you have sex with Jack, you're making love to his
radiance as much as you are to his body. Jack took off
his brace and tried doing it from on top. I had my hands
on his butt, which has absolutely no hair on it, and he
came quickly, turning over and then dozing off. I didn't
want to leave—it was only nine o'clock—so I started
reading Aldous Huxley's *The Doors of Perception* while
Jack snored lightly. Then he opened his eyes. He has
uncanny control over his sleep and waking. He asked
what I was reading. I showed him the cover. I told him
Huxley had written it after taking mescaline in West
Hollywood in 1953. He had gazed at the mystery that no
words can encapsulate and proceeded to put it into words.
Jack smiled indulgently, a smile only half the wattage
of the great gleaming of teeth the world has come to
know. It was a smile that seemed to say he was just an
Irish politician who had married upward, charged with
the incomprehensible task of protecting civilization from
nuclear annihilation, and in the name of fondling my
rosy white tits, both of which he has grown rather fond

of, he would indulge a bit of female voodoo, but not too
much.

He started dressing and suddenly seemed so
vulnerable, not at all superhuman. I wondered if I was
out of my mind, trying to extend him any further than
he already was. He bore the weight of the earth on his
shoulders, a man already sick and weakened, and here
comes this psychedelic cheerleader into the Lincoln
Bedroom, pulling off her dress, fucking him, and then
reading excerpts from *The Doors of Perception*. He was
tying his shoes—I don't know where he intended to go
after I left, but I do know him well enough to know that
wherever he is, he thinks he should be someplace else,
and I decided to read to him. I read the passage that
gave the book its title, a quotation from William Blake:
"If the doors of perception were cleansed everything
would appear to man as it is, infinite. For man has closed
himself up till he sees all things thro' narrow chinks of
his cavern."

It dawned on me that I was here in the White House,
the nerve center of the free world, and that fucking
the president was the least subversive of my acts. I
was actually proposing neurological treason at the
heart of power. As Tim Leary said, "The managers of
consciousness, from the Vatican to Harvard, have been in
this business for a long time and they're not about to give
up their monopoly."

Kenny O'Donnell knocked abruptly, and I was
suddenly out the door.

SEPTEMBER 4

My bluebirds were up early this morning, mama bird
passing on seeds and insects to her babies in the big tree
that leans toward the Potomac. Tony and I were walking
the towpath. Sisters together again. No husbands, no
spies, no luminaries, no drunks, no politicians, just sisters
walking. The ancient canal created a private pathway for
us, we were teenagers once again at Grey Towers, feeding
our horses and gathering wildflowers for the dinner table.

We haven't spent much time together of late. Tony's in
her pottery studio every day. I am painting and preparing
for a show in May. She and Ben live at the center of the
Georgetown social swirl—they are features at dinners
and parties at least four nights a week. The nights she's
not with Ben, he's in the newsroom at the *Post*, and
she's at her Gurdjieff meetings. Gurdjieff meetings are
supposed to be secret, esoteric knowledge handed down
orally by adepts through the ages, but she has told me
about them. Even spirituality is a secret in this town.

Yes, she has told me of Carlyle Le Marque, her teacher.
She spoke about me to Carlyle, and he said I could come
to a meeting. But I'm not comfortable with "teachers,"
gurus, masters, leaders, sages, enlightened nincompoops.
I'm a divorced woman. I'll restate that: I'm a free woman.
Who needs another man telling me what to do, even if
he was Gurdjieff's personal student in Paris, even if he
received "a direct transmission" of The Work from the
master himself? That's what Tony calls it. The Work.

I once asked Tim Leary if he had ever heard of

Gurdjieff. "A realized being," Tim had called him. "A marvelous rogue from the Secret Brotherhoods of Central Asia." That's all I know about Gurdjieff.

So I asked Tony how The Work was going, and she said she wasn't supposed to talk about it.

"You're getting boring," I said.

"Boring is good. Carlyle says we're nothing, our self as we conceive it really doesn't even exist, and as soon as we realize that, there's a possibility."

"Of what?"

"Of being something. Of breaking through our mechanical nature."

"How?"

"By just being present."

"OK, I'm present now. I'm walking a dirt path next to the canal, I'm watching filthy water flow, and I'm just being present. No thoughts. Is that The Work?"

"Just be present, Mary. Someone once asked Carlyle what his greatest moment was, and he said right now."

We walked silently. The topic held no more interest for me, nor apparently for Tony. Then she said: "You know, Mary, I think the president likes me."

"Really?"

"I don't want to cause any trouble—I'm trying to stay present and observe myself, because I love attention, and I don't want Ben to get jealous. But whenever the four of us are together, Ben sits with Jackie, and Jack always sits next to me with this smile—he looks at me with this big grin, as if I were his long-lost love or something. Jackie once said Jack considers me the perfect woman. How weird is that?"

I got that familiar pang again, that diabolical demon living in the solar plexus called jealousy. Abandonment. Some longing programmed into my nervous system long ago, and now the button was pressed. We are all jukeboxes filled with sad records. An ironic turn of events, jealousy and nausea erupting just seconds after a discussion of presence and freedom. Can I just be present and observe my feelings, detached? As Tim once told me, "You already know the truth about your nervous system and the worthlessness of jealousy. So when's it going to kick in?"

Timothy and Alan Watts and Carlyle whatever-his-name-is, they all say the same thing. The affairs of another person, be it Jack, Jackie, Tony, or any other sentient being on the planet, are really none of my business. And the universe tests us incessantly.

But behind the pang of jealousy, I run headlong into the wall called my relationship with Jack. It is a wall of lies that separates me from my sister, even if my silence is vital to the health of the country. Which suddenly puts me in the same league as Cord and James Jesus Angleton. I fuck, they kill, but we're all lying for national security.

Is it legitimate to wall off one fact, I wondered, but be open about everything else? Just one lie, and then flow in truthfulness in every direction around it?

We turned to head back, in unison—I'm not sure who initiated the action. Sisters in telepathy.

"Come to a meeting," Tony finally said. "Carlyle said

I could bring you. It's really a privilege. I want to share
The Work with you."

"I don't know, Tony. I'm on another path. I'm
fascinated with psychedelics and the promise they hold
for all mankind, not just working on my little self. It feels
so small. So stifling."

"Carlyle says when you work on yourself, you are
working on the world."

"Yes, Carlyle and his secret Work. I'm sick of secrets,
Tony."

SEPTEMBER 16

Today I launched Chantilly Lace, gathering the wives of
Georgetown for our great psychedelic mission. Lorraine
Cooper. Evangeline Bruce. Polly Wisner. Katharine
Graham. Pamela Harriman. Georgette LeBlanc. Anne
Truitt. A small sea of femininitude sipping afternoon
cocktails in Polly's living room. I told them we were
gathered for a unique purpose. To end the Cold War.

"Is that all, Mary?" asked Vangie Bruce. "And for that
I gave up tennis?"

Lady of the tip-top remark, long and elegant, Vangie is
the anti-Mary, so utterly at home with sheer existence is
she. I do not occur to myself as so jaunty, so intrinsically
cheerful, I who approach life as a stranger sometimes, in
vital need of instruction. I can layer colors onto canvas,
I am confident of that—I can sculpt words on paper,
I can think fiercely when the pilot light ignites in my
brain, but I wasn't built to glide through life with the

thoroughbred ease of Evangeline Bruce. To gaze into
the face of stupidity and smile. To offer more drinks as
talented people bow before mediocre ones, as intelligent
women shut their mouths while ignorant men carry
on. I cannot, and thus I find myself fascinated with
Evangeline Bruce. Perhaps she is the key to Chantilly
Lace, the secret agent who could mobilize the women
of Georgetown, endowed with a sleight of hand I don't
possess, or is it a sleight of estrogen? She grew up in
embassies. She frolicked through girlhood with curtsies
and grown-up conversations in parlors of import, at
parties of import. Hostessing is like her second skin. Can
I yoke it to acid instead of bourbon?

I told my friends that the only hope for the world
is intelligent women, and they murmured approval. I
said we are on the brink of ending life itself. How odd
it sounded, apocalyptic utterances spoken amid Polly
Wisner's pewter and candlesticks, her formal draperies,
her walls of colonial portraits, unknown people long dead.
I suddenly loathed the colonial frippery of Georgetown—
the corny nostalgia that masks the brink of nuclear
annihilation we all inhabit, undiscussed, just as we all
inhabit lives that will end, undiscussed.

But I spoke. All that I had thought about—all that had
been instilled in me by a radical family pontificating
endlessly on peace and justice, on the stench of lies and
corruption in politics that it was our job to erase, all
the genes of Pinchots past—came pouring forth like a
desperate sales pitch for the preservation of civilization.

Humanity must decide every day that it wants to live, I
said. Where danger is, there also grows the saving power.
The saving power is LSD, I said, it is the only hope we
have of stopping the men we sleep with from plunging us
into nightmare. LSD holds out a glimpse into the unity of
life that we all are blind to, consumed and buried as we
are, playing survival games.

There was silence. Pamela Harriman spoke first.
"Dear, I have a hard enough time at bridge."

The women tittered, and I realized my mistake.
Pamela Harriman could never be part of the plan. She is
devolution itself dressed in pearls.

"Isn't this all a bit artificial, taking this drug?" asked
Lorraine Cooper. "Like I solved the secret of the universe
last night, but this morning I forgot what it was!"

The cackling built, and I realized how easily
conversations get away. I was a strangely serious woman,
staking the next stage of human evolution on a group
of women committed to little more than sipping gin
and tonics and planning dinners. But Pinchots press on.
Except that when resisted, something in me shuts down
even as my mouth continues, so my explanations of LSD
felt dry even to me.

"It's about paradigms. A paradigm is the structure
we think in. Paradigms are unconscious, so it doesn't
matter what thoughts we think, because those thoughts
are shaped and filtered through our paradigm. Taking
LSD shifts our paradigm so we can think freshly, newly,
without restraint."

Lorraine Cooper: "Mary, I can't comment on his paradigms, but Sherman is a senator, and you're asking me to turn him loco. I'm in." A moment of relief.

Georgette LeBlanc: "I've been seeing Dr. Winthrop Rubenstein. You should give him a try. He's a brilliant man."

I told her therapy is fine, but the psychedelic journey is of a different order of magnitude. Dr. Leary himself is a distinguished clinical psychologist who has concluded that talking in a doctor's office is simply no match for the power of our emotional fixations. Both talking and understanding are just a spit in the ocean. We're driven by imprints from childhood, and it takes a chemical stimulus to loosen those neurological bonds.

Pamela Harriman: "Well, you've become quite the little professor, Mary. Can you imagine my Averell on some crazy drug, prancing around and doing the Twist with a lampshade on his head?"

Polly Wisner: "You know Frank hasn't been well . . . The doctors gave him some electric shock treatments. This is said in complete confidence, you all understand. His brain couldn't take another jolt like this."

Anne Truitt: "Jim will love it."

Katharine Graham: "Phil will never agree to something so mentally drastic, and he's already challenged. He would never trust me to give him something so dangerous."

I told them Dr. Leary had assured me that moderate doses of LSD were safe when taken in a tranquil, supportive environment. "Leary also said LSD is a psychedelic drug that occasionally causes psychotic behavior in people who have *not* taken it," I told them, trying to lighten the mood. But no one laughed.

"We're simply not as free and far-out as you are, Mary" was Vangie's unexpected reaction. I said I was just another wife, or ex-wife, just like them. "Ex marks the spot!" she shouted, and everyone roared. Katharine Graham, not surprisingly, uttered the final opinion. "Mary, you're a free woman, and we're not. It's as simple as that. You paint, you do men, you blast your brains out with drugs, you have no fear . . ."

We were not just women with fine houses and difficult husbands, I said. The ladies gathered here for this mission just might hold the future of the planet in their hands. With fingers I have always considered too chubby I held up the pills, tiny tablets of history emerging from a dimension far beyond the band of consciousness we all inhabit. Fabricated in some lab, they emitted a presence, like the stones of Stonehenge. Then I passed them around. Pamela walked away. The others each took one.

Lorraine Cooper deposited hers in a small silver pillbox. "I hope I don't mix it up with the Libriums."

SEPTEMBER 22

Roxanne Arcturis says we will begin to unveil the outlines of the future of the Aquarian Age in 1963. "We are currently preparing for the Wave X vortex emanating from Center. The new transmissions will travel on reverberations of light and sound codes." She says this

is especially true of the energies and teachings of the
Divine Feminine.

SEPTEMBER 28

James Angleton, I realize, found the perfect disciple in
Cord Meyer. And after our divorce, while wandering in
the wilderness of dead ideals, Cord found Jesus in James
Jesus Angleton. He believed this Jesus would save him,
but this Jesus was not in the saving business. This Jesus
pulled Cord into deep realms of fear, a frigid plunge
into the swamps of what Tim Leary calls fear-based,
ego-based biochemical secretions. There isn't much
recognizable of the sweet young man I once married who
fought so ardently for the idea of world government.

Do I miss him? I don't miss him. But I miss what
he meant. Maybe that is what we miss when we miss
people—we don't miss their bodies so much as their
meanings, the promise of a future now lying dead in the
past. It is the meanings that linger and cause pain deep
in my heart, deep at night.

I leave Cord to James Jesus and the cigarettes and
move on to a destiny bequeathed me by my father. I will
bring world peace.

And I don't want anyone to remember I had anything
to do with it.

OCTOBER 3

Many poets obsess over death, but how many actually
include it in their job description? James Angleton, in

the strange asymmetry of his nature, is actually quite a
poetic man. He once penned a short book about the wet
religion to which he serves as high priest: fly fishing.
I have not read it, but I have perused the opening
line: "As long as rivers run and trout glide and paths
lead up mountains and down hills and sunlight filters
through leaves, nothing descends so gently on water as
the lightness of a well-cast fly." So perhaps their new
godfather will take my boys fly fishing. I wish them to
enjoy "the lightness of a well-cast fly."

OCTOBER 10

The stillness after the act. He spent, she spent. The
moment when a man's drive to conquer worlds and
launch wars is momentarily released, and limbs lie
useless under sheets. Jack does not permit himself long to
recover. His *petite mort* is less *mort* than with most men,
so frighteningly inert they become after the act. He is up
and off. And my small death grows as I get up and dress,
get up and leave, go home alone.

OCTOBER 12

Autumn comes, though it is southern autumn here. No
chill as in northern air, when the jackets come out in
October and all living things sense the coming of freeze.
It is cold in my studio now in the morning, and I asked
Ben Bradlee to get me a small electric heater. I don't
want my paint to freeze on the canvas. He looked at me
skeptically. "Don't set fire to my goddam garage, now," he

growled. He's a charmer. Tony is so lucky to have found a man of such strength. She found a full-time newsman, and I found a part-time president.

OCTOBER 15

Fear grips the country. As the year of 1962 sprawls to its close, the dream of peace is slipping away, and we are glued to television sets. A U-2 spy plane has discovered missile sites in Cuba.

Jack confronted Khrushchev over the sites, threatening grave consequences if Soviet missiles ever find their way to Cuba. The generals howl that anything less than war is appeasement. That word *appeasement* tortures Jack because of his father Joe's shameful opposition to the war against Hitler. Strange that both Jack and I are children of Hitler appeasers. Even Dean Acheson is urging Jack to commence bombing immediately. The world teeters on a nuclear brink, and of course I can't get through to Jack. The accoutrements of a woman were all that gained me entrance to the White House in the first place, and female anatomy carries no weight in a missile crisis.

I try to imagine the strain engulfing Jack, but I can't. He has never dealt with a crisis of this magnitude; perhaps no human has. Kenny O'Donnell has urged me to wait. This is the crisis of his administration, and Jack can't be distracted. I need to be patient.

I asked Kenny how Jack was doing, and he said he was doing fine. "How is he really doing?" I asked then. Kenny whispered that the doctors have elevated Jack's medicine to an extraordinary degree. I asked him what they were giving him, and he said, "Mary, I can't tell you that," and I said, "Like what?" He said, "I'm not a doctor," and I repeated: "Like what?"

Kenny said Jack's taking steroids for his Addison's disease.

"Which is?"

"I don't know. Steroids are some kind of hormones. And they've beefed up the painkillers for his back."

"Is that it?"

"I think he's taking drugs for his colitis, and antibiotics for his urinary tract. Then he's got allergies. I've seen Dr. Jacobson giving him pep pills."

"Jacobson is Dr. Feelgood?"

"Yes. Jack's got fatigue and these black moods, and Jacobson's pep pills counteract them. He says that when he takes them, he doesn't need the crutches for his back. And then he has stuff for his sleep."

"Kenny, I'm worried sick about Cuba and the missiles and how Jack will get us all out of this. But I also don't know how Jack's body can take all those drugs and pills and medicines. Isn't he scared?"

"Mary, you know the boss. He doesn't do scared. When they give him another shot, he says, 'I don't care if it's horse piss. It works.'"

OCTOBER 17

My heart is in free fall. I worry for my boys, growing up in the woods far, far from Cuba and missile silos.

Far, far from a mother swerving daily off the beaten path but carrying ridiculous love for them through each adventure.

I worry for Jack, sick and smiling, waking up daily with the weight of human existence next to his two poached eggs. I worry for my sisters, the one sister of blood and the many not of blood, all gathered together last night at the Bradlees' in a solemn ceremony of concern. We are a species poised to annihilate itself over a tiny island off Florida. I turned for solace to Arthur Schlesinger because he is the bow-tied professor of Jack's entourage, and in this crisis one longs for a bow-tied professor.

He pulled a pipe from his wet mouth. Pipes play havoc with lips. He whispered in a tone of chilling secrecy that Jack is now totally isolated from the Pentagon and the generals. They see the missile confrontation as the final opportunity to eliminate Castro. They blame the president for this disaster. If he hadn't pulled the air support at the Bay of Pigs, if he'd proceeded with Operation Northwoods, there would have been a full invasion of Cuba, and we wouldn't be in this situation. The military men pulled off regime change in Iran in 1953. They did it again in Guatemala in 1954. What was the big deal about Cuba? Just go in. But this isn't Guatemala. A war with Cuba would escalate fatally. Bobby is running back-channel conversations with the Russians. He's at the center of all the negotiations; he hasn't slept for days.

I asked Arthur, How does it all end?

Bobby might pull it off, he said, if he could get Khrushchev to realize how little power Jack really has. How little he actually controls the military. How the generals might even seize power in a coup. Then he might back down and withdraw the missiles.

I wonder if I will ever speak to Jack again. Or if there will even be a world left for us to speak in. Billions of people waking up every day in small lives, pushing their hearts against small problems, and this bizarre few, so few, determining their fate, deciding the very existence of a planet spinning in space.

OCTOBER 18

Ben and Tony's living room was a waiting room in hell. We waited to hear Khrushchev's response to Jack's demand. War or peace? Sanity or psychopathy on a global scale? We waited to see if the world would continue. Ben sat heavily in his easy chair, still in his Woodward & Lothrop shirt, loosened tie, and striped suspenders. Tony was putting out trays of food, ever the dutiful woman. Joe Alsop puffed away on an ivory cigarette holder and stared straight into the room, not speaking, as if he were a secret conspirator who already knew the end of the story and was waiting for everyone else to catch up.

The phone rang, a jarring explosion of sound that penetrated our chests. I jumped an inch off the couch. What agent of destiny could be on the line? Tony picked it up, and said it was for me. When I put the strange receiver to my ear, Kenny O'Donnell was on the line.

He said ExComm had been meeting all night. ExComm was the Executive Committee of the National Security Council, handpicked by Jack to navigate the missile crisis: a dozen or so figures, including Bobby, Lyndon, Bundy, and McNamara. "Jack asked if he could see you for a few minutes. Can you come to the White House?"

I stood there, stunned, certain I could never reveal where I was going. I mumbled to all assembled that I had to handle an issue with my son.

"Is he all right?" Tony asked, so concerned, and I was struck by how utterly sweet my sister was, and how sadly removed we were from each other. We had so many secrets, though we were sisters and traveled in the same circles, though I painted every day in her garage. I felt a twinge of sadness at how life had changed us, but it dissolved when I remembered why it was I was standing up and leaving. I said it would be fine. How could I tell the journalists of Washington that I was heading for the White House?

Kenny ushered me into the small room adjoining the Oval Office. I have made out with Jack in that room—he loves that crazy sense of panic, forbidden intrigue, kissing my neck and rubbing my breasts while heads of state wait patiently on the other side of the door. I waited. This is what people do in crises and in childbirth, I thought as I stood there: they wait.

Eventually Jack came in. I had never seen him so weary, so exhausted. I hugged him, and we just stood there together a moment, hugging. Maybe that was all he wanted—a mother's love that never came from his mother, nor from an impenetrable wife, nor from streams of girls offering themselves up to a handsome president. Unconditional love, I thought, and I just held him.

"LeMay said it's appeasement," he whispered, and I nodded. "But we're going to blockade Cuba." I nodded again, not saying a word. "We're not going to invade, we're not going to bomb, we're not going to take out the missiles with air power, but we're also not going to ignore it. We're going to blockade. Sorensen suggested calling it a quarantine, and I like that. A strike would lead to nuclear retaliation, but doing nothing would put Berlin and the rest of Latin America at risk. This is a middle ground. A way through the fucking chaos back in that war room. A blockade gives us flexibility and gives Khrushchev wiggle room to back down and save face. We're going to scrap the missiles near Turkey, but that's going to remain a secret for now."

"That's a good plan," I whispered. "You've done a masterful job. I think it will work. No one will get killed. You're steering a course through the madness."

"I've got to go now, Mary," he said.

"I know."

"I'll see you soon."

"Yes."

NOVEMBER 1

When it ended, Jack was different. The blockade he mounted in defiance of the red-faced generals, his refusal to press the button of invasion on a tropical island, had succeeded. The missiles on their way to Cuba had turned around, headed back to the scrap heaps of the Soviet Union. As I walked the strangely silent streets of Georgetown, it felt as if a newer, quieter world had been born.

Jack, who had contemplated the extinction of mankind, didn't come back unchanged. He had envisioned nuclear fire broiling the planet, sweeping human existence into oblivion with no record that any of us had existed. Caroline and John John, vanished. Everybody's children erased because two middle-aged men faced off on a chessboard called the earth and, addled with testosterone and urged on by maniacs, refused to back down. They could have attempted to win a war that couldn't be won. But wisdom had prevailed, and survival had been achieved. Eased along, of course, by the secret agreement to dismantle Jupiter missiles in Turkey.

Jack emerged from the Cuban missile crisis with the aura of an invincible hero. Our work together would continue. I smiled at this, knowing how gentle he actually was; a boy who loved to read, shoved by his dad into being tough, urged on by Bobby, pounded by the generals, challenged on a global stage by Fidel Castro. It could have ended differently.

Over champagne at a White House dinner, I told Jack that there was simply no one else with the power, wisdom, and independence to end the Cold War.

Normally he recoils from such grandiose terms, and Pinchots speak in grandiose terms. But as I spoke those words last night at a party in honor of Jackie's sister, Princess Lee Radziwill, and her husband with the phony Polish title, Prince Stanislaw Radziwill, Jack just grinned and blew smoke from his cigar at me. "It's a Cuban," he said, in honor of all that we had come through. I blew some Marlboro back at him. Then, when no one was looking, we blew kisses at each other. Two people with rotten lungs blowing kisses at each other.

NOVEMBER 6
A cacophony of female tongues are unleashed by alcohol, secrets splattered over Persian carpets and rich herringbone floors. Gossip speaks in shrieks rather than whispers. Chantilly Lace has resumed, in the bedlam of Lorraine Cooper's Monday-afternoon women's salon.

I find myself becoming ever more a listener as time goes on. It is not so much an increased fascination with the wisdom and anecdotes of others as it is the sense that small talk in some ways makes you smaller—that when you waste words, you waste other parts of yourself, as well.

Sometimes I spend an entire day in the studio, talking to no one but Evangeline, my foolish cat, named for Vangie Bruce. Solitary Mary. There has always been this aspect to my nature. Even at Vassar, when other girls had departed for parts and boys unknown, I sometimes spent entire weekends at school by myself. I loved sitting alone in the dining hall, reading and eating the baked beans that Fritz cooked up especially for me.

But in the name of world peace and the cause of Chantilly Lace, I leaped into Lorraine's clacking of birds on Monday, happy to see my friends: Lorraine, Georgette, Vangie, Bebe, and Kay, all recovered from their weekend dinners and parties, all affirming the beautiful fall day with fresh new clothes, all happy to see me.

Lorraine studied me when I arrived, wrinkling up her forehead. She is ever theatrical, speaking as if to reach the last rows of some imagined theater. "Oh, Mary! Pedal pushers?" She looked down at my pants, I looked down at my pants, and then I shrugged. I hadn't realized what I was wearing; I had just come from painting.

"You can take the girl out of Pennsylvania, but you can't take Pennsylvania out of the girl," I said.

"No, but you can pull down her pants!"

I think Lorraine might be the funniest woman I know. Women aren't supposed to be funny, as a species; no one encourages us to evoke laughter, nor does it seem that evolution has selected us for wit. We have other assets that assist in the propagation of the species, and I fear I am the least funny woman I know. I have always preferred leaping headlong into adventures, and telling jokes implies a stepping back from experience.

"Leave Mary alone. She's an artiste," said Bebe Highsmith.

"No, take off her pants," said Kay Graham. "Let's finally see what it is these men are all making such a fuss over."

I told them they were making me blush, though they weren't making me blush. I was on a mission. I asked Lorraine how our LSD project went with her husband, John Sherman Cooper. "I practically had to shove the fucking pill down his throat," she said. "He kept saying he's a United States senator, and it would be unseemly. . . . I'd interrupt him and say, 'Shut up, John, you're just a hick from Kentucky, and Mommy is giving you your medicine.'"

I was actually laughing out loud. Pamela Harriman came in from the front room to inquire about the hilarity. I had to wait until we were in the garden for Lorraine to finish the psychedelic report. "Mission accomplished. I think he liked it. He has been subdued lately, meditative. He has been speaking of civil rights more often, which is astonishing for someone from Kentucky."

That was marvelous news for the planet, I said.

NOVEMBER 9
I began a new painting this morning. A circle of four muted colors against a black background. The black will suck in light from the colors, further muting them. Maybe it's indicative of a somber mood I've been in of late. But I have been inspired to keep exploring color by the artist Kenneth Noland. I met him at Bebe Highsmith's. He is a very attractive man, but a bit

arrogant. I told him I had read Clement Greenberg's essay on him in the *Journal of American Art*, and he didn't seem to care. I asked how it felt to be called the inventor of a new form of abstraction. He just shrugged and looked at me without expression. I assumed he was a genius of some kind, and geniuses sometimes have no personalities, their everyday self extinguished to make way for the new reality inhabiting them. Finally, I said I didn't understand much of the essay. What on earth did Greenberg mean, the destiny of painting was to approach pure self-referentiality?

Kenneth looked at me quizzically. "Who cares what it means? The essay did its job."

I was stunned, then laughed, then yelled: "Bebe, what's self-referentiality?"

She crunched her face. "Have another drink, Mary," she said. "You must not be feeling well."

NOVEMBER 16

Cord reappeared in my life. He arrived at the Wisners' on Saturday night with Ibbie Kenna on his arm. Ibbie is a big, simple girl of the South with a statuesque behind and the continual scent of lavender. I assume she and Cord are dating, though my ex-husband has grown so difficult, so lasciviously vulgar in his drink, so obstreperous in his political pronouncements, that I question his viability as a date, let alone a mate. I question the patience with such behavior of my fellow Georgetown divorcées, of even Ibbie Kenna, even if my CIA ex-husband may appear to the naive as some version of James Bond, albeit ridiculously flawed.

Polly Wisner is careful not to invite Cord and me to the house at the same time, as she is a hostess supreme. But I have repeatedly told her that Cord is in the past, and the past doesn't concern me. She shakes her head. "Only Mary," she says. But she knows that Cord and her husband Frank are masterminds of Operation Mockingbird. Together, they have planted the Company's hooks into journalists and organizations everywhere.

But Saturday was an exception. Saturday we coincided. Saturday we ended up in the same place at the same time, two birds standing on the same branch with drinks in our hands. I turned to leave, but he cornered me. He was not subtle in communicating that he had something to tell me; evolution has never selected men for subtlety. Secrets, yes, but not subtlety. I watched Ibbie Kenna peel off and chat up Arthur Schlesinger, who gazed way up at her approvingly. He seems fascinated by soaring women. Cord approached with the pomposity that was the air I breathed for so long, now gone like a long-absent odor from my life. He proclaimed that I have the CIA to thank for abstract art.

He rarely acknowledged that I was a painter when we were married, and has never acknowledged it since. But my days of being bullied were over.

"Well, please be kind enough to thank your comrades for their generosity," I said, invoking as much Evangeline

Bruce into my conversation as I had the capacity to muster.

"The CIA was, in fact, the world's biggest booster of Abstract Expressionism."

"Boosters of painting! And here I thought you were too busy lying and killing people!"

Cord has no ear for sarcasm. He so loves to go on, he must certainly love to go on Ibbie Kenna. But I cannot imagine what on earth he goes on about with her.

"Abstract art was our beachhead in the global war of culture."

Cord loves such phrases. *The global war of culture.*

"When abstract art began—you know, that waste of paint you and your friends indulge in with your childish doodlings—"

"Cord, I have to go speak to Lorraine. I just remembered we have a squash game to arrange."

"Hold on, hold on," he said so confidently. "Just tell me which official institution was in the perfect position to celebrate the beatniks, bums, drunks, and Communists in your New York School of Abstract Expressionism?"

"It's not my school. I work with the Washington Color School. You should come see our work sometime."

"Yes, that's right, it was all brought to you by the Company: lock, stock, and barrel. By the CIA. And your amigos Jackson Pollock and Mark Rothko and Willem de Kooning never knew a thing about it!"

He grabbed another drink from the server's tray and gulped it down, like kerosene poured onto a roaring fire. "We just promoted it all over the world. Through the Congress for Cultural Freedom, through magazines, through writers, intellectuals, historians, and artists themselves, all bought and paid for by the CIA."

The idea that this was a source of pride for him baffled me.

"And who was your greatest champion in the war to change art?" he demanded. "Who is the heavyweight champion of abstraction of the world?"

I was growing tired.

"Nelson Rockefeller. Yes, Abstract Expressionism is a Rockefeller family art form. He called it 'free enterprise painting.' He got his mummy's museum behind it: the Museum of Modern Art in New York. All the founders—Paley, Whitney, Braden—they were all CIA. So your little art form, worthy of kindergarten children and New York alcoholics, suddenly becomes the international style of art. The signature art form of global capitalism, from Shanghai to San Francisco. And none of the artists ever knew!"

He paused, pleased with himself. He had given it to Mary once again, slipped it in when she least expected it, had co-opted and invalidated her art form, an art that lets such infinity in, that I consider it freedom on canvas. He had drawn a box around contemporary art to contain it, and me with it.

"Well, you are an artist, Cord. As long as you precede it with the word *bullshit*."

I was unsprung. Restraints of deference to a man,

deference to a husband, deference to an ex-husband, the dictates of gentility, the insidious mandate of polite society to be polite, they were gone. I am unprotected, but I am free. Cord may try to infiltrate me as he has infiltrated the culture, but I have entered a life where he has no jurisdiction.

He took a long puff on his Lucky Strike, and I watched again as the vapors disappeared into his glass eye.

"So the next time you and your boyfriend Kenneth Noland paint your little circles on canvas, you can thank the CIA."

How does he know about Kenneth?

"I'll remember to. If we can ever stop fucking."

NOVEMBER 19

In bed, I told Jack I was glad to hear that Bobby had resigned from the Metropolitan Club when they refused to allow in a black man. He asked me to leave it alone, please.

"A century after slavery, they're still keeping black men out of clubs? It's sick."

He asked me to leave it. He began rubbing my breast. Stop distracting me, turning me weak when I have a serious point to make. Why hasn't Adlai Stevenson resigned from the club? Or Dean Acheson? Or Mac Bundy? Jack says he can't speak for other men. Jack says the arc of the moral universe is long, but it bends toward justice. Then he asks me to bend toward justice and nudges the back of my neck. I pull his hand away. But we lie in bed, hugging. While I have him.

NOVEMBER 20

I know what I sound like. I sound like Amos Pinchot, my
irate and irascible father. His raving nature reappears
in my cells, boiling before the world. He ranted against
war, even the war to stop Hitler. He ranted against
monopolies and what he called the aggregates of
business, assembled for the institutionalized robbery
of common people. He ranted against denial of women
of the right to vote. He was right. In each case, he was
right, ranting for the righteous cause. But in the end,
he got boring. Rants are boring. They leave no room for
anybody else. Amos got boring, and when you get boring,
you lose friends. Daddy had few when it was over. He
was a pain in the ass. And I have become a pain in the
ass. In bed with Jack, I suppose, I constitute a royal pain
in the ass. So last night I kissed him and told him I
would go easy on him from now on. "Thank the Lord,
Mary," he said.

NOVEMBER 25

I have never watched television, nor do I allow my
sons to. I grew up riding horses beside waterfalls. I
daydreamed in a castle and wandered naked through the
foliage of Grey Towers. I perfected French, a vigorous
game of tennis, and poetry. I came of age to tales of
workers' revolutions and the struggles of the proletariat,
dinners of candlelight and radical, profound thinkers.
I fail to see the hypnotic charm of flickering dots on a
screen.

But I have seen Jack often enough on television by now
to notice that he is an electronic chameleon. He seems ten
years younger on TV than in the air. It is a new world for
politicians, this TV, and he seems to have mastered it. His
cool smile pours through the electrons and straight into
your heart. Lincoln would not have been so successful
on television, he of a more biblical age. But television
seems to create a separate reality. I can't quite fathom
it, but I feel it. Someday it may become the only reality.
Last night, when I came close to Jack's skin, there was no
television to annihilate the years. The wear on his face,
the swollenness caused by medicine, the droop of his
eyes, they all betrayed a wearying sadness.

Kenny O'Donnell had called. Jack wanted to see
me, and they sent a car to pick me up. He was so tired
when I arrived at the White House, but he brightened
when I kissed him and he had a chance to smell me; a
man wants to smell his woman every day. I think he
may be smitten with me—that was the word Virginia
Goodpastor used to use after every date at Vassar. But he
seemed to have aged, even from just a week before, and
he spoke from the bottom of a deep sea of concern.

"Two hundred million people would be killed in a
confrontation with Russia," he said.

I watched him silently and nodded. Sometimes I am
simply a clearing for what he has to say.

"Two hundred million men, women, and children,
with millions more dying from radioactive fallout.
Sometimes I feel alone here, Mary."

NOVEMBER 30

I met Edie Sedgwick at Timothy Leary's office. She
is my cousin on the Minturn side, and a sprite with
dinner-plate eyes. I had flown to Boston to deliver my
psychedelic progress report, my progress with Chantilly
Lace and the wives of Washington, and when I entered
Tim's office on Divinity Avenue, Edie Sedgwick was
there. She is part of a tribe who float in and out of Tim's
orbit these days, sharing a sort of drug haze. It is in fact
quite fashionable now among young people to be passive
and zombielike, and considered square to be bright and
alert.

No wonder Tim's situation with Harvard grows ever
more precarious. He told me there is a dean who considers
him a drug fiend and is determined to cut off his research
funding. "This character wants to throw me out on the
street—lock, stock, and consciousness!" Tim smiled, still
appearing to know something everyone else doesn't.

I whisper that Edie Sedgwick is my cousin, and
that she appears not to have eaten for a while, and he
whispers that she's been institutionalized for anorexia.
He's attempting to cure her with LSD. I said maybe you
could cure her with food, but he didn't seem to hear. I
remember him saying once his hearing was challenged,
a souvenir of the war. He grinned at Edie as she placed
a record on the hi-fi. She said she bought it in London,
where it is all the rage, a band of four young British
boys with long hair singing in harmony. It sounded a bit

childish to me, but Tim was enthralled by it. Is he an open channel to the universe now, or have his faculties of discernment simply been permanently eroded? Edie sang along with the British boys as if in a trance.

She apparently spends a great deal of time in Harvard Square. It's a new trend among kids to don odd outfits and inhabit the street doing nothing whatsoever, a kind of proclamation that all traditional purposes and activities are dead, and they await without impatience what comes next. She says she studies sculpture, and when I ask her what kind, she says, "Kinetic."

Edie is a skinny boy-girl who seems disconnected from gravity. Maybe she is the model for a new kind of human, sprung free from the machinery of personality. I mention the Minturns, Daddy Amos's family by marriage, but she says she is unconcerned with the accidents and fictional construct of family. I know there has been great wealth but also a heavy family destiny laid on her tiny shoulders, and the death gene that claimed the soul of my sister Rosamond seems to circulate in our family. Both of Edie's brothers have committed suicide, and I worry about her. I kiss her in a sudden flare-up of tenderness and because she is family, but she is cold and unresponsive. She says LSD has taught her there is no purpose in identifying with the story that inhabits your body—it is all quite foolish, and soon she will be leaving for New York to become a model. She is a flora and faun of these times, and I wonder what destiny awaits her in Manhattan.

DECEMBER 2

Jack exploded in me. It was a rage inside him, exaggerated
I am convinced by the drugs they're shooting into him.
To Jack's catalog of illness, Kenny says they have added
autoimmune disease, for which they are injecting massive
doses of hydrocortisone and steroids. So I may simply be the
object of pharmaceutically induced passion, but Jack pounds
with a force akin to desperation and is spent very quickly.
Robin Nightingale once whispered to me at a party that sex
with Jack Kennedy was the best twenty seconds of her life.

DECEMBER 8

Vangie Bruce is a woman endowed with such élan and
elegance, Christian Dior personally designed a maternity
dress for her. I stopped in to see her at her brick castle for
a progress report on Chantilly Lace. When I climbed the
tiny flight of exterior stairs and walked through the door
with the half-round window above, it was like entering
a new world. Actually, it was like entering an old world.
She and Ambassador Bruce maintain a punishing
entertainment schedule, in a salon redolent of an ancient
European grandeur.

Vangie's home and her body are permanently
magazine-ready. All traces of this tawdry twentieth
century have been banished from her living room. The
silk taffeta curtains that camouflage her windows are
from England. The tawny-pink walls carry heavy, murky
classical paintings. The house feels more like a dusty
museum than a home. And even as I visited at noon and

she sat reclining on her divan, her commanding head of hair was perfectly styled and she sat in repose in a moss-green dress, her long legs propped in front of her.

"Well, we did it," she said. I hugged her because I knew we had accomplished an important step. "David took the LSD, I hovered around him, and he actually enjoyed it. I had no idea this acid or what you call it was something you could actually enjoy. He falls asleep when he drinks red wine. I thought it was some kind of endurance test that scrambled your brains, and you hope, when it's over, you can still recognize your name. I sat by the phone the entire time, ready to call who knows who, but David just grinned and looked around, bemused.

"He said it made normal life seem rather shabby. I played Mahler's Sixth Symphony the whole time, and he sat in his big fluffy armchair. At one point he said the orchestra was playing inside him, his body was a concert hall, that in fact everything was inside him, or outside him, he didn't really know the difference."

I told Vangie what a great a job she had done, that we were changing the trajectory of the world, turning on one important man at a time. "I'm so glad something turns him on," she said with her big laugh and cloud of cigarette smoke. "We almost did it, if you know what I mean, but he couldn't find it!"

CHRISTMAS DAY 1962
Quentin and Mark are asleep upstairs. The sweaters I knitted sit unopened under the tree. My sons will sneer

when they open the boxes; Mark wants a Meccano robot man, and who knows what Quentin wants, what does a seventeen-year-old want these days? But I don't believe in frivolous presents.

Later we will go to the Bruces' for Christmas open house. For now, I sit with Evangeline on my lap and think about another New Year. How do I bring myself into sharper focus, unblurred by men? I have been blurred by two men, two soldiers who returned from war with pieces missing. Some of the missing pieces were biological, pertaining to functions of anatomy. Others were invisible, pertaining to the delicate capacity to allow life to soak through you and feel it. Neither Cord Meyer nor Jack Kennedy possesses the capacity to be intimate with a woman. My good fortune. And indeed, it is the fortune of most of my friends. Pain closes hearts. War builds armor. And the women of my generation have been trained to accept these limitations as eternal masculine truths. But I have always judged the paralyzed psyches of both my husband and my lover as casualties of war rather than imperatives of evolution.

Cord and Jack were each hailed as the promise of their generation, growing up in the spotlight of attention. They were discussed, they were profiled, they were written about. How odd to live in both their shadows, first one and then the other. When Cord lost his eye in Guam, and his twin brother in Okinawa, and his dreams of world peace in the brutal machinations of a cold war, his youthful promise degenerated, a promise ultimately measurable in cigarettes, alcohol, and espionage.

Jack's fall from a golden youth never seemed as steep, Jack never having felt so deeply, perhaps, in the first place. And it became my destiny to love this man, a man who hated being touched. Whose sexual obsessions had no time or inclination to honor the desires of a woman.

Such were the men of our generation who came home from war. As Lorraine Cooper says, we await the men of the future with open legs.

1963

JANUARY 2

Jackie's in Greece. Kenny O'Donnell called last night, asking me to return to the White House. Climbing into the car taking me to Pennsylvania Avenue, I pictured Jackie navigating the islands of Homer with giant sunglasses and a silk scarf wrapped tightly around her head, a mummy in sunlight. We all have our paradises to bear.

Jack was in the rocking chair when I arrived. It is a beautiful old rocker, but someone sewed what looks like tiny seat cushions onto the armrests. Now it is an odd-looking specimen of furniture. Jack was in a reflective mood, the force field of male electricity that usually sets off sparks in my body absent. Had we moved from the fugitive fields of Eros to the cozy meadows of companionship without first passing through a marriage license?

He lit a cigar and said that little Caroline was madly

in love with a puppy that Khrushchev had sent for her birthday.

"A Bolshevik beagle?" I asked.

"No, I think it's a Dachshund."

Jack has the worst German accent I have ever heard.

He grew solemn. I kissed him on the cheek and lit a cigarette. He said he would not preside over the destruction of humanity, and I nodded, eager to listen. But . . . there is always a *but*. The word seems inherent in the design of human thought. "But despite what you and Sorensen and Stevenson keep telling me, there's no turning back in Berlin. We can't turn back. Berlin is like a shining island in this grim ocean of Communism. We can't turn back the clock and run."

I could hear Joe Alsop's voice speaking through him. Joe is a soft man pushing a hard line, and Jack listens to him. He's just a newspaper columnist and a pigheaded opinionmonger at that, but I think Jack finds him comforting. The patrician speech, the haughty aspect, the pompous WASPness—I think they all remind Jack of the other Joe in his life, Daddy Joe Kennedy.

"I think you're listening to Joe Alsop too much. He's a broken record. Nobody likes Communism, but despite its dangers, once in while you have to shut up."

My friend Joe's bellicose views on Russia are putting us all in danger, but I know the source of his hatred. I know Joe Alsop's dark secret, and he doesn't know I know. I abhor secrets, I believe secrets defy the grace of living, but I inhabit a community of secrets, so many secrets surround me, and one of them pertains to Joe Alsop.

It is just this: the KGB set Joe up one day when he was in Russia. That's it. They secretly photographed him in a hotel room off Red Square, sucking the cock of a handsome young Bolshevik. The photo now hangs over Joe Alsop's head, the blow job of Damocles. Encouraged to come clean by the CIA operatives for whom he works—ah yes, the cascading disclosure of secrets within secrets—he informed both the FBI and the CIA of the incident. It diminished the threat of blackmail, but he knows that one day the photograph will show up in the wrong mailbox. Until then, all Joe can do is hate Russians and employ his newspaper column and the salons of Georgetown to ratchet up the vehemence of the Cold War.

"I think I have to go to Berlin," Jack said.

JANUARY 5

Fucking orchids. I have always loathed orchids. This is my floral peculiarity, even as it is James Angleton's peculiar obsession to cultivate them. I wrote a short story in college where a woman stands horrified at the orchids she beholds in the window of a flower shop. "They look as though they had been grown in damp underground caves by demons. They're evil sickly flowers with no life of their own, living on borrowed strength."

At Vonnie Klaxton's poetry reading last night, as Cicely and I leafed through the program, James turned to me and said: "Did you know that deception is the saving grace of orchids?"

"The saving grace of orchids," I repeated. "Now that's a good title for a poem."

"It's not the fittest orchid that survives. It's the most deceptive." James seemed delighted that the need for deception extends to the flowery realm. "The perpetuation of the orchid species depends on an orchid's ability to misrepresent itself to insects."

"Have you read Vonnie's new collection, *Marginalia from Paris*?" I said, trying to deflect him, but his insane intensity, his paean to the deceit of orchids, continued.

"Orchids have no food to offer insects," he said. "So they have to deceive them into landing on them and carrying their pollen to another orchid in the tribe. Don't you love that?"

"Enough about orchids, James," said Cicely. "Vonnie's about to read."

But he continued. "To accomplish their deception, orchids use their color, their shape, and their odor to attract insects to their pollen." He looked at me intimately through his owlish spectacles. "Orchids play on the sexual instincts of insects."

An auspicious beginning to the new year: listening to the CIA head of counterintelligence utter the words "Orchids play on the sexual instincts of insects." But James Jesus Angleton is singular. As Cicely devotes herself to the cultivation and breeding of words in her poetry, James traffics in a twisted netherworld of motives. I realized that besides the fervent pursuit of double agents, his two great loves are fly fishing and orchids. Fly fishing is the art of fooling fish into believing artificial flies are real. Orchids survive only by deceiving insects into carrying their pollen. James is a creature born of immaculate deception.

JANUARY 6

I am leafing through the poems in *Marginalia from Paris*. They are so delicate and subtly observed. I love this one.

As We Vanish

As we vanish
I speak to your eyelids
and tell them I'm glad
they're there,
unwitnessed
and meekly following
some organic plan
of composition.
And yet your eyelids
(as we vanish)
move sometimes
and witness
through historical air
the stones and Parisian statues
also vanishing
but majestically.
I will tell them so
next time I see your eyes.

JANUARY 9

Crisis alters the trajectory of thought. As the Cuban missiles recede into history and the world offers us a new beginning called 1963, I have begun to rethink Cord's turning. I have come to think of idealism not so much as a virtue Cord lost on the way down but as the very cause of his descent.

Idealism is simply a state of mind where the representation becomes more important than the reality. (Have these lectures I conduct regularly in my head grown boring?) Cord always considered women singularly unsuited for abstract thought, his wife especially so, but I recognize that Cord's views on thought say more about his brain than mine. I am an abstract painter who also entertains abstract ideas.

Idealism, then, is a state of mind where life is forced into a straitjacket constructed purely of thought. And reality is sacrificed at the altar of a picture. The picture doesn't in fact exist; it is a figment of the neurons of the brain. In the diabolical brain of my ex-husband, the neurons coagulated into a dark picture entitled *The Communist Menace*, and then they recoagulated into a picture called *The American Way of Life*. Within his mind, the two pictures are engaged in holy war, and in the name of those pictures, Cord would do some bad things. Good people do good things, they say, and bad people do bad things, but when good people do bad things, that takes idealism.

Maybe Timothy Leary knew this back in 1946. Tim

Leary and Cord Meyer actually crossed paths back then, at veterans' meetings in Berkeley where the boys who served in war came home to build a peace. They tried to work together, but Cord fought with everyone. He imposed his cranky opinions mercilessly; he thwarted Tim at every turn. He proved to be an impossible partner. That realization still awaited my discovery many years later in marriage, but back then, in Berkeley, Timothy Leary finally quit. "Cord is an absolute fanatic," he said of the man who would one day become my ex-husband. "A real monster-machine."

The day would come when I would meet Timothy Leary and explore LSD with him, and together we would envision a new future for our planet. I would never tell him who I had been married to.

JANUARY 14

"What does Adlai Stevenson have, anyway?" Jack asks me. He is fascinated by the sex lives of other men. Sometimes I think he is still the boy with scarlet fever, stranded in his bed alone, reading Sir Walter Scott, dreaming of playing outside with his big brother Joe and the other boys.

"This guy is half bald," he complains. "He wears dumpy suits, has this giant paunch, yet women love him. He has a harem."

"Adlai actually cares about women," I tell him. "He actually listens when they speak. He thinks they're intelligent."

"I knew there was something wrong with him," Jack says.

"As a matter of fact," I reply, "I'm on my way to see Adlai right now. All the way with Adlai! That was his slogan, right?"

Jack shifts focus effortlessly and instantaneously, and Cuba far outweighs Adlai Stevenson's paunch in his preoccupations. "I'm going through back channels to Castro," he says quietly. He is entrusting me with secrets, and I am honoring the trust. "Bill Attwood is in Havana talking to him now. If this got out, we'd be barbecued."

I tell him my peace-crusading daddy always said that as long as you're talking, you're not shooting. But I can't help remembering a dance at Choate so long ago, when Bill Atwood was my date and Jack an interloper, a lecherous snot who kept cutting in on us. Now Bill is in secret negotiations with Fidel Castro, and Jack is lying next to me in a White House bed. How frivolously time juggles us all.

JANUARY 16

Roxanne Arcturis says the gates of ether are opening, and women will have an intimate relationship with the Divine Feminine. "This intimacy creates escalating awareness in the realms of love, beauty, and relationship," she says. I have known skirt chasers, lotharios, suave seducers, grabbers, gropers, Don Juans, and feeler-uppers, but I never met a man who would call the feminine divine. Maybe I have looked in all the wrong places. How lovely it would be to experience the Divine Feminine while I still breathed on earth.

JANUARY 21

Jack and I lounged on fur in the yellow Oval Room. It was once Truman's study, till Jackie redecorated it. Now it has a big white couch in the center, engulfed by a luscious blanket of yellow fur. I don't wear fur, but I love lying on it, especially after pulling Jack's shoes off, especially after pushing him down and snuggling with him. I was wondering who else might Jack snuggle with on a blanket of fur. Nobody, I was convinced. Then my mouth ruined the mood. My mouth does many things, and one of them is ruin moods. I mentioned Berlin.

I told him I knew the German city was this great citadel of freedom—I sounded like Joe Alsop orating at the dinner table—and I know Berlin is Jack's gorgeous shop window for capitalism, but it was no excuse for war. War is obsolete in the atomic age.

I could feel Jack stiffen on the fur and pull away. "You can't appease the Russians," he said quietly.

I'm not trying to appease the Russians, I felt like saying, but it would have sounded absurd.

"But I don't think Khrushchev wants to annihilate seventy million people in ten minutes. He has to posture for the hardliners in the Kremlin, just like I have to deal with Curtis LeMay and the loon Lemnitzer. 'Bomb the fucking enemy into submission!' That's all these SOBs know. 'You have nukes, so nuke the bastards!' And these guys sleep very well at night."

I told Jack that presidents have always led their countries to glory through war. It would be his destiny to reverse history and lead his country to glory by avoiding war, by fending off the maniacs in the Pentagon and old fossils in the Senate who liked sending other people's sons to die. Strontium-90 from nuclear testing was already showing up in the bones and teeth of children.

"Mary, I've had McNamara make it clear innumerable times that we would use nuclear weapons only in response to a major attack against the US or its allies. We are not contemplating preventative war." Jack said this as if he were at a press conference, though we still lay looking up at the chandelier and holding hands.

Then he told me his back was bad, and we lay in silence. I love being so comfortable together we don't have to say anything. I wondered if he has these moments with Jackie, and then realized that I keep comparing myself to her, and that these thoughts are automatic. Comparisons arise from fear and weakness, so I took two marijuana cigarettes from my purse and handed one to Jack. We sat up against the back of the couch, and he took a silver lighter from his pocket. I watched the presidential seal on the lighter glow in flame, here in the holy of holies, and I had a sudden fear of fur igniting in the White House and the world holding me responsible for killing the president. He held out the lighter for me, and I inhaled long and deep. It burned my throat, and I coughed.

"I've done cocaine at Peter Lawford's in Santa Monica," he said, "but pot is my special form of fun with you."

"It's for your back."

"You're a bad girl, Mary, Mary."

"Life's either a great adventure or nothing much at all. That's what my daddy used to say."

One joint was quite enough, almost too much. Any more, and I would have felt my brain dissolve. There's that point with pot where the senses are alive one moment, and the next, you are suddenly in anguish. My senses did spring to life, the chatter in my mind stopped, my body felt wrapped in fur from the inside as well as the outside, and Jack seemed far away. I suddenly ached to be filled. I lay back and pulled Jack on top of me, he was shining into my eyes, he was smiling like a little Irish boy on his first date, it was so crazy doing it on a couch in this round room. All these circles. We were in an oval room, and I stared up at a round chandelier, an avalanche of gold and crystal hanging down over our heads, though Jack didn't see it because he saw only my face, and not even that, because his mouth and mine were joined.

JANUARY 24

Of course, I could spend my time knitting sweaters for the boys. I could travel to the playing fields of Massachusetts and cheer lacrosse games. I could immerse myself in painting, slurp bourbon, flirt with men, and call it a day. But something haunts me.

I was a tiny girl at Grey Towers—I don't remember how old I was, it must have been summertime. A man named Bob La Follette was staying at the house, visiting Amos. Later, they told me he had run for president. Later, they told me he was a great man who fought his entire life to end child labor, to preserve civil liberties, to end US imperialism in Latin America. But I don't remember any of those things. All I remember is that Bob La Follette lifted me up that day, hoisted me on his shoulders, and took me out walking to the waterfalls. They were the loudest crashing thing I had ever heard, and I was frightened by the sheer power of water. Then he swung me up in the air in front of him. I felt like I was flying, the cool water was crashing behind me, and Bob La Follette said to me: "Nothing is done. Everything in the world remains to be done. Or done over. Will you remember that?"

I promised him I would remember, even though I hadn't the slightest idea what he was talking about. But I remember. I promised.

The only hope for the world is intelligent women.

JANUARY 30

I was drinking a strawberry milkshake at Packer's and reading *Look* magazine. What is more blissful than a smooth sweet drink and a magazine? Arnie, the soda jerk, puts extra sugar in my shake, which probably goes directly to my hips, if the articles I read are correct, but I am addicted to sugar. Other articles say sugar is good for you, but I believe they are written by the sugar industry. Why are humans the only species who crave what isn't good for them?

Jackie was on the cover of *Look*. The piece was entitled: "The First Lady inspires the new international look." Having been a journalist, I can attest that this is what's called filler in the business, an illusion of news having no more substance than my milkshake. Then Pamela Harriman walked by.

Pamela is an intimidating presence, even if she reached her exalted status climbing a ladder built of men. Who said "Pamela Harriman has become a world expert on rich men's bedroom ceilings"?

"Mary, I think you should leave this drug business alone," she said.

I was taken aback. I told her the world was about to shift on its axis, and we either change with the world or the world will change without us.

"You talk like a beatnik, Mary, which is cute, but I must say you and your CIA ex-husband suffer from the same disease."

"Which is?"

"The belief that there is actually a secret to life. And that it is discoverable. And that in finding it out, we can escape."

"Escape from what?"

"Life. Reality. Mary, you actually think you can rewrite the rules. You think there is an escape route out of here, and there isn't, my dear, there isn't. Utopias and rainbowism are the province of children, drunks, and madmen. Here's the secret, Mary: You just get on with it. That's the secret. You get on with it. You can take drugs, you can meditate, you can levitate, you can go to Tibet, you can go with your sister to her Gurdjieff meetings. But you won't find out why we suffer. And you surely won't find out why we die."

"You have become cynical, Pamela."

"And what precisely does cynical mean, my dear? The insistence on seeing things as they are rather than how they should be? Yes, I learned a long time ago how to please a man. Because that's the only way a woman can get ahead. I wanted wealth, and I wanted power, and those are big ambitions. Am I a startling beauty, dear? Are you enthralled by my formidable wit? I know who I am. I just got on with it. I never stopped. I played the cards I was dealt, if you want to put it vulgarly, Mary."

"I think things can change."

"That's where you are wrong and hopelessly naive. But I won't burst your bubble. That is not my job. Please don't take this as criticism. A woman has to get by any way she can. You have chosen a childish route. When you come down from your LSD, the world will still be the world, and you will have to carry on."

She walked off, and I continued to sip the milkshake, stunned yet aware that criticism is the first reward for those who seek change. All revolutions fail, they say. Except the last one.

FEBRUARY 3

All is synchronicity. At random moments, an underlying
pattern emerges, an apparency of predestination. Why
was my ex-husband led down the path to skullduggery
while I was led to expose it?

I still consider it an omen that Timothy Leary and
Cord Meyer had met each other a long time ago in
Berkeley, California. Omens are a form of magical
thinking, but then isn't all thinking magical?

Each of these two returning veterans had left a sense
on the fields of butchery. Tim had forsaken part of his
hearing. Cord relinquished half of his sight, the promise
of a generation returning home with a glass eye—a lump
of ceramic that never moved within its socket, even as the
waves of thought vibrated in his brain.

Once, after watching cigarette smoke curl into his
ceramic eye and die there, I gave him a copy of the
Platters recording of "Smoke Gets in Your Eyes." Cord
never got the joke; he is among those not constituted to
get jokes. I've always believed humor an indication of
intelligence, humor being the ability to hold a single
thought on two different levels at the same time. But the
humorless overcompensate in other areas and achieve
great heights, unburdened by either ambivalence or
irony. Such was Cord Meyer, driven by the idea of world
government, a dream I shared with him. Sovereignty was
the enemy. I agreed. When you have sovereignty, you will
eventually have war.

But it would not be long before Cord's mission would change, when instead of a marching band for peace he would become a killer in the cause of sovereignty. When James Jesus Angleton would recruit him into the CIA, along with all the other fine young men in Langley committed to World War III. And my worship died there, like the vapors of his cigarette.

And following that, it would not be long before they broke into my house.

FEBRUARY 4

They are speaking the language of objects. They are piercing the invisible walls that are the true walls of a house, my little house on Thirty-Fourth Street, three windows wide. I came home last night, and the African mask from MacDougal Street in Greenwich Village was no longer attached to the wall. It lay on the bookshelf, staring up at the ceiling. My heart pounded. With a simple shift of location, the mask had gone from exotic artifact to bloodcurdling demon. The Harry Belafonte and Ray Charles albums I had left on the floor by the record player were now carefully placed atop each other on the coffee table. My *Circle #3 in Indigo and Green*, the only painting of mine I hang in my own home, was no longer on the wall. It had been removed. It sat on the floor, leaning up against the coffee table.

The cold men have entered my home, besmirching my possessions with a careful dusting of threat, as if to deny that I possess them. Because I know too much? Talk too much? Will never be Cord Meyer's again, ever? Have trespassed on the body and mind of the president?

Have the cold men issued a cease-and-desist order for my life?

Where is the dictionary for the language of objects?

FEBRUARY 8

How odd, suddenly, to dream my death. Who is dreaming? Who is dying?

I am shattered by the break-in, the violation of my home that is a violation of my self, a female self that I will not allow to be silenced. My mind unravels. I tell myself a tale of erasure, a tale of two sons shorn of their mother and my brother-in-law Ben Bradlee left to convey the sad news to my friend Anne Truitt, living all the way over in Japan.

I envision an apartment in Tokyo, on straw mats, in a room divided by shoji screens, where my friend will buckle over in tears. And when she recovers, she will tell Ben there is a diary. There is a book. There are secret thoughts and forbidden adventures scribbled in plain ink in a journal of French *papier de luxe*. I have scribbled this saga with great pain. Who would not avoid the burden of writing if they could?

So Ben will receive news of a diary from Anne (my mind continues to unravel) and place a call to his secret master at the Agency, Mr. James Jesus Angleton. Yes, I add one more secret to the pile, a secret even Anne doesn't know. This sleeves-rolled-up journalist with blue blood running through his veins, dear brother-in-law Ben, was recruited for the Company by James Angleton himself and is a foot soldier among the recruited writers and journalists. Assets of intelligence. Slaves with pens.

James Angleton will then hear the news of a diary and take off in pursuit. Alone. The story of a free woman kicking and screaming her way through an enslaved era will enflame his brain. A tale of sex beneath presidential sheets, chemical explosions in the consciousness of a president, a tiny hot breath a single woman breathed against the entire edifice of the Cold War, secrets falling like leaves out of the files of Georgetown and into the lap of a CIA leader's ex-wife . . . it will all prove too explosive to assign to an underling. James will hunt down my diary himself.

Yes, James Jesus Angleton will break and enter my studio. He is a master of breaking and entering. He was taught by Kim Philby himself, or else by some assassin, or some Mafia thug, I don't know who taught him. But he will break and enter. And what will he make of my painting studio as he wanders among the unventilated smells of paint in his black suit, his crisp white shirt and tie? Will his cigarette accidentally ignite my turpentine? Will my death ironically culminate in a chemical explosion and the death of the CIA head of counterintelligence, vaporized in a bizarre turpentine fire? Or perhaps James will be distracted by my explorations of the optical field. Will he gaze at my paintings, the circles and triangles ablaze with reds and greens and blues on my round and rectangular canvases?

Will he come upon the wooden box of brushes, slide it carefully aside, and discover the mahogany box that protects this journal? Will he read the story of a woman whose destiny it was to be alive at the fulcrum of time?

Yes, he will enter my studio effortlessly when brother-in-law Ben Bradlee informs him of my diary. A woman's padlock has no chance against the CIA head of counterintelligence.

FEBRUARY 10

And suddenly I'm reminded of the hole where a son used to be. It's an ache you wake with, the thought that things are not right, will never be right, it's a gripping of the lungs that connects upward to the tear ducts. I could cry but perhaps will not. Where does this pain arise in the midst of sleep, as if you were accidentally born into the wrong person and now have to march forward living the wrong person's life, chatting with the wrong person's friends?

The Tragedy. My sweet Michael is gone six years now. A mom cooking spaghetti, just like every mom in every kitchen in America. A knock that shatters the world. Policemen, young men in grown-up blue uniforms with the grave look of the grave on their faces, they are talking to you but you don't hear them. Not really. A car has hit a boy on the blind curve of a country road. No one can know the blow of outliving a child. It makes you doubt the sanctity of the universe. I keep his teddy bear in my studio, on the shelf beside the brushes and cans of turpentine. I paint in the presence of the teddy bear. I paint amid the innocence of what remains of my son. Alan Watts relays the Zen koan. Chop wood and draw water. Chop wood and draw water. After the unspeakable you simply continue. This is the title of life: simply continue.

FEBRUARY 16

How many times have we met? I have lost count, but it has reached some invisible number where a shift occurs: from a kind of lover to a kind of wife. A kind of wife who will never be recorded in history, never be seen smiling and waving in the black-and-white footage of a presidency as it replays till the end of time.

But we walked out into the Rose Garden on Saturday, a kind of husband and a kind of wife, on a rare afternoon together when the bristling cold hit our uncoated bodies. Jack never seems to feel the cold, never bundles up properly—is it the warrior in him, or the drugs? I looked at rosebushes waiting out a long winter until they bloomed again, and he told me he wasn't the brother who was supposed to be the politician. A family needs only one politician. Older brother Joe had been groomed since childhood to be the president. Jack smiled sadly, speaking of his lost brother. I knew the story. I was aware he'd died a useless death in a suicide mission over England in 1944. He was carrying a massive payload of explosives that detonated through sheer electrical malfunction. A pointless, senseless death, it seemed to me, but you don't say that to Kennedys. They are queer in matters of death, so I didn't. Daddy Joe turned to the next son, and Jack had no chance to say no to the presidency, Jack who grew up skinny and sickly in the shadow of his big brother, the blue-eyed first son who was quite mean to his younger brother, a vicious competitor. And that was how Jack came to be in the White House, a bit ashen now next to bushes where the roses had disappeared.

"Sometimes I feel so alone here, Mary." It embarrasses me when people repeat themselves, and Jack has said the same words to me before.

"You're never alone as long as I live," I said, and he smiled with a bit of pain.

"Lemnitzer wants to launch a preemptive strike against Russia. A nuclear strike. He'd launch a world war tonight if I gave him the go-ahead. Wipe out millions of people, just like that. Can you believe what I'm up against with these generals?"

I took his hand in mine, the strange freckled Irish skin giving it the look of a hand that never grew up, no matter how much pain its owner endured. I will reveal my secret plan to him soon. Meanwhile, I smiled when he quoted a line from a poem written by a Spanish matador.

Only one is there who knows,
And he's the man who fights the bull.

FEBRUARY 19
Another sleepless night. Something jangling in my chest like anxiety or excitement or foreboding. I got out of bed

and headed to Clyde's for a bourbon, and when I arrived,
C was there, the Wildroot Cream–oiled Cold War man I
fucked last summer.

There had been no second time—I had seen no need—
but he was electrified to see me at Clyde's at that late
hour. It's a short story. I had two bourbons, he had two
Scotches, I felt like he would never leave, nor ever leave
me alone, I suddenly saw no need to be left alone, I'm a
free woman, I must have said to myself, and I took him
home. Voilà, as my French nanny used to say.

It was all rather impersonal, but as I was reminded,
he is a smooth machine. Highly practiced. And it felt
extremely good, for a brief, limited period of time. Then
I felt what might be called nothing. I told him to leave.
I was rather blasé about it. He asked to see me again,
and I told him no conversation, he had to go. And he was
quite a gentleman about it, smooth even in the closing.
He put his tie back on carefully, quite meticulously for
such a ridiculously late hour, and as his head barely
cleared my little front door, I noticed not a greasy hair
out of place. Who was he? I asked when the door closed,
and had no immediate answer. Another cold warrior
with a dick.

But who are we when we fuck, anyway? Not the
personality life has thrown together in order to get by.
The identity for which the government issues a social
security number. We are primordial in the sexual act, we
escape identity, and as such all sex is anonymous.

FEBRUARY 28

Memories of violation. Memories of the Tragedy.
Memories of the pain that Jack bears. I am haunted by
ghosts. I haven't painted for a few days, and just when
I think perhaps I can start again, memories return
of a back seat in a LaSalle Series 50. That was where
she left her body, my ghost sister Rosamond, in the
back seat of a LaSalle Series 50. She breathed a last
breath of carbon fumes on that seat till there was no
more oxygen to break down sugar in her cells. She was
the loveliest woman in America. They wrote that. The
theater critics wrote that when she acted onstage. The
newspaper writers wrote that when she acted in French
films.

She taught me to swim. She taught me to lie naked
in the sunlight with high green branches fanning our
behinds, and not to care who saw. She taught me to ride.
She stormed through the woods of Grey Towers on her
stallion in the moonlight. I would hear the galloping
clip-clop outside when they thought I was sleeping, and
I said one day I would ride with Rosamond.

She left her body in the back seat of a LaSalle wearing
a white evening gown, silver slippers, and white ermine
wrap. We don't know her mind, and now there is no
longer a mind that answers to the name Rosamond
Pinchot.

Ghost sister. Discovered on a ship when her days as an
actress began. Discovered in car when they were over.

MARCH 2

Chop wood and draw water. So says Alan Watts in *The Way of Zen*. Life continues, and it's time to break the spell. I called Lorraine Cooper and told her I needed to break out of a really blue mood.

"Get your girdle on and meet me at Le Bistro. One o'clock," she said.

"How about a walk on the towpath?"

"What? I'm at two with nature. See you at Le Bistro."

She hung up, so I had no choice but to put on a fresh pair of pedal pushers, a pink angora sweater, and flats, not sneakers. Le Bistro is a bit stuffy. It's Jackie's favorite lunch place, but she's French, I think, or at least has this strong French bent.

I was thrilled to see Lorraine at the bar in a blue Dior dress and hat, already sipping her Tom Collins. "I'm just having a chat with my friend Tom over here," she said, raising her glass. "You've got to meet him. Alfred? One more."

Alfred brought me the first in what would be a series of Tom Collinses, and I started venturing far, far from my blue mood.

"Sherman tells me he's introducing this bill in the Senate to cut deficit spending, and I tell him I understand it perfectly, I've been doing deficit spending my whole life and it's worked out very well. But what on earth is balance of payments? Sherman scrunches up his face, the killjoy, so I tell him to run along to Capitol Hill because

I'm going to have a Tom Collins with Mary. I tell him, if you decide you like deficit spending after all, you know where to find me."

I'm laughing, Lorraine is laughing, even Alfred is laughing, I think he's from South America. Then I notice James Jesus Angleton sitting at a table in the rear with none other than Cord.

"Lorraine, Cord and James Angleton are in the back having lunch together!"

"That's their problem, sweetheart, we've got drinking to do," she says, and we crack up again.

"You want some rabbit stew, Mary? It's to die for at this place."

"I'd love some. But I don't think I've ever seen you eat."

"Sparingly, my dear. Sparingly. I grew up in Italy, and I decided early on you either choose men or cakes, you can't have both, and I've never deviated. Do you take vitamins, Mary?"

I was taken aback. "No. I take LSD, though!" I burst out laughing again.

"We've got to talk. François! I think we're ready to sit down, if you'd be kind enough to show us to a table. But not in the back, please."

We followed François to a table by the window.

"We'll both have the rabbit stew, and two more Tom Collinses, please," I heard Lorraine telling the waiter, but I was feeling swirly and looking out the window onto M Street and grinning.

MARCH 4

Jackie's in Paris with her sister, hunting for clothes, and Jack was lonely. So Jack and Ben and sister Tony and William Walton and I boarded the big plane for dinner at Hyannis Port. The staff made meat loaf again—Jack loves that meat loaf, though it may not be about what he loves so much as what his delicate stomach can bear. There was a full moon shining on Cape Cod, churning the sea waves into a surfer's dream, but inside, the fireplace crackled and conversation was cozy.

"Tell Mary about your paintings, Billy Boy," Jack said to William. "She's quite a painter too. And you're a sculptor, right, Tony?" He turned suddenly to my sister, not giving William a chance to speak, and beamed in her direction. Tony blushed—she is so much more shy than I am, so much thinner, so much quieter, so much everything that is ladylike, and it haunted me: Does Jack prefer her? Tony spoke of her pottery. "I'm only happy when I have wet clay on my hands."

"And you, Benjie," he said to Ben Bradlee. "No talent whatsoever!"

"That's it, Jack. I live off the backs of people with talent."

"And other parts of them too, no doubt." Jack was feeling frisky, and I suddenly asked him to show me the ocean, to show me the places where he began sailing as a boy, a sickly boy pushed by his father out into the deep. He paused, then looked at me and smiled. Tony seemed confused, her eyes darting back and forth between Jack and me. Ben smiled into his martini glass, and William Walton turned to Tony and began describing how he had redecorated the Oval Office, choosing a copper-painted bust of Saint Thomas More as the centerpiece.

Jack and I rose—I desperately hoped it wouldn't generate rumors—and we walked outside onto the carpet of the full moon. We held hands as we walked to the water but said nothing, as if silence was proof to others that nothing was really afoot. But as we looked at the white churn of surf in the charcoal night, I had an impulse. I unzipped my dress, pulled off my bra, and wriggled out of the girdle I had worn to look thin. I stood naked, a moon-bathing statue, and Jack stared at me. "It seems like Christmas has come early." He smiled, looking between my legs, and suddenly he was on the ground licking me. Unusual indeed for Jack; the full moon must have affected his brain. Jack's mouth between my legs, the roar of Atlantic surf penetrating my ears, I stood in that night of salty wind and orgasmed. All went quiet. Then Jack said we needed to get back. Jack always needs to get back, so I wriggled back into my clothes, all these things a woman is forced to wear so that polite society remains polite.

"It's beautiful out there, isn't it?" said William as we resumed our places at the table, damping the conversation to a safe neutrality. I said surely that it is, that now I knew where Jack had sailed his boats as a young boy on the Atlantic, that they should all go outside and witness the full moon themselves, but I'm not sure Tony cared.

MARCH 23

Timothy Leary called and announced that he is now an
official exile of the American imperium. He and Richard
Alpert have been kicked out of Harvard. In its place
they have commandeered a resort on the Pacific coast of
Mexico and established an acid utopia there. I should see
it, he implored. I should visit. So I did. Last Friday I flew
to Zihuatanejo to take acid.

It took me an entire day to get there. I had to fly
to Mexico City and then hop a little twin-engine to a
fishing village in the jungles north of Acapulco. Who
could have discovered such a place except Timothy Leary,
or maybe some pirates?

The open-air hotel perched upon a cliff bore the lovely
name Hotel Catalina, and in synchronicity, I carried with
me in my suitcase my red Catalina bathing suit.

Tim seemed ecstatic to see me, his gleaming teeth
and electric smile clearly arriving intact to the jungles of
Mexico. He was bare-chested and wore Bermuda shorts
and a captain's hat perched lopsided on his head. He held
a gin and tonic, as if he had arrived in Mexico, but his
hand was still back at a faculty party in Harvard.

"Welcome to psychedelic summer camp!" he said in
the melodious voice I had missed. He was, as always,
in his own bubble of space independent somehow of his
surroundings. When I finally gazed around, psychedelic
summer camp seemed more like an island of shipwrecked
eccentrics—dazed-looking students, strange characters
with hairstyles run amok, playing flutes and strumming

guitars, and Harvard professors who seemed dazzled by the exotic classroom they suddenly found themselves in.

Tim beckoned me to follow him down a long, winding staircase, an endless cascade of wooden steps you had to traverse carefully one step at a time until you finally set foot on a beach of pure white sugar. I wondered how anyone on LSD could possibly walk that staircase without a catastrophe. Then we strolled happily along the beach, green water lapping at our feet. Tim smiled broadly, and I could see he was at some pure moment. It was a moment poised fragilely in time between what would inevitably be debacles: his professor's life lay in ruins behind him, while assaults of law and media scandals were closing in on him from the future. But for the moment he walked free, infinity opening itself up to him like a flower, a lord of some tropical paradise encountered typically in British novels.

All was fresh in Zihuatanejo, all was primal. There was no electricity, no intrusions of man's geometry; we were no longer even under the domination of Anglo-Saxon culture. All was pure air, scented with salt breezes and the perfume of flowers. "There are no clocks here," he said proudly. "Time is measured by the ancient timepiece our cells have been listening to for millions of years, the surf."

Two people approached us hand in hand, giggling like teenagers. They were Richard Alpert, Tim's Harvard partner in psychedelia, and Prissy Hickock, a beautiful girl in her twenties with wheat-colored hair that floated freely in the salt breeze.

Later, I would learn that Richard Alpert was homosexual, and his real love was Tim.

Later, I would learn that Prissy was an heiress to the Mellon fortune, and her real love was Tim.

Even later, I would learn that she and I were linked by currency and history: just as she bankrolled Timothy Leary's LSD adventures with the money of her ancestors, those same Mellons of Pittsburgh had also bankrolled my uncle Gifford Pinchot when he was governor of Pennsylvania.

But in those first moments in Zihuatenejo, I felt my cells decompressing on a Mexican beach, and Richard Alpert was hugging me. I assumed hugging was a ritual of LSD culture; trippers all shared a realm where separations between people were considered an illusion. He introduced himself as Tim's partner in a victorious expulsion from Harvard University. "Contrary to historical precedent, we were expelled to Paradise, not from it!"

"Dick is my partner in this spiritual oasis," Tim said, extending his arm in a wide arc as if to indicate that the whole tableau of sea and sun and sky, it was all there by his careful design. "It is an ecstatic place in which we're very serious."

"We're very serious about our ecstasy, aren't we, Dickie?" Prissy Hickock said with a stoned giggle, but Tim remained in professorial mode. I assume he often plays that role.

"We are scientists here. Our main business is

continuing our explorations of LSD. At any moment you can see one-third of the group planning their session for the night. Another third will be in sessions, sprawled out on the sand or floating in the water watching the sunrise. Another third will look bedazzled because they have come down from LSD and are reporting the results of their sessions. We're very productive, right, Dick? Scientific reports, essays, articles for scientific journals."

Prissy ignored him. She came up to me and softly rubbed my cheeks and mouth, as if she were blind and trying to discern the lineaments of my face. "In the Nahuatl language, Zihuatanejo means 'Place of the Goddess Women,'" she said. "We're home, Mary!" I smiled and hugged her, yielding to the embrace of LSD culture, and felt a warmth emanating from her young body. A thin man with a bedraggled beard and a turbulent growth of hair passed us on the beach, his body covered in what appeared no more substantial than a loincloth.

"Rolf von Ekkelsberg." Prissy laughed. "He was my accountant until I turned him on to acid."

"Now he's a no-count!" said Richard energetically.

Acid Fragment 1
It is a beautiful Saturday morning. In a blaze of hot sunshine, on a long carpet of white sand, I take 300 micrograms of Heavenly Blue. I can feel the sun radiating its heat into my cells, can feel my body turn into sunshine. I stand up and remove my Catalina

bathing suit. I am a creature unburdened with identity, moving slow, slow into wet green liquid, changing composition from sunshine to seawater.

I become an amphibian, propelled with frog legs through lapping waves. I transform into four-legs, a creature of my racial memory treading some dim pool a billion years ago. Legs, eyes, feathers, eggs, placentas, flowers, I metamorphose into a two-legged human being, an upright person leaving the water and returning to sand. I am a sea nymph. I am a goddess, and Tim is there to greet me, smiling. We start kissing. It is effortless, it requires no setup, it is an act of nature no more significant than the sea rolling in, we fall down, gravity sucks us downward onto sand, and we begin making love in the rolling surf. Am I in a famous movie? Do the movies of life simply imitate the movies of cinema?

Suddenly, Prissy Hickock is there. She's been watching over us. She seems a bird at first, and then I see her as an Aztec statue, and then she is a woman who is upset, and I think she must be joking, all human dramas are clearly a joke to me, but she seems serious. She appears to be overcome with jealousy at Tim and me being together. It seems utterly ridiculous—she is enacting a part—but we disentangle and sit up on the sand as water rolls in over us. "I'm not tripping, now, OK," Prissy says, "and I know that everything is everything and all that, but you know, it's not OK with me you're with her."

"I'm just dancing with the living situation," Tim says

to her in his melodious voice of quiet authority, and he
seems reasonable, but I am naked and a million miles
away. I put my bathing suit back on and race into the
water, swimming as fast as I can, I don't know why, and
suddenly I don't know where I am, I am upside down, I
am upside up, I'm not sure where the water stops and the
air begins, and I decide it is time to panic. And then I am
grabbed, lifted up, I am raised by hands of iron. Rolf von
Ekkelsberg has picked me up and is carrying me through
the water. I feel surely he is a god, I have never met
anyone more godlike before, I know it is some version of
Valhalla. A part of me knows I might have died then and
there, I might have breathed water until I was no longer
among the breathing, but I am alive and Rolf is laying
me on the sand and covering me with a Mexican blanket.
Tim leans over me, looking deeply into my eyes. "You're
trying very hard to be a mermaid!" he says. His eyes
are twinkling, he is serene, he keeps saying "You're all
right, you're all right," and I try to tell him I know, I'm
all right, but the words don't come, or perhaps they come
and I simply don't hear them.

Acid Fragment 2

I lie on the beach, and Prissy Hickock comes over to
cradle my head in her arms. I am so sorry, she says, but
the word *sorry* doesn't mean anything to me, I look at
her and see the wheat-colored hair, her freckly white
skin turning red from the sun because it has no defense
against it, and she looks like my family, she looks like

the girls I went to school with, and I kiss her on the lips.
She kisses me back, and I just say "Prissy," and she says
"Mary, I love you," and I rest my head on her legs and
just become aware of breathing for a while. You need to
rest, she says, and I lie in the sun, the hot Mexican sun
that bleaches the sand and turns the frangipani white
and yellow.

Acid Fragment 3
The next day was Prissy's day to take LSD and mine to
recover and record my experiences. I lay on the beach
for hours, healing in the sun, holding trembly hands
with Rolf von Ekkelsberg's forceful fingers. My "Acid
Fragments" were written in the moments in between,
when we released hands and I was free to write. Tim
demands it. He is a scientist, and everyone in Zihuatanejo
must keep a journal. What will become of all these
rapturous reports, ecstatic recountings, and delirious
diaries about lysergic acid dissolving the mind, erasing
the barrier between self and the universe, laying bare
the empty hollow air of words and things? A psychedelic
journal is a contradiction in terms. At the moment in
question, there is no such thing as a Tim Leary, let alone
a scientist. At any rate, I am writing. And no one but Tim
will ever read these fragments.

MARCH 24
At campfire, the group gathered under tropical stars to
stare into flames and listen to Tim orate in the role of, as

he describes it, not completely seriously, the High Priest. I record what he said.

"We're all anthropologists journeying back in time from the twenty-first century. This little place on the Pacific coast of Mexico is a time capsule, set in the dark ages of the 1960s. What do we learn here? That we inhabit a universe made up of a small number of elements, of particles, of bits that swirl in chaotic clouds, occasionally clustering together in geometrically logical temporary configurations. We are those configurations. Turn to the fellow temporary configuration next to you and say hello!"

Perhaps he was driven by Prissy's outburst on the beach, but Tim excoriated human emotions:

"Emotions are the lowest form of consciousness. Romantic poetry and flowery fiction have blinded us to the fact that emotions are a harmful form of stupor. Emotions are simply fear-based, ego-based biochemical secretions in the body, designed to serve during states of acute emergency. An emotional person is a blind, crazed maniac. My advice to our group here: check your emotions at the door to paradise."

I suddenly felt spent. Exhausted. Perhaps using chemicals to expand consciousness beyond the normal human state is simply an unnatural process, one detonating unnecessary strain on the organism. Somewhere on the frontier—where exactly is that frontier?—somewhere on the frontier where physical body meets spirit, the body is stretched or reconfigured and needs time to recover. Maybe my body was simply not ready for the doors of perception to be cleansed. Maybe we live in the comfort of dirty windows. I felt like sleeping for a week.

And once again, bathed in the heat of the roaring fire, I felt the chill of my isolation. I am a creature of the WASP ascendancy sitting on the sand with a group of eccentrics, bohemians, and misfits in the jungles of Mexico. I am too loud for the cold warriors of Georgetown. Too emotional for Timothy Leary's icy new chemical version of the human. Too creative for the bourbon-drinking spies at my parties. Too weird for Katharine Graham and Pamela Harriman, even Evangeline Bruce. And too headstrong for my own good. I am deep in Mexico and deep in the in-between.

I kissed Prissy good night. "All we're trying to do is see and hear the world as the artist or musician sees it," she said. I left Zihuatanejo the next morning.

APRIL 14

History is accelerating. Nineteen sixty-three hides itself beneath a verdant spring but I can hear the wheels whirring. Strange rumblings begin to emerge from the cozy stage set of Georgetown.

Last night we feasted on soft-shell crabs. The Wisner house vibrated with the energy of a pink moon, the first full moon of spring, and the energy of those who founded, promulgated, and chronicled the Cold War. Why was

Clover Dulles suddenly so friendly? Lorraine Cooper and Kay Graham sat on either side me, yet Clover saw fit to zero in, hug me, and make sure I noticed her pale blue eyes peering into mine. What was the language of her pale eyes?

Phil Graham had been drinking continuously, his habit of late, and had reached the state of disregard for civilized propriety. He remains brilliant and magnetic—most women would still go upstairs with him in a heartbeat—and he still presides over the *Washington Post*, but his behavior has grown manic. According to Lorraine, he suddenly bought *Newsweek* one day, handing them a two-million-dollar personal check on the spot for the deposit. He simply pulled a check from his wallet, asked for a pen, crossed out his own name, and scribbled on it "The Washington Post Company." Katharine is urging him to get tests.

Is it a career lived too close to the burning core of power? A black spot on Phil's soul that whispers that his success derives more from marriage than merit? Is the abuse showered on his long-suffering Katharine simply rage against the fact that her family owns the *Post*, and he, in the end, is simply an editor-in-law?

Phil suddenly tapped a metal pitcher to get the room's attention and raised his glass in a toast to Frank Wisner. Frank was wary of the attention, the inventor of covert operations naturally phobic about commanding the limelight himself. I have always loved Frank. He too has a manic energy, molded years ago into a bizarre obsession with Communism, but he is an awfully sincere man, a dutiful soldier who happened to be present at the birth of our Intelligence. And he is not the man he once was. Secrets attach naturally to a man of secrets. Intimations of breakdowns, of electric shock treatments, of the Agency's relieving him of his duties quietly and graciously. So Phil Graham, a damaged man, drew the room's attention to Frank, another damaged man.

"Ladies and . . . non-ladies! Welcome to another party at the Wisners', otherwise known as government by invitation!" He unfolded a piece of paper and began reciting a doggerel poem he had penned in tribute to Frank Wisner.

> *I write this with no mania / Nor Princess from Romania . . .*

A shock wave pierced the room. Phil had dropped a bomb with the first sentence, an embarrassing allusion to Frank Wisner's not-so-secret affair with Princess Caradja of Romania, back when he was stationed in Bucharest with the Office of Strategic Services. The affair had been brutally revealed by J. Edgar Hoover, who alleged that the princess was a Soviet agent, and the scandal had nearly ended the Wisners' marriage.

Polly Wisner left the room abruptly. Kay Graham shouted, "That's enough, Phil." Frank Wisner watched Phil with a pained attempt at a grin, but Phil continued:

*This is for Frank, our gentle host / Far too secretive to
    boast.*
Let's pull out the stops / and celebrate his black ops!

Frank stiffened, the sad memory of a smile frozen on
his cheeks.

Here's to Albania, the Al-Bane of your existence,
And Guatemala, which offered minimal resistance.

It was a directory in rhyme of the CIA coups and
assassinations orchestrated by Frank Wisner.

Here's to Iran / It went according to plan,
And Brazil / How unfortunate those leaders fell ill!
Anyone in the house / Like what we did to Laos?
*And how about Chile? / Where you got a bit
    silly.*
*But, Frank, we all wish you well / Which is more than
    we can say for Fidel.*

Phil Graham was struggling to focus on the scrap
of paper in his hand, and it was James Angleton, of all
people, who stopped him. He suggested another drink,
which of course was the last thing Phil needed, and led
Phil from the room and into the garden. The chill of
embarrassment remained, but in a room of diplomats,
spies, and the women who keep their secrets, stiff drinks
and even stiffer upper lips prevailed. Joe Alsop tried to

lighten the mood. "Anybody have any hobbies?" he said with a grin, sitting down beside me.

"I think it's an omen," I said very quietly. "Things are falling apart."

"Things are always falling apart, and we are constantly putting them back together. It's been ever thus," he said, sucking on his ivory cigarette holder and blowing smoke calmly into the air as if blowing away the discomfort of the evening.

"Joe, we have so many secrets." I touched his arm softly, realizing that I had never touched his arm before—what woman has? "We live in secrets, and I'm afraid we're all going to die in secrets." He looked at me without expression. It was a simple meeting of eyes, communicating somehow that he knew that I knew his deepest secret, and that it was all right with him that I knew. I wondered if his eyes also communicated that he knew my deepest secret.

"Joe, your friend and I are in love with each other."
I had said it.

"I have so many friends," he said gaily, turning away abruptly and smiling at Allen Dulles. My reading of the unspoken continued, and I took his statement to mean: you can make insignificant things significant, which is what occupies us most of the time, or you can make significant things insignificant, which is a far rarer and more important endeavor.

"You're not a big fan of love, are you, Joe?" I asked.

"Love?" he repeated, turning the word over in his mind. "Love is infinity made available to poodles."

MAY 5

Kentucky Derby Sunday at the Wisners', and the hats proliferated. Polly's living room became a bestiary of birds and flowers, the heads of my friends bedecked with lace and feathers. I hid beneath a tan pillbox with matching veil.

The Kentucky Derby is a hallowed event in Georgetown, for reasons I have never quite fathomed. A full day of ritual and revelry over a horse race that lasts two minutes. It's like sex.

I sipped a mint julep, thinking about the nature of horses, thinking of the thoroughbreds grazing everywhere in the fields of Kentucky, dreaming of the Derby, thinking of my old black Arabian, Comanche, and my ghost sister Rosamond's midnight stallion, Excalibur. After two juleps, to the wild applause of a crowd ready to go berserk over horses, Polly and I stood up and sang a rousing rendition of my favorite song, "Chantilly Lace." No one knew its hidden meaning except me. The Big Bopper spoke in teenage code on that 45 rpm record for the cellular evolution of mankind.

"Chantilly Lace, and a pretty face and a ponytail, hanging down . . ." While everyone clapped, James Angleton did a maniacal version of the Twist—I believe he had downed an entire bottle of Glenlivet at that point—and staggered over to where Lorraine Cooper sat. Lorraine lifted her veil and gazed at the cadaverous figure swaying like a samba to the drums of alcohol. I anticipated a meaningful pronouncement of some sort, but all Lorraine said was: "Down, boy."

I waited for some sort of inebriated praise for our performance of "Chantilly Lace," but James had something else in mind. He struggled to retrieve it from a world beyond his skull, but it was mired, it seemed, in some internal tableau. Finally, it surfaced.

"I met E. E. Cummings at Yale, you know," he slurred. "We invited him to address our gallant little literary magazine *Furioso*, and he showed up to read, even though he was Harvard."

"Yale," I said. "Fucking Yale. My father was Yale, my uncle was Yale, my ex-husband was Yale, most of my dates at Brearley were Yale. Hey, all my favorite spies walking around this party right now, you all went to Yale too!" I don't know the source of this outburst, but Vangie Bruce shook her finger at me. She has begun tapping me at parties, I notice, indicating that my mouth betrays me. I tread too carelessly over the unwritten rules of the secretively powerful and the powerfully secretive. Evangeline protects me—she is like Isabelle, my French nanny back at Grey Towers who also tried to protect me, who also detected an urgent need for me to behave.

"Who's your horse, James?" I asked, steering the conversation back to the Derby. "I figure you for Crimson Satan!"

"So E. E. Cummings addressed our little literary band," he continued and began reciting from memory:

> *if I should sleep with a lady called death*
> *get another man with firmer lips*
> *to take your new mouth in his teeth*
> *(hips pumping pleasure into hips).*

"A lady called death?" I blew a puff of Marlboro in his direction, a protective smokescreen no doubt, and called out to Frank Wisner, "Frank, am I a lady called death?"

"I've heard it said," Frank answered quietly, noncommittal right down to his quips. To which I responded: "From the Big Bopper to E. E. Cummings in one afternoon. Who says Washington is a cultural wasteland?"

I realized the double entendre inherent in this sexual poet's name, Cummings, and James repeated the lascivious phrase: "Hips . . . pumping . . . pleasure . . . into . . . hips." He popped the *p*'s for emphasis, and I knew something was coming that would need handling, and I preferred it didn't.

"Mary, Mary," he said. "I should have been with you instead of with your roommate from Vassar."

It is a woman's job to stop men when they get stupid. I stood up and told him to shut up, I spoke it to penetrate his drunken stupor: "Cicely is a poet and a treasure, and she has put up with you, James, all these many years."

His body laughed, his face didn't join, and I sensed the great unburdening he longed for from the fortress of secrets he carried in his scrawny body. "Mary, Mary," he repeated, but before he could venture onto a new tangent, I stood up and said: "Let's go for a walk."

I led him through the French doors and out into the Wisner garden, Venetian lanterns splashing light through the foliage though it was still daylight. How sweet the flowers smelled in Georgetown! I felt like James Angleton's guide on some secret rendezvous as I pushed his long, almost comically angular body onto a concrete bench.

"Mary," he said, not missing a beat, "you know how I got to be in charge of counterintelligence?" His breath was rancid with liquor.

"Are you sure you want to be telling me this, James?" I asked, a familiar chill returning to my chest. I recalled Polly Wisner saying she made a point of never learning anything about Frank's clandestine work so she could never accidentally reveal a secret. I wished to know nothing more about James's squalid business, this ridiculous omnipresence of James Angleton in my life.

He ignored me, and the unburdening proceeded of its own weight. "I got to be head of counterintelligence because I agreed not to polygraph Allen Dulles." The statement hung in the warm night. His body swayed on the bench. "I agreed to ignore all the background checks on Mr. Allen Dulles and his closest friends. They were petrified that their intimate business dealings with

Hitler's pals would come spilling out like vomit onto their shiny shoes, along with their business dealings, along with their care and feeding of Nazi criminals. Along with the obstructions and impediments they put in place to hinder the Nuremberg trials. Along with the ratlines they built to Chile and Argentina for their Nazi friends who never repented. You want some names? I'll give you names. Wolff. Dollman. Rauff. The CIA got tens of thousands of brave people killed."

I stopped him: "You sure you want to be telling me this? Are you hoping I'll unremember it?"

I suddenly felt a wave of foreboding. Was it his men who were entering my house and moving things? Was he trying to warn me, signal me, threaten me? And what would happen tomorrow when the alcohol wore off, when James Jesus Angleton sat again in his dark office, lit up a Virginia Slim, and remembered what he had whispered to Cord Meyer's ex-wife in a Georgetown garden?

"The founding fathers of US intelligence were liars," he said. I could not tell if he was confessing or boasting. "The better you lied, the more you betrayed, the more likely you would be promoted, and they all had an overriding trait in common: a desire for absolute power. Allen Dulles. Richard Helms, our gracious host standing in that living room, Mr. Frank Wisner—they're all grandmasters of mendacity. I'm telling you all this, Mary, even though I've never told your roommate from Vassar."

I stopped him again. "Please leave Cicely out of this."

"I'm a part of it, Mary, Mary. If you were in a room

with these men, you had to believe you were in a room full of people that would deservedly end up in hell. And I've loved every minute of it."

MAY 7

I was invited to Kay Graham's mansion for tea. She is intrigued by Chantilly Lace, and she has a nose for news. She asked me once again to review my ideas for world peace. I hope she will help me; the *Washington Post* is growing in influence.

I lightened the mood by complimenting her on her lawn. Who in tiny old Georgetown, with all the old Federalist houses built flush up to the street, can boast such a lush front lawn? She is a depressive sort of person, saying Phil certainly won't mow it, so it's another burden. The burden of a big house, which always falls on a woman. As does the continual hosting of parties, choreographing and casting them perfectly so you have the right mix of age, professions, nationalities, and always a few beautiful young women thrown in.

"You know, Mary," she said, "historically a woman had only three options in Washington, DC. You could be a political wife, you could run a boardinghouse, or you could be a madam. Put them all together, and you have a Washington hostess!"

MAY 13

In the book of these times, when the chapter called "Cold War" is written, ten thousand years from now, they will

say: It has come to pass. For it *has* come to pass. The deed
has been done. The occurrence has occurred. Chantilly
Lace is realized. I have led the most powerful man on
earth on to the next step in cellular evolution. Jack and I
took LSD.

It was Sunday at Joe Alsop's house on Dumbarton.
Jackie was at a farm in Virginia. Jack told her he would
be in National Security meetings all day, he told the Joint
Chiefs he would be in Virginia, and Kenny O'Donnell
made it all work. The Secret Service sat outside in a van
all day, with one red-faced skinny block of stone stationed
in the garden next to Joe Alsop's bronze statue.

Jack wanted to turn on here because he loves Joe's
queenly presence. This is where he came to smoke cigars
and chat the night of the inauguration, when he couldn't
sleep and wanted to pretend for just a moment that
nothing in his life had changed.

Sunday was a shimmering blossoming of May in
Georgetown. Joe Alsop hovered over us like a mother hen
in his bow tie and slippers, waving his cigarette holder in
the air like a wind instrument.

Jack was unusually frightened. "What if the Russians
attack while I'm on this?"

I laughed.

"What if I don't come back all the way?"

I told him Tim Leary had given me a hypodermic
packed with Thorazine.

"Mary, Mary, quite contrary," he said, remembering
the first time we met and danced in 1936. He has no

fear in the outer world, pushing his ship through the
storms in the Pacific, running the nation in the face of
pain and illness. A warrior prince. But Kennedys don't do
inner lives very well. They are trained to attack in the
outer world. What lives inside leaves them lost, so this
psychedelic journey may be the biggest challenge of his
life. Mine too.

And then the time came. I trembled because
somewhere I knew the fate of the world had slipped onto
my shoulders. I took two tablets, each one containing
300 micrograms of Owsley lysergic acid diethylamide,
and placed one on his tongue and one on mine. He is
no stranger to concoctions racing in his bloodstream. I
have seen him racing on amphetamines after a shot from
Dr. Feelgood, and I've seen his face puffed up from who
knows what chemical interactions, but this was different.
It was 11:00 a.m. when we swallowed the pills.

We waited for the drug to take effect, silent and
nervous. He looked deeply at me and grinned. Jack was
always up for a grin for me. I took his hand. He lit a cigar,
and I began to feel the chemicals take hold of my nervous
system, like a slow melt into the Garden of Eden. I was
becoming a new human, and suddenly the cigar smoke
smelled foul, and I felt like throwing up.

I picked up Tim Leary's version of *The Tibetan Book
of the Dead* and began to read aloud. "Liberation is the
nervous system devoid of mental-conceptual activity.
Realization of the Voidness, the Unbecome, the Unborn,
the Unmade, the Unformed, implies Buddhahood, Perfect

Enlightenment—the state of the divine mind of the Buddha."

Joe Alsop sat beside us with his arms folded, amused and fascinated. A parakeet chirped in a cage above his head. I saw the Greek vase on the table in front of him, and suddenly I knew we were in Greece. I couldn't explain it in a trillion years, but Washington was Greece, and I had the idea we were doing it over because we didn't do it right the first time.

We stood up, both at the same time—it just happened, we didn't discuss it—and walked out to the little pool in the garden. The pool was tucked neatly against a brick wall tangled with a hair of vines. The Secret Service man was sweating profusely, looking back and forth at me and Jack. He knew something was odd, but we had told no one of our purpose here, not even Secret Service. I looked at his aviator sunglasses, and suddenly it all seemed so fake. He was a big little boy with pink skin, exuding fear like a wave of poison gas. I could see that he couldn't see through himself, as I could now see through myself and through Jack, and all the Secret Service man could do was hide behind the mirrors of sunglasses.

Jack wore shades too so no one could see his eyes. I held his hand as we walked the winding brick lane that Joe had designed for his garden. "You won't leave me," he said suddenly, the same words I had once said to Allen Ginsberg. I truly don't believe Jack had ever uttered those words to any human being in his life. "I'll never leave you," I said, and started pulling off my blouse and pulling down my capri pants and then my panties so I was naked and the Secret Service man tried desperately to look away. I jumped into the pool and splashed the water at Jack. He kept laughing. "Why are you in there?" he muttered, though the words didn't come out right, and he repeated them a second time. This time, what came out sounded more like "Where are you there?" which we knew made no sense, and we laughed hysterically because human speech was suddenly so abysmally funny. Then Jack stepped into the pool at the shallow end, shoes and all in the blue-green water. "Water isn't really wet," he said, and I nodded. "Water isn't even really water." Nodded again. "We should invite Khrushchev to jump in the pool with us," I said, and splashed a giant splash out to the Secret Service man, who just sat there like a stone, baking in the sunshine in his white shirt and pretending I hadn't splashed him.

"I think Fidel Castro would have a good time here," Jack said. "We could settle everything. Have some tacos and enchiladas here for him—I don't know what they eat in Cuba. Do you know what they eat in Cuba, Mary?" and I said, "Beans. Human beans." We burst out laughing again.

I remember it all as if remembering the day through a huge fabric of gauze. It was as if on acid I could see the foolishness of objects; I saw the filter we live through and how everyone agrees to live in the filter and that's how we have a world and then everyone forgets they're living in a filter. And when you go to the other side of the filter, words mean nothing, so you don't try. Words are just more stuff in the context of everything else, rather than some superior construct that is outside everything else and defines it. I'm sure that makes no sense. So you laugh, but the laughter is not humor. Laughter is a gasp of overwhelm. Laughter is the sound of the mind dying.

I put my clothes back on, and we walked to the brick patio. We looked at the bronze god in the birdbath, and Jack took off his shoes. Joe had built this house because he's an amateur architect and wanted a modern house. He did not believe in re-creating a Georgian house like all the other homes in Georgetown. He thinks re-creating historical styles is fakery.

We sat in a wisteria-covered loggia, and the full dose hit. I took a piece of paper from my pocket and began to read aloud to Jack, though I wasn't sure how my mind was reading and how my mouth was forming speech. They were words I had copied down from the French poet Rimbaud:

> *I dreamed of Crusades, senseless voyages of discovery,*
> *republics without a history, moral revolution,*
> *displacement of races and continents. I believed in all*
> *the magics. What was unutterable, I wrote down. I*
> *made the whirling world stand still.*

I saw Jack smiling, crying—I don't know if he heard the words or what he was feeling, but he kept disappearing and appearing. It was like a roller coaster when you reach the top so slowly, slowly, then suddenly drop into free fall. The terror of freedom. The terror of gravity unleashed, of not knowing where you will land or where it will end. I felt a fool for not having a guide, for not having Tim here with his soothing voice. I experienced my birth, I experienced my death. So much work, I kept saying to myself. So much work. Was I ready to die? I saw the fierce attachment that kept me here, that made me fear death, that made myriads of people fear death, and I knew one inch further, just another inch, and I would never fear death again.

Eventually we came down, came back to ourselves, sat there on the stone bench by the pond, exhausted. I stared at Jack as if for the first time because whoever I was before, I no longer was, and we were both sitting together as if for the first time. Jack said he needed to get back to work, and I told him to stay and breathe, the world was turning without him. He said "Really?"

I said: "Really."

"Mary, Mary, quite contrary."

Quietly, quietly, the president of the United States and I reentered what is commonly called reality.

MAY 15

I returned to the White House on Tuesday, two days after the acid, fearing what I would encounter when I hugged America's first psychedelicized president. I wondered if I was insane; had Amos and Ruth's headstrong daughter put the entire Planet Earth in peril by leading Jack

Kennedy into a cataclysmic shattering of self in Joe Alsop's garden?

My fears were allayed when Jack entered the lounge adjoining the Oval Office, a place he likes to smoke cigars and relax. His commitment to control was clearly in command, the commitment that had overridden a shipwreck at sea, a catalog of pain and illness, the exhaustion of marshaling an entire nation to vote him in as a leader, an election some whisper he had actually lost. And now it overrode what LSD plainly reveals: the illusion of the self.

Jack was in control, but he was also in a mood; I can tell by the way his eyes droop back in a weird angle in their sockets. He said the world hadn't changed during our trip, and that Khrushchev was still driving him crazy. He asked how I was, and I said that I was quite fine, that reentry from LSD is always a challenge, that somehow you have to return to yourself and carry on but remember the lessons.

"I don't know what to make of it," he said. "It's like I was shipwrecked again and had to float back again, and now I have to ignore it so I can carry on."

He looked at me tenderly for a moment, and I kissed him. We were silently acknowledging that we had undergone something profound together, all the more profound because it would remain a secret to history. A secret he could reveal to no one, not to his family, nor his closest ally, Kenny O'Donnell, not even to Bobby. Then he spoke of Khrushchev and said he had been rethinking his posture toward the Soviets. He wants to propose a nuclear test ban. It's a beginning, he said, and he's considering a speech that will set us out in a new direction. That, instead of demonizing Russians, will uphold our common humanity. Why leave people more frightened than they already are? he said. I hugged him.

He walked back into the office, took a document from his desk, and brought it out. "I asked Ted Sorensen to write this. I told him to write the speech he would deliver if he wanted to end the Cold War, if he wanted to save humanity. This is what he wrote."

I glanced at a paragraph in the middle. That's how I read. I never seem to begin at the beginning. I scribbled down what I read on a yellow pad beside the couch.

"Every thoughtful citizen who despairs of war and wishes to bring peace should begin by looking inward, by examining his own attitude toward the possibilities of peace, toward freedom and peace at home, toward the Soviet Union."

"This is wonderful," I said. "They're going to kill you." I laughed. Jack hadn't shown the speech to anybody. He had not cleared it with the war machine for approval, he had not shared it with Central Intelligence, he had not conferred with the Joint Chiefs. "All I need is that son of a bitch LeMay eyeballing this and throwing up all over it. I'm just going to deliver it. Read what Ted wrote at the end."

I read the end over several times, and Jack let me scribble it down. "Now don't show it to anybody, Mary.

The future of peace in this world just landed on your shoulders. Don't fuck it up!"

This is what I wrote down, what I still have on my desk on a scrap of lined yellow paper:

We all inhabit this small planet. We all breathe the same air. We all cherish our children's future. And we are all mortal.

"It's beautiful."

"I have to find the right time and place to deliver the speech."

"Why not deliver it at a college commencement? You're allowed to be visionary when you're talking to students. You can be inspirational. You're allowed to dream, and you don't have to clear it with anybody."

I knew I had touched a nerve. I quoted the phrase back to him: "Jack, we're all mortal."

JUNE 11

Jack gave the speech yesterday. He delivered the commencement address at American University, pronouncing the words exactly as I had read them in the White House. Wearing a graduation gown and looking so happy in the sunshine of a Washington spring, Jack announced the Nuclear Test Ban Treaty. I realized I had only seen him in daylight once before. At my urging, he has struck a blow against the cold men that they will not soon forget. He has threatened their livelihood, more precisely their deathlihood. He has departed from the script, and intelligence professionals are men who read scripts, written for the most part in blood.

He reframed the argument with words that will halt, if but for a moment, the suicidal hatred of Russians we have all been programmed to bear. "For in the final analysis, our most basic common link is that we all inhabit this small planet. We all breathe the same air. We all cherish our children's future. And we are all mortal." The words of Ted Sorensen, the devout Unitarian, the megaphone of Jack's mind, a poet of politics.

There was no approval for the speech from the Pentagon, no input from the Joint Chiefs, no cooperation from the CIA. Jack stood there on his own, his own man, and delivered the address, leaving the cold men out in the cold. I quietly slipped in and out of the university to watch history, in which I had played my part, though as with so many women in history, anonymously.

Afterward I walked back along Massachusetts Avenue, back toward the cozy streets of Georgetown, thinking the world was now a different place by the sheer act of declaring it so. How lucky I was to be present as the world tilted ever so slightly on its axis toward peace. How lucky I felt to be wearing new tennis sneakers and walking in glittering Washington sunshine past mansions so breathtaking they now belonged to countries instead of people.

And then I noticed three men walking behind me. I felt them suddenly and whirled around. They were not close enough to intrude, but not too far to distinguish their features. Why did I think they were the three who'd huddled with Kirkland Jennings at the Wisners' party? A deep cold slowly climbed my legs. *I've lost a son!* I felt like shouting at them, screaming at them. *You can leave me alone!*

I walked faster. I crossed the street. I wondered how fiercely the men in National Security would react to a president urging us to reexamine our natures rather than build more weapons. And what indeed would they say if they knew that shaping the speech at American University, the call for a nuclear test ban treaty, was their own psychedelic drug of choice, LSD?

JUNE 14

Revelation is the natural tendency of information. When a critical mass of secrecy is reached, it seems, secrecy itself begins to unravel and disclosure erupts on a massive scale. This is my only explanation for a note left in my mailbox this morning, signed "V."

> *Too many lives have been destroyed.*
> *Meet me at the Key Bridge on the towpath 2 PM Saturday.*

Two possible lives diverged from the vortex of that note: the threatened life and the humdrum life. The threatened life, so much more real and vivid a sort of life than the routine one most of us choose. The threatened

life, so addicting in its bodily charge, has claimed cloak-
and-dagger men like Cord and James, has claimed rebels
of spirit like Tim Leary; something in him too must set
itself on fire rather than succumb to the deadliness of
routine.

I did not choose the threatened life. I simply have a
big mouth. And now I must accept threat as an air that I
breathe. Now, the nauseating scent of peril mixes with the
hydrangeas in the summer air of Georgetown. I read and
reread the note, first in disbelief, then with the realization
that it is a telegram from the next level of danger. The
kind of note they find crumpled up on floors next to bodies.

JUNE 17

I met the young man called V under the Key Bridge
by the canal on Saturday, beneath the hum of traffic
to Virginia. I will say little about him. He told me he
worked in the CIA in the Directorate of Plans, Cord's
department, the department responsible for covert action.
I thought the bizarrely banal and bureaucratic name
"Directorate of Plans" itself was a form of covert action.

"Why me?" I asked him.

"Many in the Agency feel it has all gone too far. And
there are rumors of plans that will go even further. Much
further than you can imagine."

"Why me?" I asked him again.

"We know about you. Everyone knows about you,
and we know that you know people. In fact, you know
everybody, and we believe you are the only person in

such a position of influence who is sympathetic to our thinking."

"So I'm the designated loudmouth?"

"You can do what you will with the information. My job is to share it. It has never been divulged before."

What V told me, I accepted. I will bear the truth.

What V told me, I write down from memory, feverishly.

What he told me is the secret history of LSD.

JUNE 18

Allen Dulles unleashed LSD on the world to reengineer the human mind. That was how V began his story. He said Allen Dulles considered the war against Communism a battle for men's minds, hence mind control the logical mission of the CIA. LSD was the tool of choice for the mission, a mission he code-named MKUltra. "MK" indicates that the operation emerged from the technical services division; "Ultra," that it carried the highest classification of secrecy.

As the truth of MKUltra spilled out along the towpath, I wondered if rather than being liberated by our acid trips, Timothy Leary and I had simply been dupes in some vast truth serum experiment engineered by Satan himself, Allen Dulles.

For a moment, I felt I could bear no more secrets. I wished to place my forty-two-year-old woman's body, the body of the mother of two remaining sons, not one inch farther into the realm of danger. The breeze blew gently through my hair and past all the souls of Georgetown, the trees swayed extraordinarily green and silent, the water of the canal flowed along its liquid way. The world was really quite beautiful, and I could simply choose to enjoy it. Real human beings perished in the wake of Joe Alsop's wine, James Angleton's cigarettes, my ex-husband's glass eye. I was qualified to swirl color on canvas and knit winter scarves for my sons in boarding school, but not to bring down Central Intelligence. Not to end the Cold War.

But I am a Pinchot. So I listened to V.

Here is the story he related:

LSD was an accident of chemistry. In a laboratory in Switzerland in 1943, experimenting with a derivative of the ergot fungus known as lysergic acid, Dr. Albert Hofmann accidentally underwent the world's first acid trip. When he swallowed his concoction, the boundaries between his mind and the universe dissolved. He had pierced the mystery at the heart of existence, the state of final truth that visionary seekers have pursued since the dawn of time. Dazzled by the discovery, he came to call lysergic acid diethylamide "medicine for the soul." He happened to pass the formula on to Dr. Harris Isbell, who happened to work with Allen Dulles, at which point the notion of "soul" was dropped from the equation.

Project MKUltra was launched in Lexington, Kentucky, under the guise of the first government drug treatment hospital. Famous black heroin addicts sent there to dry out now became human guinea pigs in

JULY 1

V and I walked up Wisconsin Avenue toward the
cathedral, the revelations of MKUltra continuing.
Information may be the underlying thread connecting
all phenomena, as stated in a *Scientific American* article I
read, and information may be the basic building block of
reality. But I have become a repository for information I
never wanted to know.

I told V that they broke into my house, that they
moved things. I asked if I was at risk, and he didn't
answer. He simply looked at me and asked if he should
continue. Yes. I saw that I was still on my own, so I
nodded for him to proceed, and he spoke of Operation
Midnight Climax. It was the creation of federal narcotics
agent and CIA operative George Hunter White, and
what he did, I did not want to hear. White created CIA-
financed bordellos and sent drug-addicted prostitutes
to pick up men, bring them back to the safe house, and
ply them with drinks laced with LSD. Psychological
research, CIA-style. Poising himself behind a one-way
mirror, guzzling martinis from a pitcher and surrounded
by photos of manacled women being tortured and
whipped, White watched the hallucinating men perform
sex with prostitutes, in a bizarre attempt to measure
the impact of psychedelic drugs on the human nervous
system. George Hunter White was famous for writing:
"Where else could a red-blooded American boy lie, kill,
cheat, steal, rape, and pillage with the sanction and
blessing of the All-Highest?" George Hunter White was

the man who trained Richard Helms and James Jesus
Angleton.

Double-hoodwinked, I said, these poor men, seeking
nothing more than relief from the unrelievable
urge nature has given the male body. Fooled first by
prostitutes, then by our government, winding up in an
unconsenting state of schizophrenia in a CIA whorehouse.

V told me something else he thought I might find
interesting. During the span of MKUltra, as the CIA
unleashed LSD on the world, they administered a routine
standardized test to prospective employees to gauge
their fitness for the CIA. The test had been written by a
clinical psychologist named Dr. Timothy Leary.

JULY 12

V left another message in my mailbox. There was a story
untold that deserved disclosure before taking its place in
the oblivion of a CIA file cabinet. He said it would be the
final message left in the mailbox. Any future messages
would be left behind the shutter nearest my front door.
So once again we walked the towpath from Key Bridge
toward Fletcher's Cove.

The canal flowed on, a wet, silent servant of
American history, and V began his story. It concerned
a bacteriologist named Frank Olson who helped the
CIA conduct experiments in chemical warfare. In one
such experiment, it seems, they dosed an unsuspecting
town in the south of France with LSD, transforming the
unconsenting village of Pont-Saint-Esprit into a tiny,

picturesque insane asylum. Suicides, people hurling themselves from rooftops, ripping off clothes and thrashing wildly, people screaming with hallucinations as flowers and snakes arose from their bodies.

To head off an investigation into the bizarre occurrences at Pont-Saint-Esprit, Allen Dulles launched a campaign of disinformation. The sudden outbreak of insanity, according to the explanation, was merely the result of fungus in the bread.

But Frank Olson suffered an affliction unforgivable to Allen Dulles: remorse. Possessing no such faculty himself, Dulles virulently suppressed it in the soldiers of his secret army. So to stop a whistle-blower from raising an explosive whistle to his lips, they plied Frank Olson with LSD for days of reprogramming at a secret CIA facility in the woods. But the acid failed to reinvigorate his Company spirit. In fact, it accelerated his confusion. A week later he mysteriously fell from the twelfth-floor window of a hotel onto the sidewalks of New York.

The official story was that Olson was simply another suicide. Who can fathom the demons that lurk within a human mind? This is the question upon which the CIA has built its citadel. Frank Olson was another perfectly executed CIA suicide.

I looked at V. "Do you think I might end up a suicide? Do you think I may succumb to a massive heart attack one sunny morning in Georgetown? Or accidentally fall from a train in Niagara Falls? There's no one else I can ask."

"I can't worry about you," V said abruptly. "I'm sorry. I can only tell the tale."

I am once again unprotected. With a suitcase of secrets to carry, and no one to help me with the luggage.

JULY 17

It's amazing how much we rely on the people we once enslaved to free us. Kenneth took me to Bohemian Caverns to hear a black saxophone player who had inspired his painting.

I was thrilled to find myself in the Negro precincts of Washington again, feeling more at home here than under the chandeliers of Georgetown. When I was a young journalist in New York, I went to Minton's and the Cotton Club in Harlem, and friends were always shocked when they heard it, but I knew I had nothing to fear.

It was midnight when we arrived, and all you could make out in the violet haze of cigarette smoke was silhouettes. A black man wearing an impeccably tight purple suit and pink tie led us to a table near the stage. A musician named John Coltrane was wailing on the saxophone—that is the only word I can find for it, wailing; it was not a sound I had heard before. It was a primal sound, a prehistoric beast screaming in a primeval landscape of earth rather than what we have come to call music. I realized that jazz is abstract art applied to air.

A pianist, a drummer, and a bass player accompanied John Coltrane, but each appeared to be in his own musical world, each emitting sounds through his instrument that seemed random and unstructured, not pertaining to what anyone else was playing, sound with no obvious rhythm to tap your foot to nor melody to hum on your way home. Yet it all seemed to jell. Like Ad Reinhardt's black paintings, it forced you to listen to what was there in the moment rather than rely on recognition of sounds familiar from the past.

I let the sounds wash over me. At times the saxophone sounded melodic, with a jaunty rhythm; then it would lose its footing and approach cacophony, as if it had jumped the tracks of music, and some human voice was screaming at you through the brass tube. Toward the end, the drummer began a stately rolling of drums, like the rolling cadence of timpani in a symphony orchestra, and for a moment the saxophone became melodic, almost biblical. It had a kind of sad, religious feeling to it, and John Coltrane gave me the impression that he wasn't trying to play, he was just playing, that there was no longer a separation between him and the saxophone, and that is how I would like to paint. The audience seemed transfixed, nodding their heads, and clapped loudly when John Coltrane left the stage. The man in the purple suit jumped to the microphone and in almost a whisper, said: "Ladies and gentlemen. 'A Love Supreme.'"

JULY 20
I am navigating lovers, the fate of a woman who has traded marriage's ritualized boredom for the madness of love unsanctioned by the state.

I have dismissed C. There was nothing further to explore, no deeper erotic upheaval to uncover, and I enshrine our encounters as a permanent exhibit in the Mary Museum of Flesh.

Kenneth Noland remains a lover, appropriate for a teacher and mentor. I consume his essence both bodily and intellectually, and our relationship takes shape in the shapes I conjure on canvas.

Stewart Z remains an occasional occasional. He is a funny writer, I laugh at his twists of words, but I am unaccustomed to men who do not take charge. Easy to say when the president is your lover. I have never been accused of being old-fashioned, but as willful and prone to adventure as I am, I do not want to lead a man, so Stewart will probably become even less occasional. I will miss the humor. I once went off on the threat of nuclear annihilation as we kissed, and since that night he has referred to me as "Apocalips."

As for Jack, he remains a walled garden of the heart. He is a future that dangles ever out of reach, but he is the north star in all my imaginings. It is his face that smiles when I imagine companionship.

It has been a while. You have no rights when you're a mistress. To a married man. Who is president of the United States. And I have been diverted by an atmosphere of threat, and the revelations of V, none of which I can share with Jack, so even my hidden life has a hidden life. But Kenny called me last night. Jack wanted to see me. I told him I was devouring *The Group*, I was

obsessed by this novel about Vassar girls just like me—
well, sort of just like me—and Kenny said there was
no one just like me. I laughed and told him I would put
down the novel for an evening, but Jack better make it
worth my while.

At the White House, Kenny said Jack wanted me to
meet him at the swimming pool. I told him I didn't know
there was a swimming pool, and he said FDR had had it
installed by a terrace off the west wing. "Polio."

Jack was alone, sitting in a deck chair by the pool,
surrounded by a glass pavilion and a long arcade of half-
round windows.

"You miss me?" He grinned, blowing out some cigar
smoke.

"How can I miss you? I see you on the cover of the
newspaper every day."

"How do I look?"

"You look better here. You're a little flat in
newspapers."

I sat down on his lap, and our lips joined. I am
tired of wondering if this love will become more than
sporadic flashes of desire, each event ignoring the chasms
between.

"Let's go for a swim," he said, ripping off his robe
and bathing suit. In the half-light, his body was still
remarkably boyish and thin. He climbed the ladder
carefully down into the pool as I dropped my clothes onto
the cement, not caring where they landed. Then I did a
massive cannonball into the water as we did as kids at

Grey Towers, sending a tidal wave that submerged him
for a moment.

I asked Jack how he could bear being in water after
what he'd gone through.

"You mean being on the Harvard swim team?" He
grinned, and I pushed his head underwater. He came
bobbing up, held me in his arms, and with a surprising
burst of strength, threw me several feet. I sank like
a boulder. When I resurfaced, I splashed him, and he
splashed me back.

"I meant during the war," I said. He said that after
swimming for hours through a Pacific Ocean crawling
with Japanese boats, all the while dragging his mate
Patrick behind him, the White House pool presented no
great challenge.

I enveloped him. I wrapped my legs around him and
kissed him, kissed the Irish teeth, kissed the weird mix
of cigar smoke and chlorine that hit my nostrils. There's
just no elegant way to be romantic in a pool. We rocked
in the water, and then he reached between my legs and
began fingering me. I wondered if the chlorine irritates
private parts. Then he tried getting inside me. It was
impossible. Then he lost his erection. "This is worse than
the Pacific," he said, and I answered, "You weren't trying
to do this with Patrick in the Pacific, were you?" He tried
coming into me again, jamming his cock against my
bush, but it was soft, so I began rubbing him.

"I am not going to dive down and use my mouth for
this," I said. "It won't work. I'm just too buoyant."

"Yes, Mary, you've always been too buoyant," he said, and we laughed and splashed and I said I would take care of him when we got back upstairs. Which I did.

That is a kind of status report on love. A progress report. Or a regress report. A Pinchot on the playing field of love. Only sister Tony has found happiness in marriage.

AUGUST 31

Bobby Kennedy invited me to an end-of-summer party at Hickory Hill, and I brought Kenneth Noland along as my date. Bobby made his usual whirlwind appearance in the middle of the evening. He gave every person an overenergized hello, as if it were one more campaign rally, except there were no more campaign rallies; they had won. Bobby always gives the impression he has desperately pulled himself away from something monumental in order to acknowledge your presence, and perhaps he has. He further gives the impression that he would like nothing better than to help you attain whatever it is you need, if he had but the time. So different from Jack, Jack who always seems removed from the hurly-burly of life, while Bobby seems commander in chief of the hurly-burly. The seventh or eighth kid in an Irish family, scrapping desperately to make it with his older brothers.

Jackie appeared, greeted the guests graciously, shaking hands with Kenneth as if she were welcoming Picasso himself. Having come from a similar breeding ground, I am fully aware of the code instilled in girls like us:

at each moment, whoever is in front of you is the most important person in your life.

Ethel has stopped drinking; she's sober and out of rehab for a month now, and she tells us LSD therapy has cured her alcoholism. It seems to have been a small dose, but potent enough to give her the distance on the levers of addiction. I felt like telling her addictions are delusions, tedious configurations of loss, rejection, and inadequacy frozen into us as children and carried thereafter to the grave. But I didn't. I congratulated her, saying I too have had experience with psychedelic chemicals and am more aware of the miracle of life every day. She seemed uncomfortable with that sentiment, old starry-eyed Mary once again introducing her voodoo, so instead of sharing the magnitude of my ambitions for world peace through LSD, I joked that she should turn Bobby on to acid. She laughed at the ridiculousness of the notion. She would leave that job to me, she said—she has a hard enough time getting him to come to dinner with the children.

I felt like circulating. I ride energies and sometimes, I can be a charm boat at parties, but I am accustomed to being alone, and when you're alone you are free. Even if you are lonely, you are free. But at Bobby's party I felt anchored down by Kenneth Noland. Like many artists who attain comfort only in a world controlled and created by themselves, he is awkward in social gatherings. His discipline and methodical nature have helped make him a painter of renown, though no one in this crowd

cares the slightest about his renown, but I suddenly
saw him as a bit of a bore. The night had a starry
magnificence, liquor flowed, Peter Duchin's band played
the songs that defined the century and my youth—
"Jeepers Creepers"!—and I had the urge to soar. But I
felt responsible for handling Kenneth, and I'm sick of
handling. Let the world handle itself.

So I peeled off my clothes and jumped into Bobby's
pool, utterly naked. I called out for everyone to strip and
join me, and I could hear Kenneth in the background
screaming, demanding I get out of the pool and put my
clothes back on. Daddy Amos, your daughter is naked in
the pool of the attorney general of the United States and
has just been ordered to behave by a pioneer of abstract
art! You have raised an interesting daughter.

"This is how it all started!" I shouted, and started
splashing water in Kenneth's direction. "We came
into this world naked and in water. I wasn't born in
tights and peasant blouses!" Kenneth yelled that I was
embarrassing him, and I shouted back: "You mean, I'm
bare-assing you!" Others leaped into the pool to join
me, many becoming as unhinged as I in the childhood
freedom of water, but whether they took their clothes off
or not, I don't know. Kenneth stormed out of Hickory Hill
and left me there alone.

SEPTEMBER 2

We buried the incident. That's what humans do, isn't
it? . . . bury the dead and go on. But Kenneth Noland

remains a glum presence in my life. Had he not been an artist I revered and indispensable to my development as a painter, I would have sent him the way of Cord and C.

Kenneth always says the paint will reveal what it wants you to do, so I have been listening closely. The paint has whispered "circle" to me, and I have begun working with circular shapes and circular canvases. A circle is infinite. Such a simple shape, yet so perfect. I cooked dinner last night for Kenneth and told him I have a new set of paintings. They are circular. He said he was not interested in seeing them. A pain arose in my midsection, and tears fell into the sink as I turned my back to him. The latest in a chain of men who are not there for me, who do not honor my devotion and what I consider my childlike sincerity.

My happiness is not dependent on Kenneth Noland, I reminded myself. I breathed deeply and set a plate of pasta down in front of him. My happiness is not dependent on Jack either, I reminded myself, is not dependent on any man. Obvious yet impossible to apply when the pain of need has overtaken your body. Such a declaration of independence from men would be a radical thought for the girls I grew up with, and an occasion for ridicule from women I know now. Am I suffering for them so that one day they will not have to suffer?

SEPTEMBER 16

Hot autumn is purely magical in Manhattan, the rough decay of New York covered over in a warm yellow light.

I needed release from threat. I needed to walk streets unknown and unwatched, in a city where possession of knowledge was not grounds for a funeral. So I traveled to New York.

Anne Truitt is back from Japan for a month, readjusting from Tokyo, or what she calls Mars with tea, so she joined me. We went to see one of the most important exhibits of 1963: Ad Reinhardt's black paintings at the Museum of Modern Art.

On the way to the museum, we stopped off at a restaurant called Max's Kansas City, where artists were said to congregate. There apparently is no Max and no Kansas City, but the steaks were excellent. A rather effeminate young man wearing large sunglasses held court at the table next to us. Anne asked if he was an artist—she is forthcoming, whereas I would never bother a stranger—and he said he was a painter and his name was Andy. When I asked what he painted, he said soup cans. Beside him was a man named Roushenburg or some such Jewish-sounding name. He answered the same question quite philosophically. "What is the separation between art and life? There's no reason not to consider the world as one gigantic painting." He said he is experimenting with placing junk and random objects on his canvases. Is he a sculptor or a painter?

Sitting beside him was a striking blond woman who appeared upset with the others. Isolated in her own mood, she paid no attention to us, working her way through a large steak and a strangely colored cocktail. Anne persevered and asked if she was an artist too, and the blonde mumbled in a deep, smoky voice shaped by a heavy German accent. All I could gather was that she was a model, and that Andy was urging her to sing in a band.

We took a taxi up to the Museum of Modern Art and the city was ablaze with sunlight, a radical contrast to what we would soon encounter in Ad Reinhardt's black works. I was so moved. They seem like nothing more than canvases of black paint until you look closely, until you look not at what you think is there but what is actually there. A moment comes when the invisible becomes visible. You gaze at a field of black, and suddenly you're not seeing a field of black, you're seeing ten distinct squares of color, each a different shade of black. They have been there all along, but your seeing didn't see it. "These are the last paintings anybody can paint," Reinhardt wrote in the program.

OCTOBER 2

Jack is going to Dallas. I didn't want to hear it. I told him not to go. You can feel these things. There is a blast furnace of hatred directed at him now, smoldering most intensely in the South.

Jack laughs when I talk this way and I suddenly see him as some kind of stubborn, naive fool, come of age on fairy tales of heroism. But really, are there heroes? I have a sudden urge to kiss him, to protect him—for a thousandth of a second I even pretend he is my husband—but I leave him be, he prefers not being touched, and I let him keep smiling. Untouched but knowing that I love him, he says gently that he is president of the entire country and must act accordingly. I tell him too many people have left me, and I couldn't live if I lost him too.

He puffed on his cigar, and I sat down on his lap. I looked up at an oil painting of James Madison. Someday, I thought, we will be gone, and new people will occupy the White House, as indifferent to us as we are to James Madison. "You're now at the seat of power," he said, as I shuffled my ass on his lap.

OCTOBER 4

After Dallas, Jackie will be going to Paris. Jack wants us to vanish someplace together when she is away, to Cape Cod perhaps, but I told him I don't want to talk about what happens after Dallas, I want to live right now. I told him our minds are curiously designed to keep living in the future, even though we never reach it. "We spend our lives right here, but we're never here."

Jack says: "Mary, you're giving me a headache."

Jack says: "Mary, you're the most philosophical blonde in the United States. What if we met at Camp David? What would Ike think of that?" He is unrelenting. I tell him I don't want to be hustled out of Washington to hide in the country at some government compound.

"In fact," I say, "I don't need to follow someone wherever they go, even you. Otherwise, I'm living their life, not mine."

Jack says he is not accustomed to being told no, and I tell him it's good for him to hear the word.

"Well, Mary"—he smiles—"maybe I have been missing out on the value of hearing the word *no*, or maybe you should be more loving after all we've been through together."

I have grown tense. As if I must end the Cold War before it ends me.

OCTOBER 7

Roxanne Arcturis speaks about the Divine Feminine in the Aquarian Age. She says: "Venus is opening portals for us to receive transmissions directly from her. We will enter a period called Venus in Retrograde. Retrograde will make Venus appear to be traveling backward in the heavens, but this stretch of time will bestow on women a revelation of our ability to heal the entire planet."

Venus in retrograde. It seems more a summation of an age that is ending than a future we are living into. Why have we been in retrograde for so long? Someone conceived this arrangement eons ago in some forest as a means to facilitate war. And we have agreed to bear children in retrograde, prepare meals in retrograde, devise fashionable hairstyles in retrograde, laugh at the foolishness of men—all in retrograde.

I am in retrograde. Is it my destiny to be up to my neck in the final realm of the Cold War and fade to my forgotten end along with it?

OCTOBER 15

My birthday. Joe Alsop phoned and wished me love and
a life filled with beauty and champagne for a hundred
years. Then he said he had a surprise for me.

"Diamonds?" I asked, we both knowing I care nothing
for rocks and metal on my skin.

"Bigger," he said.

"A Jaguar?" I asked, we both knowing I love my little
Studebaker and see cars much the way eternity does: as
boxes of metal with wheels, rusting their way to oblivion.

"More powerful."

"I'm tired of playing," I finally told him, and he
said: "Be here seven sharp tonight, and don't be tired of
playing when you get here."

"Maybe I'll get a second wind," I said.

So I arrived at seven, expecting a party, expecting the
regulars and certainly Ben and my sister, figuring I would
feign surprise when they sang "Happy Birthday," a song I
loathe, but when I opened the door there was no one there.
Joe came up and hugged me. "Ready for your surprise?"

"I'm already surprised," I said.

"Close your eyes, my dear, close your eyes," and the
next thing I knew he was blindfolding me, he was tying
a piece of silk across my eyes as gracefully as if it were
routine: "Trust, my dear, just trust and all will be well."

He held my arm and led me gently through the house.
I had no idea where I was, and then we walked through a
door.

"I will leave you now," he said, and pulled off the

blindfold as he exited through the door behind me. When I came to my senses, Jack was sitting there. I don't think human smiles get more joyous, more enveloping, his or mine. I was stunned, I fell into his arms and kissed him deeply. Surely this is what was meant by love.

"They let you out!" I said into his eyes.

"Kenny gives me one night off a year for good behavior."

"We're all alone!"

"All alone except for Joe Alsop, and he has orders from the commander in chief to stay on his side of the house or face charges of treason."

Why isn't life like this always? I thought, my mind already trying to possess, to hold on, to freeze the moment. Why can't we live like this forever?

We fell together on the couch, like teenagers in their parents' house alone for the first time and hungry beyond hunger for each other. I don't think he stopped smiling, I don't think his back ached or his stomach or his endocrine system or any of the other problems that normally ailed him.

I didn't know if he was coming into me or I was coming into him.

It was that kind of night.

It was my forty-third birthday.

NOVEMBER 27

I was painting. It's really all I know how to do. I was in my studio when I heard. When Anne Truitt called me with the news. It was a week ago. I don't know what

I've done for a week. I'm not sure I want to write this. I'm writing on empty. There is no desire expressed in these words. I'm not even sure why I bother. The diary doesn't concern me now. He is gone. It occurs to me every few hours and then it leaves me every few hours, it is a dream and I am quite ready to wake up. I have watched the proceedings on Anne's TV, they keep replaying the ceremony of flags and sadness, they keep replaying the fat gangster shooting Lee Harvey Oswald, they keep replaying John John saluting, and who can bear it?

I think that everyone I love will be taken from me. It is not logical, it is not rational, yet that is the thought that arises from deep within me, that is the summation of my life. I lose Rosamond and then I lose Michael and then I lose Jack and everything feels so ephemeral, thinner than air, and there is no place to stand.

I will keep painting because paintings make no sense and there is no way to make sense of this life, and I am not special. Everyone in the country cries and everyone is in shock, except for those who did this thing, and I am just one more person crying. I am just one more person crying. I could keep writing that. I will never forget my painting *Half-Light*, a wheel of four colors on a field of black, unfinished on the canvas in front of me when Anne called. It felt funny, the phone ringing, so I picked it up right in the middle of my work when I don't pick up phones, and I knew everything, everything was there in the way Anne said "Mary." He's gone. And life happens just like that, life happens at the speed of death, and an

empty space is borne by those still carrying on, there
are missing persons and we have the punishment to be
present. Yes, I read it in French, it was a French poet who
wrote: "The true tomb of the dead is the heart of the
living."

NOVEMBER 28

Days of emptiness. Dallas never leaves me now. First a
son, and now him. With a cataclysm, the cause of peace
was lost and my lover erased. Am I to blame somehow,
pushing him where they did not want him to go, pushing
him where he himself didn't want to go, or am I insane
to assume even a modicum of blame? I, anonymous and
inconsequential to a tragedy that will span generations
and history to come.

Today was foggy and overcast, too much of a cliché
to say that heaven was crying, and yet the earth was
intensely sad. I decided to go to the towpath. Whenever
I am lost, I walk by the canal, and in a wet gray world I
walked the path, unable to see the waters of the Potomac
for the mist. I simply walked, urged on by the force
that makes people walk in the rain, battered by spray
in my gray trench coat. Water scoured my eyes, now too
wet to cry. And then I saw a figure approach. Perhaps I
hallucinated it, two people lost in the storm at the same
point and time—when I looked at the face, it was Jackie
Kennedy. We had walked this towpath together before,
and here we were again, naked to each other, and we
hugged. We sobbed and hugged, a thousand miles away

from any words that could be spoken, only a sorrow. Is it only a woman who can feel such sorrow, who is allowed to feel such sorrow, two women crying over a husband who is gone, as women have cried over men taken from them since the birth of time? We cried for all the wives and all the women who have been left when a man has gone, and it felt like I held her in the rain forever.

NOVEMBER 29
Kenny O'Donnell, emissary from a man no longer there, invited me to Hickory Hill. It is the first Thanksgiving without Jack, a mournful Thanksgiving. The family was gathered for the holiday, there being nothing else for them to do except gather, a massive Irish family sharing their special relationship with death by virtue of a Catholic faith. Death had crept up on me too—you never notice death until it's there, driven as you are by the ceaseless rumble of dreams. And then one day your son is gone, and your marriage is gone, which is a form of death, and Jack is gone, and I say yes to Kenny; I will go to Hickory Hill. I am the character in a play I saw in New York City who said "I can't go on, I will go on." I say yes to Kenny and he tells me the family wants everyone to be together, but I can feel, unstated, that he does not want me excluded. The strange exile of mistresses. The death of the man you love, and you have no place in the proceedings; his proper family and official wife enact the rituals of mourning and you are left, breathing alone, in a vast chasm in which nothing is present but yourself.

We entered the living room, and Jackie was sitting next to Ethel, holding hands. I felt spectral, as if it was I who had died, that my soul was watching a film the way the dead apparently do, the way Roxanne Arcturis wrote of the Akashic records. I had the bizarre thought that each death transports you to the Hall of Records, and they are all here, Daddy Amos and ghost sister Rosamond and dear little Michael, chasing his big brother across the highway so as not to be late for dinner, but all I see is Kennedys.

I nodded quietly, and others nodded quietly to me, and I sat down beside Jack's sister Eunice. Kenny went and spoke to Ted, who seemed very young and very confused. Then Bobby came over, and I bolted up to hug him. He seemed like some young priest, so different from his brother, who had always exuded a sense of nobility and royalty. A very spartan and righteous young man, whose basic sadness had been transmuted into a posture of unyielding toughness. An avenging angel staring straight in my eyes. "Thank you for coming, Mary," he said, and I knew he continued to be generous, even in grief. He was acknowledging what I was to Jack—it was obvious he knew, I never knew he knew, and now no words came from me. I was deep in myself and hadn't even taken off my sunglasses. Then he said, and he seemed so vulnerable saying it: "I thought they would get me instead of the president." I just nodded and hugged him and he moved on. I don't know why he told me that, but I have never been so aware of the danger we were all in, the wineglasses and leafy boughs of Georgetown no more than a dream inside a horror of death and evil, monsters and serpents just waiting for us somewhere beyond M Street.

A Negro serving maid in black dress and frilly white apron asked me if I wanted a plate with turkey and stuffing, and I just shook my head, looking into the sad world of her brown eyes. "When they brought him home," she said slowly, "Mrs. Kennedy was still wearing that suit with the blood all over it. She wouldn't take that thing off her body. She just kept wearing it, and I said let me take that thing off you, but she just said 'No. Let them see what they've done.'"

DECEMBER 5

Post-Dallas winter days are gray enclosures surrounding pieces of the world, a visual representation of the emptiness at the root of all things. I think of loss, of what might have been after he left office, when perhaps we would finally have been together, when his brutal catalog of ailments might finally begin healing. But it is impossible. There is no way to picture him other than as he was, smiling at a nation and walking briskly down paths toward helicopters, or lying in my arms eager and throbbing in unofficial hours of passion. Could he have been a professor? A writer? A free-floating intellectual free from his father's command? A shining ambassador for peace through the kingdoms of the world?

I went to the towpath again yesterday. I looked

through gray fog out to the undulating Potomac and thought Jack had become like a poem now, though he was not a poetic man. He was actually quite shy, and in his desperation never to be alone, in his mad obsession with fucking, he was, I have come to realize, a somewhat sad character. I came to love him later than he came to love me. Sometimes love catches up. And sometimes too late.

DECEMBER 12

I am hollow. The organism with which I meet the atmosphere has receded, maybe I hover two inches from myself. How many people have to leave you before you refuse to stand there and be left again? I hold my brush in my hand and allow the paint to speak.

I am left with pure optical truth. I retain that as a gift from Kenneth. In a life when meaning is too brutal, I embrace a form of painting with the meaning removed. Painting with no claim to represent some separate reality existing outside the frame. The frame is the crossroads, the place where the painting meets everything in the universe that is not the painting.

Because I am hollow, because I have learned my lessons from Kenneth Noland well, I am removing all gesture and all texture and all emotion from my work, letting color and not the design carry the painting.

My arm moves and shapes just float on the canvas as we human beings just float in the world, shapes without meaning. And what we don't know is that we have no meaning.

1964

JANUARY 11

Quentin and Mark are home for winter break, this winter when the losses accumulate like the wisps of snow that dust the yards of Georgetown. They are just wisps. We are too far south for the white winters of my childhood, and the calendar's turning to 1964 brings no renewal. But at least my sons are back, happy and fidgety, back in the little house with their long-lost mom.

I cooked up spaghetti and meatballs. It brings them back to their childhood, the days when Michael was still with us and we were all still a family. As I watch them devour the spaghetti, I cannot help but think of the strange fate of mothers and sons. I was there when they were born and there when they were young, but I won't be there when they are old. They will grow old without me; I will become a distant memory of diminishing significance, a photograph in a frame in some room that they will not particularly take notice of after a while, except when they pack it up to move to a new house. Your children replace you, and then they themselves become the next generation of the forgotten.

So now Michael is not with us, the Tragedy without end; Cord is gone, buried in secrets; and my sons spend their days in boarding schools far up north in the woods of Massachusetts. Their childhood is a lost memory.

I do not like to write about my sons, and will not do so again. They belong to a private realm beyond the conversation recorded in these pages.

But yesterday, Quentin brought home a pile of papers from Cord's house for me to sign. School reports, health records, the paperwork parents get used to signing as part of the job of being parents. I have never been comfortable with paperwork. Cord is much more thorough. He relishes controlling events through indications written on paper. He is accustomed to the weight and significance of documents, while I am more comfortable with canvas and color. Nevertheless, dreading the tedium, I went through the papers this morning at the kitchen table. Buried in the pile, I found a document that did not seem to pertain to Quentin and Mark. Nor did it seem to emanate from a school office.

The document was a diagram, an organizational chart written in what seemed like strange code. I asked Quentin if there was supposed to be a diagram or chart among the papers Cord wanted me to sign, and he said he had no idea. His father had told him to take the papers on his desk to his mother. Quentin had gone into Cord's home office and taken all the papers on the desk and piled them into his briefcase. He took every paper he could find because he could not bear his father scolding him for leaving anything behind. I looked at the document and suddenly knew I would never show it to Quentin.

JANUARY 17

Jack always loved Kenny O'Donnell, and so did I. Kenny was the beating heart of the Irish mafia surrounding Jack—best friend, confidant, chief political guru. Ted Sorensen once said if Jack Kennedy ever ordered Kenny O'Donnell to jump off the Empire State Building, Kenny would ask for a towel to be put down so he wouldn't mess up the sidewalk.

Kenny is a tortured man now. He blames himself for the assassination. It was he who organized the trip to Dallas. He phoned me up to say he was ready to talk if I was, and I was so happy to hear from him. Kenny was always affectionate and respectful. I think he knew that had Jack served out his two terms, he might have divorced Jackie and married me.

I told him we should meet somewhere private, someplace no one would see us. I've begun to live as a spy. Clandestine has become second nature to me, as if prowling through the chambers of a secret life was bequeathed to me by my ex-husband, along with child support. But I am also a contradiction: a covert operator with an overt mouth. A woman without restraint, which is inconvenient to the cold men. They don't like women without restraint. So I don't know what they have in mind for me. I don't know if they have anything in mind for me. I don't even know who they are. Is an invisible threat more insidious than a visible one? Or am I the threat? My family has troubled the status quo of things for generations, and now I have come to know things, secrets, more than I ever wanted to know. There is also a part of me numb to the onrush of events, a part that simply doesn't care anymore. Too many people have died and left me now. I notice myself walking over the carcass of their memories.

Kenny told me to meet him at Don Luigi's in McLean at five.

JANUARY 19

Kenny was seated when I arrived, had already begun the daily regimen of gin martinis. Three more would disappear inside him before the evening was out. We hugged, he lingered that extra millisecond, he was hugging the memories of the past. A hug can offer a split-second illusion that the past can be held on to if you but squeeze hard enough, even though it has already disappeared into the vacuum of time. His skin was as I remembered, pasty and freckled, so dry, as if no moisture ever entered him though he drank incessantly. The dark circles and sad pouches were new.

He told me he was working for LBJ and planning an exit strategy. He was considering a run for governor of

Massachusetts. You'd make a good one, I told him, though I knew Kenny was never a man for the spotlight. He is a backstage man. We are some of us born to shine, and some of us born to polish those who shine.

I myself am a private person. I know in fact that I am peculiarly private. I do not allow myself to be photographed, for instance. There are no pictures of me. I will not let a false image of myself be frozen permanently onto paper. Yet my life has continually been cast with public figures. My parents were public figures, I grew up surrounded by public figures, virtually everyone I know today is a public figure. Only I am not.

Kenny shook his head, and tears flooded his eyes. "It's a nightmare," he said.

Poor bloodshot Irish eyes. "We lost our best friend," I told Kenny, and burning memory condensed to tears in my eyes.

Kenny and Dave Powers were in the motorcade behind Jack. Jack had wanted them to ride behind him, wanted them to sense the crowd, wanted to know if the people loved him. Jack always wanted to know things; he exhausted people with questions, he especially needed to know how much he was loved. Maybe that's what made him a deft politician.

Kenny said that when the cars turned onto Elm Street, it was like riding into an ambush. He heard four or five shots. Two of them came from the front, from somewhere near the fence on the grassy knoll. He later reported that to the FBI, but the FBI was under orders not to hear it. The FBI agents said it couldn't have happened that way. "I told them I flew B-17 bombardiers. I flew thirty missions against Nazi Germany. I was shot down and escaped from enemy prison. I know what a bullet sounds like, and I can tell what direction it's coming from. They said I must be imagining things, please rethink it and tell us where the bullets came from. The whole thing was an excruciating exercise. They didn't want to know the truth. And I didn't want to stir up any more pain or trouble for the family, so I testified the way the FBI wanted me to. I'm on record saying all the shots came from behind, from the Book Depository. But it's a fucking lie."

I told Kenny I've been working my way through the newspaper reports, official announcements, marking things up, ripping out pages, scribbling comments, underlining lies, but finally I stopped. It was just too hard, and I had lost the point. I told him that when the ground is composed of lies, it's like gravity has been suspended, and I'm tempted to just continue painting and stop thinking. Plus, I keep getting warnings.

"I don't think they will bother you," he said. "But how do I know? I know what they're capable of, and their faces are well hidden."

"Cord used to tell me I was being protected. I took it for granted. Now I'm no longer being protected."

"Mary, Oswald tested negative for firing a rifle."

He spoke it simply and then let it hang in the air, as if it were the summary of his testimony. As if it were the signature fact his life would then turn on. We remained quiet as the waiter laid two dishes of pasta on the table. Kenny said no more. Our best friend was gone, and there was no more to say. He was crying. What becomes of a woman who doesn't shut up? I wondered. Kenny is busy crying. Cord and James Jesus are off somewhere smoking and smirking. Bobby is in a pit of despair, waiting for his moment to strike, or not sure that moment will ever come. That leaves me. Can a blonde go up against the whole world?

JANUARY 22
I am looking at the document that mysteriously appeared amid the school papers. At the top of the page is a title:

JM/RESET.

I have no idea what this means, or what language it refers to. At the top of the organization chart is a box that says:

M.

A line extends from this box to the right that says:

HELM.

Another line leads down from M. that says:

HARV.

From HARV, three lines descend downward to three separate sections:

AGENCY.   **MOB.**   **CUBANS.**

Under AGENCY, three lines extend to three boxes that say:

EHH.   **DATPHIL.**   **DFITZ.**

Under MOB, three lines extend to three separate boxes:

STRAF.   **CMAR.**   **JROS.**

Under CUBANS, three lines extend to three separate boxes:

DMORAL.   **MANART.**   **RCUB.**

Under AGENCY, another line extends to a separate box:

PONTCHARTRAIN

Under PONTCHARTRAIN, two lines extend to two separate boxes:

FERR.   GUYB.

Under CUBANS, a line extends to a separate box:

CORSICA LSART.

Was it a mistake, or did someone want me to find this page?

JANUARY 25

What if you came upon a code? That's what I asked the code man himself, Frank Wisner, the CIA's father of black ops. We were sitting in his garden as he sipped an old-fashioned. I could see the load of woe he bore behind his eyes, eyes trained to reveal nothing, trained by the forces of our nation for cipherhood.

What if you came upon a code?

I asked it casually, but in my sweat there sat a lie, discernible perhaps to the lie detector hidden in his nostrils. He stared blankly, and my eyes disappeared into the slice of lemon in his glass, such a bright yellow against the brown whiskey. I said the code begins with two capital letters, J and M, and they are followed by a slash, and the slash is followed by the word *reset*, spelled out in capital letters.

"JM slash RESET?"

I nodded. He asked me where I had seen such a code, and my body registered that a mistake had been made. Frank is customarily quite light with me, quite comforted in some way by my presence. I occur to him differently from the other women in our circles. His electroshocked Cold War psyche seems at ease with me, a woman who demands nothing of him, who brings her own happiness to the occasion. But the mention of a code had set off flash warnings, so I made light of it, sick to death of danger and a life where lives are lived under cover. I laughed that the code was simply something overheard at a party. "There's nothing but codes at some of these parties," I said, an absurd attempt at whimsy. "They have more codes than hors d'oeuvre!"

Frank was quiet. Many things transpire at parties in Georgetown. Cases of hard liquor flow without end. Assignations occur secretly in walk-in closets and pantries. An Amazon River of gossip, rumor, truth, and untruth flows through the conversations of men who run the government, men who spy, men who scribble opinions in newsprint, and all the women who accompany them, like mothers overseeing an alcoholic playground. But the casual tossing about of secret codes is simply not a staple of these parties.

"JM slash RESET?" he asked once again.

"Yes, that's it, I think."

"It's a CIA cryptonym." He said it wearily.

"Of course," I said, wondering if he could hear the blood racing down a speedway in my head, wondering how many more friends and how many more enemies I would be condemned to irritate before the world has had enough of me.

"It's a code name. That's how we designate operations in the Agency. Names always begin with a digraph. A two-letter prefix. A prefix indicating the geographical or functional area of the operation."

He asked me to repeat the prefix, though I knew he remembered it. "JM. Which stands for . . ." I paused.

"Yes," he said. "Cuba."

JANUARY 27

I took out the organization chart and laid it on my desk. Frank Wisner had provided the key, and suddenly the language of code became obvious. It was the architectural blueprint for a CIA operation in Cuba. "Cubans" had been there all along, but just as with Ad Reinhardt's black squares, I hadn't seen it. Now I could see there were three groups comprising this mission: AGENCY referred to the CIA operatives; MOB, the mobsters working in partnership with the CIA; and CUBANS, the anti-Castro Cuban underground working in confederacy with both groups. There is a shooter with CORSICA in front of his name, but I don't know what CORSICA is code for.

JM/RESET is the name of the operation. They are doing a reset. Of course. they are doing a reset of Cuba. After the fiasco at the Bay of Pigs . . . after Jack's refusal to be maneuvered by Allen Dulles into sending in air support that would have turned the invasion of Cuba into an

official US government action . . . after abandoning 1,400
soldiers on a beach in Cuba . . . after adding the fury
of anti-Castro Cubans to the blood oaths already sworn
against Jack and Bobby by mobsters . . . after all this, they
are at it again. I have uncovered a CIA plan to assassinate
Castro.

FEBRUARY 4

Just when I thought I could bear no more secrets, I
noticed the shutter ajar by my front door. When I looked
closely, I saw a message taped to it.

> *Connect the dots.*
> *National Cathedral 2 PM Thursday.*
> *V*

I thought V was gone. I thought he had done his job,
had explicated the dark, sad story of LSD gone wrong and
then moved on, leaving me helpless with the information.
What can I do about MKUltra? But he was back, the first
contact since the assassination, and I headed to meet him
at the cathedral yesterday, carrying a heart of loss. The
time comes when you long for the world to be the world,
and not a vast intrigue where pieces of evil keep falling
into your lap.

The cathedral is a house of death, I thought, unsure
why, looking up at the vast assemblage of gray stones. A
strange music box built for eternity. And now it would
become a house of truth and lies. In its shadows, in the

shadows of the Washington National Cathedral, I sat on a park bench and saw V walk toward me.

"Frank Olson."

"Yes?"

"I told you Frank Olson fell from that hotel window? Dead on the streets of New York. Well, the man who pushed him was a hit man, a drug runner and intelligence asset named Pierre Lafitte. Now you must follow the string. Massive crimes succeed because people do not follow strings. Here is the string. Pierre Lafitte once worked at William B. Reily, a coffee company in New Orleans. William Reily was a fanatical anti-Communist and financier of a CIA-funded propaganda outfit called the Crusade to Free Cuba. He had worked for the CIA for years.

"So here is this thug and intelligence asset, Pierre Lafitte, working with another intelligence asset named Reily in a business smack in the center of the intelligence community in New Orleans. So who else is working at that coffee company at exactly the same time as Lafitte? Lee Harvey Oswald. This supposed Communist who supposedly defected to Russia at the height of Cold War anti-Communist hysteria, when people are practically being arrested for attending socialist meetings, this guy comes back from Russia after proclaiming that he gave secrets to the Russians, and what does the US government do to him? Nothing."

"He was an asset," I said.

"He was an asset."

I looked over. A group of children were filing into the side of the cathedral, all holding a rope as they walked. They were an organism, and the rope was their spine. They entered the cathedral innocent and uncomprehending. Innocence was their job for the moment, I thought, but our jobs change, and they will lose their innocence in due course. That is the way it is. And in Washington, DC, they may lose it in dramatic fashion.

"I'll run this by you again," said V. "Lafitte and Oswald are both working for the same CIA-affiliated, Kennedy-hating, anti-Castro fanatic in New Orleans. Now follow this. As an assassin, Pierre Lafitte uses all sorts of pseudonyms. One pseudonym is Louis Hidell. So in March of 1963, Lee Harvey Oswald purchases a mail-order Carcano Model 91/38 carbine rifle with a telescopic sight, using the alias A. Hidell.

Both Lafitte and Oswald used the same alias: Hidell.

I told V I had heard enough. There was another matter I needed to discuss. I told him a document had come into my possession that I needed to decipher. He said he would meet me back at the cathedral in three days.

"Are you in any danger?" I asked him.

"I'm already dead," he said.

FEBRUARY 17

Why are you dead? I asked V when we met again in the shadows of the cathedral. I was haunted by his ominous remark, and he stared in his typical fashion, without

aspect. He said two words: "Operation Cleanse." Ever
since the assassination, agents had been disappearing.
Agents who knew things, agents who felt that the
obsession with Cuba had distorted the mission of the
agency, had rendered the CIA indistinguishable from the
criminal underworld it had joined hands with. V said that
his time was limited, he was certain of it, and his job was
to tell the tale while he still could.

"To make the invisible visible" were the words that
suddenly flashed through my mind, like the Force That
Has No Name who has delivered us all out of invisibility.
Maybe I had a fever. Maybe my LSD trips were flashing
back. Maybe I could not process what was taking place.
One more person was being taken away from me, and I
didn't even know his name.

I told V I had come upon an organization chart,
written in code. I needed to understand it. I was not
ready to share the original document with him, I couldn't
even tell him why, but I had written out some names for
him. He took the page and said to meet him on the same
bench in two days.

I turned to go, but V said he had something else to
say. Someone had told him that James Angleton and
Katharine Graham had been seen having dinner together
over the weekend, and this person had overheard her
discussing my plan to turn the men of power on to LSD.

I felt sick to my stomach. An unbearable heat of blood
flooded the veins of my temples. "The witness said
Katharine appeared amused, telling Angleton something

to the effect: 'Could you imagine Phil whacked out on LSD and bringing peace to the world!' Whereupon James Angleton replied quietly, referring to me: 'Well, you know, Mary's an artist, and artists come up with the most creative solutions to things!' My contact felt he wasn't being truthful. That something had stunned him about the LSD experiments, and it may be in your interest to rethink them."

Chantilly Lace was dead.

FEBRUARY 22

The Hindu goddess has blue skin and wears an impenetrable smile. She sits beatifically on the skin of a dead tiger, while a candy-colored landscape soars backward toward a fairy-tale infinity. She is focused on me.

The postcard of the goddess arrived several weeks ago. I taped it to the refrigerator, hoping for whatever blessings the blue goddess had to deliver—I am so blessing-deprived of late. On the back of the postcard was a phone number and a short note. "All is flux. Timothy Leary."

So Tim returns to my life. We are both misfits, both targets of the invisible power that I first married into, then divorced from, the power that stands immovably in the way of human evolution. Tim seems to ride above the power like a surfer on turbulent waters, while I feel earthbound and weary. I dialed the number on the postcard this morning.

I no longer felt the fiercely determined woman who

had phoned him at Harvard what seems like an awfully long time ago. A man with an Indian accent answered. I asked for Timothy Leary, the phone was handed over, and there was the mellifluous voice once again. I exploded. I told him I'd been betrayed. I told him I had been naive, had not realized the dangers of trust, I had unwittingly been a bull in a china shop of secrets. Someone had spread word of the psychedelic wives' project, and it had now reached the highest echelons of the CIA. He asked if I was in danger, and I told him I didn't know anymore. You can't trust anybody, I told him, not even women, or especially women—it was a woman who had betrayed me, so be careful. I never thought I would be saying that. I had never thought of myself as anything but an artist and a mom, simply that, a mom with eccentric tastes perhaps, because normal moms don't generally sleep with married men who run the world, but a mom nonetheless. And then it all explodes in your face, like you are vomiting into a storm and you realize you are naked.

Tim said he lived in a mansion now, on an estate surrounded by verdant woods. He had opened it up to a rather bohemian cast of characters who continued the psychedelic quest, who were imbibing the latest iterations of chemical expansions both indoors and out . . . LSD, DMT, mescaline, mushrooms, peyote . . . strange people showing up at the estate every day from who knows where, dancing naked on the roofs with bare-chested rock 'n' roll bands blaring away on the lawns, playing to nobody and everybody and the woods. He told me to

escape Washington once and for all. Leave the hellhole
of the power delusion and come to paradise in Millbrook,
New York, he said. I could stay as long as I wanted. And
paint. There were all sorts of artists there, he said, many
of them painting on the walls. Jasper Johns had taken
acid there one day and painted the piano pink.

I told him I would think about it, I would figure it out,
I would contemplate my next move. I would be in touch.
I didn't know anymore.

"Remember—" He laughed as I hung up. "The
universe is an intelligence test."

MARCH 15

We are guests in a private world of occurrence; my life is
what occurs to me, your life is what occurs to you, and we
are all making do until everything is washed away, till
no one remembers you, no one remembers me, till new
people live in our houses and repaint them accordingly.

I walked the leafy sidewalks of untruth this morning,
in this town named for a forgotten king. I waved hello to
Anne Chamberlain on her daily jog. She is such a physical
specimen. She will live a long time. I contemplated
the nature of facts and asked the trees: Is the CIA
eliminating the existence of truth, or is life a conspiracy
even more diabolical?

MARCH 18

The assassination has wiped the smile off the face of
Georgetown. There are still dinners in stuffy living

rooms, people still jabber incessantly about politics and
drink themselves sick, Lorraine and Vangie and Bebe
still gossip and judge breaches of decorum harshly—but
my heart is not in any of it. I have too little spirit and
too many secrets. My Georgetown adventures among the
drunk and powerful have faded to an unremembered
series of cigarettes and salons. My dreams of Planet
LSD seem embarrassingly naive. My plans for love are
buried in Arlington Cemetery. All I have is a chart.
The breakers-in, the hidden watchmen, the clandestine
brotherhood of Cord Meyer and James Angleton and
Kirkland Jennings . . . they are no longer kidding with
me, they are charmed neither by my breasts nor my
paintings nor the aristocratic pronouncements that flow
from my lips. They are unthrilled with my performance
as a supporting female on the stage of Georgetown, and
they would commit the unspeakable to get this diary. Out
of breath, out of ideas, all I have left against them is a
chart.

MARCH 21
This chart exerts a kind of totemic power over me, with a
code that substitutes for language just as lies substitute for
truth. It is as if my life ebbed and flowed like a Mississippi
River through the middle years of the twentieth century
and culminated in a chart. It has dawned on me that
with this chart, this unofficial official document, with
this indisputable proof, I could bring down the entire
apparatus of Central Intelligence. The entire assassination

machine. And then, perhaps, with the house of lies in smoking ruins behind me, I could gather up my paints and brushes and sons and move on. Back to Grey Towers?

"I will show you the original document next time," I told V, still unclear of my own reticence. "I just need verification of what this chart means. I need to know who these people are."

"Nobody can know you have this document," he said, and when I nodded, the revelations of information began.

"HARV stands for William Harvey, head of the assassination apparatus of the Agency. Executive Action—those are the code words for assassination. Harvey is a drunken beast, a thug of the first rank who happens to be a legend in the CIA." I nodded and scribbled some notes. "William Harvey was up to his eyeballs in the Bay of Pigs and every one of the Company's anti-Castro operations, the ones Kennedy knew about and the ones he didn't. This whole initiative was code-named ZR/RIFLE, and Harvey was still organizing raids on Cuba at the height of the missile crisis, while Kennedy was negotiating with Khrushchev. When Bobby Kennedy got wind of it, he almost tore Harvey's lungs out. Harvey was exiled to Rome to run the CIA office there but Company guys never disappear. They just forge new secrets. Rome is where Bill Harvey became intimate with the Mafia.

"OK, the men under the heading AGENCY. EHH stands for E. Howard Hunt. He's like a black-ops popinjay, active throughout Latin America, but he turns up everywhere some covert action is going down. He was in Dallas on November twenty-second. That's all I'm going to say about him. Now DATPHIL—that's David Atlee Phillips, director of Western Hemisphere operations for the CIA. The guy in charge of Cuban operations for the CIA in Mexico. I'm told he was a case officer for Oswald and met with him in Mexico City shortly before Dallas. DFITZ is Desmond FitzGerald. He is a guide for the new director, McCone. OK?" I wrote swiftly, as if I was back in class, taking notes. I was overwhelmed. He said he would have more for me in two days, on the towpath by the Key Bridge.

MARCH 28

I handed V the document, an evil configuration of codes that entered my life through the innocent hands of my son. Something gripped my chest as he took possession of the paper; the transfer was the crossing of a line. On the other side of the line, V would carry the document back where it came from, back to Central Intelligence, where he would ask questions no one wanted to answer. He studied the chart, and I became aware of the steady hum of traffic on the bridge above us, like the hum of the universe that is always there since the beginning of time but we never hear it.

He held up the document and pointed to names.

"First, under the heading MOB, JROS stands for Johnny

Rosselli, the Silver Fox of Las Vegas, one of the heads of the mob in America. He is William Harvey's link to the Mafia. He organized the meeting at the Fontainebleau Hotel that launched the underworld plot to kill Fidel Castro. Rosselli, Sam Giancana, and Santo Trafficante all met in Rosselli's suite with John T. McRogers, operations chief of the security division of the CIA. STRAF stands for Santo Trafficante, who ran the casinos in Havana until Castro seized them and evicted Trafficante along with the full complement of American gangsters and executives of the United Fruit Company. Trafficante heads the mob in Florida now.

"CMAR stands for Carlos Marcello, head of the mob in New Orleans and Texas. He is crucial here, in case that wasn't obvious. He must be paid attention to. His empire includes Dallas, in case that wasn't obvious either. Bobby Kennedy went after Marcello ruthlessly, relentlessly, finally deporting him one day with no warning. Marcello didn't even have a chance to say goodbye to his family. That's when he swore a blood oath against the Kennedys.

"Under the heading of CUBANS, DMORAL stands for David Sánchez Morales. He's an assassin, pure and simple—a cold-blooded killer and CIA operative in the Directorate of Plans, the department responsible for Executive Actions. His nickname is El Indio, because he's dark-skinned and Mexican and he was a close associate of Bill Harvey on ZR/RIFLE. Morales was sighted in Dallas. You can draw your own conclusions. Finally, MANART stands for Manuel Artime, one of the most vociferous

Cuban exiles in the war against Castro. He led one of the brigades in the Bay of Pigs."

Everything seems to come down to the Bay of Pigs. That's what I told V. The Bay of Pigs is like a giant force field emanating from a swamp in Cuba. He looked at me without comment.

APRIL 5

The Company has crept into the veins of power, the plodding machinery of government replaced by the silvery apparatus of assassination. Jack was ready to dismantle the whole stinking house of lies. Only I know this footnote to a colossal tragedy.

APRIL 6

Only I know that an infinitesimally small particle of loss among the infinity of loss in Dallas was a skinny boy's love for a girl.

APRIL 12

V and I met at the Zoological Park yesterday, inside the Reptile House. When we dream of horror, we dream in reptile. Lizards and snakes! You are innocent! You are simply victims of our metaphors! And then it all came pouring out.

I told V once again that I was being followed. My phone was bugged. My house had been entered, my possessions rearranged for no apparent reason. There was no longer safe ground for me to walk on. My ex-husband had removed whatever protection I had. Even Katharine Graham had betrayed my mission to transform the world with LSD. But I promised V that I would tell the tale, our dangerous tale, however I could.

V listened without reaction; there is that in him which I will never reach. He pulled the document from his pocket. "Pontchartrain is a lake in southern Louisiana. The CIA set up a guerilla training camp there, an assassination school for Cuban exiles. The Pontchartrain training camp is overseen by the two men listed below. FERR is David Ferrie—a vicious character, an anti-Castro zealot with long ties to the Marcello family in New Orleans. He's connected to every part of the mob-connected Cuban exile underground. GUYB is Guy Banister, a private detective and former FBI man who works with Ferrie. These are rabid, right-wing operatives headquartered in New Orleans and up to their asses in CIA anti-Castro operations."

"Who is CORSICA LSART?"

"I don't know."

"HELM?"

"That's obvious. Richard Helms. The Kahuna. He heads all the Cuban efforts at the Agency."

"And M?"

"I don't know."

I watched a crocodile undulate and ooze through murky green water, separated from the air of Washington, DC, by nothing more than a thin pane of glass.

APRIL 18

I am making a point of not describing V. I am making
a point of allowing him to remain a cipher to history.
Whatever may become of me, whatever may become of
this diary, his journey will be faceless and anonymous,
even as he removed the ciphers from an organization
chart and rendered them human for history. I am hoping
he was wrong about Operation Cleanse.

We met for the last time on a little bridge in
Dumbarton Oaks Park. "I've got LSART for you," he said.
"It stands for Lucien Sarti."

"And who is Lucien Sarti?"

V was quiet, looking down at the water. "An assassin
and drug runner for the Corsican mafia," he said finally.

"The Corsican mafia?"

"William Harvey was booted out of the Company by
Bobby Kennedy during the missile crisis. But Harvey
ended up in Rome, not hell, where Bobby would have
preferred he go. While he was based at the Rome bureau
of the CIA, Harvey made connections to the Italian
mob through his friend Johnny Rosselli. And the Italian
mob connected him to the Corsican mafia, based out of
Marseilles. The Corsicans are very useful as assassins.
They're legendarily ruthless, barely civilized, in fact, and
far enough removed from the fray to remain invisible.
Bill Harvey uses Lucien Sarti for his 'wet work.'"

I listened to the words "wet work" and suddenly heard
the gurgling waters churning below the stone bridge.
How did a Vassar girl from Grey Towers end up on a

bridge, conversing about wet work and Corsican assassins rather than Emily Dickinson and Egyptian archaeology?

V handed me back the document. He didn't need it anymore. I looked once more at the name on top: JM/ RESET. "It's obvious to me," I said. "They're planning another invasion of Cuba. They're planning another assassination attempt on Castro. This is the team. This is the organization chart. How do we stop them?"

V looked at me without emotion. As if he wasn't even hearing me. "I thought we could stop it. The Big Event."

"The Big Event?"

"Dallas. That's why I started talking to you in the first place. MKUltra was just a place to start. We thought if the secrets started pouring out, we could gum up the works. Confuse them. You know the principle that if even so much as one detail shifts, you can alter history? We failed."

"We failed. And you think you're on their list?"

"I know I am."

I hugged him. It was all I could think of to do. He stood frozen, motionless, as I wrapped my arms around him and placed my cheek against his. Yet another son I was powerless to save.

"Why don't you just leave?" I asked him.

"Where would I go?"

"You could see the world."

"I've seen it."

He looked at me as if his personal nature had ceased to exist. Then he walked off, and I was alone again on a bridge.

APRIL 24

This morning, I found a message taped to the back of my shutter.

M stands for Cord Meyer.
Now the picture is complete.
Veritas

MAY 4

I dreamed of Jack. We were on a sailboat heading far, far out to sea. He was so confident and so happy, turning the wheel and pulling those ropes—I'm not sure of the nautical terms, and we were never on a boat together. But the waves grew bigger, and I said we should turn back. He said he didn't know which way was back and kept grinning. Suddenly my ghost sister Rosamond appeared: she was sitting with her long legs stretched out in front of her, sipping a glass of wine and relishing the wind that splayed her hair back against the sky. I noticed her bare feet, so long and so beautiful, much more beautiful than mine, and she wasn't scared. We're never getting back to land! I cried, but she just smiled and said, Jack is a sailor. A wave pounded the side of the boat and drenched us, but Jack kept steering, and I woke up.

SEPTEMBER 1

If you are reading this, Anne, and I am now composed of the cells of memory rather than the cells of biology, please let my sons know that in her own peculiar way, their mother fought in the first fusillades of the battle to restore America. Perhaps they should know that I was a woman alone in that fight, if you care to add that. That the forces of war could not allow the struggle for peace because, as my father, Amos, said when I was very little, war is the business of business. So I will offer up what I know in these pages of high-quality French paper, with my Waterman fountain pen recording the facts and my heart stilled to courage.

SEPTEMBER 7

This morning I passed Packer's on my way down to the towpath. As I passed, Kirkland Jennings was standing in front of the entrance, staring out at me, just smoking a cigarette, just staring. Why was he there? I nodded ever so slightly, and he nodded back, just as slightly, and just kept looking.

SEPTEMBER 13

Once, under the purple skies of Mexico, I sat by a campfire and heard Timothy Leary say that emotions are the lowest form of consciousness. Emotions, the driver of our race, the subject behind the subject of every work of literature, every song on the hit parade, the quivering sensations that we honor, suppress, analyze in therapy sessions, divulge in secret tête-à-têtes, and reveal publicly when our children walk onto stages in caps and gowns, the whole fucking morass and motion of emotions, they're all nothing but biochemical secretions meant to serve the body in states of emergency.

An emotional person is a blind, crazed maniac, Tim said, and it has come to pass. I am no longer a dignified daughter of the WASP ascendancy. I am a blind, crazed maniac. I have abandoned the starry realms of psychedelic freedom, and I am back in the rented room of my biochemical secretions. I am an angry woman, taking my place in a long lineage of angry women.

They killed the love of my life and covered up the deed. An accidental document—and was it really an accident?—says they are at it again, another operation to assassinate Fidel Castro. And V has disappeared. Where is V? I want to talk to him one more time, need to talk to him one more time; who else can I talk to safely? I left a message behind my shutter, then another one in the mailbox, but he hasn't answered. It is two weeks now. The biochemicals will no longer allow me to remain silent, will no longer allow me to play the role of Georgetown wife, or Georgetown ex-wife, shoving the next drink down my throat and pretending not to know what my husband is up to. Or ex-husband. I call Cord's office repeatedly, and Darlene hands me over to Cord's assistant, Ray, who sends me back to Darlene. I paint triangles, circles, squares, as the vortex of forces closes in, but my own ex-husband at Central Intelligence will not take my calls.

I walked with Lorraine Cooper along M Street and

said I could not get through to Cord; he would not answer calls, and I was backtracking in my commitment to world peace because I wished nothing more than to strangle him until there was no breath left in his body. Lorraine is a woman, which means that, quietly and calmly, she knows things. With a strange strength in her dark eyes, she said, "Darling, Cord attends the waltz group every Thursday night at the Sulgrave Club near Dupont Circle." Then she smiled.

Cord is now a ballroom dancer as well as an assassination planner.

SEPTEMBER 18

The revelation of the waltz group detonated in me, and I arrived at the Sulgrave Club last night at eight o'clock, unsuitably dressed. I stormed the sumptuous Beaux-Arts mansion near Dupont Circle in the little beige silk dress of my great-grandmother. Unsuccessful once at a White House banquet, it would be a fashion faux pas a second time at the Sulgrave Club, but I hadn't come to dance. And what exactly is the dress code for assassins?

I crossed the lobby, crushing in my hand a slip of paper covered with strange names. I pushed open the doors and burst into the ballroom, plunging into a hot, sweaty wedding cake. White moldings dripped like frosting up and down the cream-colored walls and continued in swirls across the ceiling. Heavy purple drapes shielded the glittering ballroom from sunlight, and a gold chandelier the size of my painting studio hovered below the ceiling. Beneath crystal lights, men in white tie and tails waltzed with women in fairy-tale gowns, all to the music of a sweating Viennese orchestra. And there was Cord among the dancers, heavy and slow of foot, dragging a skinny woman across the floor. Her skeletal face was frozen in the grimace of a smile, the smile that corpses hold out to eternity, and she appeared desperate in her attempt to follow Cord's lead. Cord, certain of a grace and panache that was not there, seemed barely to notice his emaciated partner. He appeared drunk, his cummerbund askew, and I walked up to him and read from the crushed paper in my hand. "Cord, is your friend E. Howard Hunt here?"

He turned to me, shocked.

"Oh, Howard?" I called the name sweetly, gazing around the ballroom. "I know you're covert, so maybe you're here and I don't see you?"

Cord spun around and froze.

"How about William Harvey, Cord? Is your friend William Harvey here? You know, Harvey the assassin? Harvey! I mean William! Are you waltzing around this room somewhere, or are you back in Cuba?"

Cord began quivering, his sense of dignity woefully fragile at the best of times, his toleration for embarrassment nonexistent, while I have never been implanted with the gene for embarrassment. We will all be vacating the stage soon enough. Cord screamed for me to leave, but I was just getting started. I thought of John Coltrane blowing into his saxophone, all that air unrestrained, and I yelled: "Is your friend David Atlee Phillips here, Cord, honey? Mr. David Atlee Phillips, your man in Mexico. Didn't he handle a client of yours, a young man named—what was his name again? Yes: Lee Harvey Oswald! And what about your friend Santo Trafficante! Your *paisan*! Santo, are you hiding out somewhere in this room?"

I didn't care that the gowned and white-tailed of Washington had stopped waltzing and stood staring at me. Or that Marge Babbington, president of the waltz group, was bounding over to throttle me. Her drunk husband had once slavered all over me at a party in Georgetown—he had fat wet lips that were disgusting—so I was not at all impressed with Marge Babbington.

"Mary, you must not be feeling well," she said. "You must leave this place now. We're just a dance group."

"Cord, honey! Is your friend Johnny Rosselli here? Does he like to dance, too, or is it only murder that gets him off? You and Johnny Rosselli and William Harvey, the three of you are all planning outings. I don't mean outings of spies—that's a funny play on words, isn't it?—I mean outings like picnics, right? Hey, wait a minute, let's not forget about David Morales. What's an outing without David Morales? Where are you, David Morales, Bill Harvey's boy? You're a damn good shot, they say!"

Two gorillas in tuxedos tried to rip the arms from my sockets as they dragged me across the floor, leaving Cord standing there, watching me disappear backward from his evening and his life. I continued to shout, 'Is your friend Carlos Marcello here? Your business partner? You know, head of the Mafia in New Orleans? You're both Skull and Bones, right? Of course, his experience of skull and bones is a little more literal than yours, right, Cord? And what about V, Cord, what about V? The young fellow from your office. What did you do to V?"

My last picture of Cord was of a very small man with only one eye and a falling cummerbund, and I wondered how this brilliant young boy I once married could have accumulated so much evil as to be part, when he wasn't waltzing, of a plan to assassinate Fidel Castro.

SEPTEMBER 27

Entropy is the natural bent of the universe. All explodes, all descends to chaos: that's the law of thermodynamics, as explained in an article I read in *Scientific American*. Entropy must be the explanation for the Warren Commission report, a report that would be more accurately entitled "Fictions from an Assassination." It has arrived in bookstores with the smell of fresh paper and ink and the promise that each new book brings, that of a world made more vivid or at least more comprehensible. It is how Jack must have felt when the fresh copy of *Ivanhoe* was brought to his room on his tenth birthday, inscribed to him by his mother and father in the handwriting of a servant. He still keeps that copy of *Ivanhoe* on his shelf in the White House. He showed it to me proudly one night; we kissed tenderly, and I said he was my hero, my Ivanhoe, making an assumption, since I am unfamiliar with the plot.

But the book I hold is no book of heroes. The book I just purchased from the Savile bookstore was not written by heroes. Its purpose is to conceal rather than reveal, printed up in the millions and dispatched to bookstores everywhere. Perhaps only the Bible will exceed it in sales. Yes, the Warren Commission report was released today.

SEPTEMBER 29

The Group is abandoned. I will finish that novel someday. Now I am underlining the Warren report to mad death, dog-earing its pages, scribbling on it, defacing it with questions. With accusations. I write notes in the margins, notes of a madwoman, desperate to return the report back down the vortex from which it arose.

What about the shots from the front? What about the mob and the Cubans and Lucien Sarti and William Harvey and E. Howard Hunt and Carlos Marcello and Jack Ruby and David Ferrie? You don't think I know? Once again I stand against the grain of the universe, confronting the narrative they have constructed to replace truth, to replace the facts as they occurred to a man whom no one will ever know I loved.

Earl Warren lent his name, but Allen Dulles lent his shame. He is behind this. How could this have come to pass, a man who hated Jack, a man whom Jack fired, a man who continued to control the apparatus of secret intelligence, taking control of the history of Jack's death?

It is a fable and a cover-up. I stand against the grain and wonder how many grains they will allow me to stand against before they revoke my license. I will pursue facts, and there are consequences to a fact-based existence. As it further states in *Scientific American*, information is a measure of order in the universe rescued from randomness. I will pursue information.

SEPTEMBER 30

I am an insomniac. I am a citizen of the nation of sleepless, the ones whose minds do not release them even as the moon releases the day. I carry dread to the sheets. One more night when consciousness will not spare me. My brain is a jukebox, and I have no control over the quarters.

And now this report has come to deny me sleep once again, to deny me—how did Edgar Allan Poe put it?—"surcease of sorrow." I read the Warren report all evening, a substitute nightmare, and once again it feels like they are entering my home, once again they are moving things around, but this time through a book.

Last night I dressed and walked the hill down to Clyde's on M Street. It was one thirty in the morning and people were still gathered at the old oak bar, forgotten refugees from some Dante's hell, adjusting their neurochemistry with strong alcohol.

I ordered a bourbon and noticed Lukas Vorst, an attorney for the Justice Department, and moved to the stool beside him, imagining he sleeps no more than I do. "Have you read it?" I asked, with no need to elucidate.

"The Warren Commission report?" he asked. "I mean, the Warren Omission report?"

I nodded. "Yes, one of the great works of fiction this year."

Chazz, the bartender, set down the bourbon and looked at me, it seemed, mournfully. His life was an immersion in smoke and darkness and secrets; the bags under his eyes suddenly seemed like pouches of secrets, the lies of Washington entering the skin below his eyes and dying there. Was he warning me subliminally not to speak? Was I turning permanently paranoid?

"Not really an investigation at all. They knew the outcome they wanted and built a case to support it, ignoring an encyclopedia of evidence that goes contrary to their conclusion. James Jesus Angleton is front and center, of course."

"He always is," I said of my sons' godfather. "He wasn't even an official member of the commission."

Lukas downed his drink. It seemed to explode momentarily in his throat and GI tract, but he recovered quickly and held his glass up for Chazz to refill.

"The CIA erased all links to the assassination," he said. "Angleton called Bill Sullivan of the FBI and rehearsed the questions and answers he'd give to the Warren Commission. Who else but the head of counterintelligence could ensure a national security cover-up of a counterintelligence nightmare?"

I didn't bother to ask him how he knew. There's a time to ask questions and a time not to ask questions, and the time not to ask is far more important than the time to ask.

"Oswald had handlers, Mary. He was overseen when he defected to Russia, he was overseen when he came back to New Orleans, and when he moved on to Dallas, they got him a job at the Texas Book Depository. Listen to this. The book depository was owned by an oil millionaire named D. H. Byrd. Who was Byrd? He was the founder of the Civil Air Patrol. Lee Harvey Oswald joined the Civil Air Patrol when he was a teenager."

"Oh, what a tangled web," I said.

"In the Civil Air Patrol, Oswald met a pilot named David Ferrie, a semi-deranged right-wing fanatic. They grew close, and then less close, because Ferrie was also queer and couldn't always separate business from pleasure in the matter of young men. But Ferrie was the personal pilot of Carlos Marcello and the New Orleans mob. More important, he was a central figure in the Bay of Pigs invasion force, and was immersed in the anti-Castro Cuban underground in Miami."

"Oh, what a tangled web," I repeated, and lit a cigarette.

Lukas was now in overdrive. Chazz stood listening intently. "More than once, Ferrie was heard to proclaim that JFK was a dead man, but he was simply echoing a universal feeling down there since the betrayal at the Bay of Pigs. So . . . Lee Harvey Oswald pretended to be part of a bogus chapter of the Fair Play for Cuba Committee, a stunt meant to create a false impression of him as a

Marxist. What was the address of his chapter of Fair Play for Cuba? The same address as David Ferrie's office, on Camp Street in New Orleans."

"They won't get away with it," I said.

"You notice no one asks why Oswald was in Dallas. Or how he got the job. Or how he was able to defect to Russia. Or how he was able to come back at the height of the Cold War and receive financial support rather than punishment. No one asks. But who ran the fake defectors program, and who served as general manager for all of Oswald's various handlers? Yes, James Jesus Angleton."

I used to read from Aldous Huxley to Jack, back when there seemed a world we could change, but I never read him the line I now quoted from memory.

"Maybe this world is another planet's hell."

OCTOBER 5

I'm nobody! Who are you? So said Emily Dickinson. She wrote it in a poem I read at Vassar, and I understand her perfectly, sweet Emily who never went out and lived in her thoughts. Last night I lay with my fat tabby Evangeline, free of the burden of having to be someone. The social mirage of this town eventually feels like hard work, the nightly constructing of yourself into a someone in order to meet all the other someones.

Evangeline and I luxuriated in being no one in particular; we were free, except she was free to doze, to be no more than a blob of fur with eyes, while I was compelled to pick up my mangled, dog-eared copy of the

Warren Commission report. Eventually I will put this book down and confront Cord and James. Eventually I will not let them get away with it. In the meantime, I assemble data. I scour facts, building a case no one wants built. Which is why I finally got up, the confusion growing in Evangeline's little marble eyes, and headed down the hill again to Clyde's.

When the sounds of the closing door echoed and then died on a deserted M Street, I saw Lukas waiting, as if he had no one else to talk to either. I nodded to this big burly man whose glasses slip down his nose from perspiration, and he came to the stool beside me.

Chazz was wiping up the bar next to us, and I nodded to him.

"Who the fuck was Jack Ruby?" I asked. Information is a measure of order in the universe rescued from randomness.

Lukas pushed his glasses up his nose, pausing for about a thousandth of a second to assemble his thoughts, and then spoke. "A mobster. A Mafia operative. Clearly doing the bidding of Carlos Marcello in New Orleans. Dallas falls under Marcello's jurisdiction, don't forget."

"Why did he kill Oswald?"

"Why indeed? Something must have gotten fucked up."

"Fucked up."

"Yes, Oswald was apparently meant to be eliminated immediately, but something got fucked up."

"And how was Ruby allowed so easily into the police station?"

"How indeed?"

"And here's something I've wondered. Have you seen the photographs? They were moving Oswald through the tumult and crowd in the police station right before Ruby ran up to shoot him. All the officials in the police station were wearing black suits and black cowboy hats. All except one. The single officer walking right beside Oswald in the chaos of the police station, the one escorting him to the area where Jack Ruby waited, was wearing a white suit and white cowboy hat. Am I the only one who noticed that?"

"You're very observant."

"I'm a visual person."

OCTOBER 9

Sometimes being alone hits you, as if absence itself is the presence of something malevolent. I walked down Warren Commission Hill again toward Clyde's. This is my absurd new name for Thirty-Fourth Street. It was late, late in the Georgetown evening, and I was aware that in Washington, a putrid saloon in the deathly hours of the morning may be one of the few places truth could live.

Lukas was at the bar, lost in desperate chatter around some young blonde. Her drifting attention veered between boredom and bemusement, a woman's unconcern with a man's rat-tat-tat.

When will men learn that need is toxic? Fumbling pursuit preceded by no sign of interest tells a woman

you are after her, and if you are after her, she knows
you perceive her as having high value, and if her
value is high, your value will be low, and you have
just telegraphed yourself as unworthy of consideration.
I decided to save Lukas from further failure in the
evolutionary game and beckoned him to the other side of
the bar.

"I heard a story from a reporter in Texas," he said.
"There's this man named Virgil Pennebaker, and he
happens to be on the overpass as the motorcade arrives,
a few hundred feet away from the grassy knoll. He sees
two men in the railroad yard behind the wooden fence
at the top of the knoll, and something strikes him as
odd. They are in a heated discussion and dressed rather
strangely: one wears a dark business suit with white shirt,
tie, and fedora, the other the striped overalls and cap
of a railroad worker. Virgil turns toward the motorcade
just as Kennedy's limousine turns onto Elm Street, and
when he looks back to the knoll, Suit Man is holding up
a rifle perched on the pickets of the wooden fence. Boom.
A spark of light erupts, a puff of white smoke, as if a
cigarette were being lit, but Virgil knows it's the rifle
firing. He watches as Suit Man throws the rifle to Train
Man, who starts running north into the railroad yards.
Virgil looks down and sees Kennedy's car roaring beneath
the overpass, heading for the entrance to the freeway. He
can clearly see the president and Jackie slumped down,
he sees blood everywhere, he can even see what's left of
the head . . ."

I told Lukas it was enough. I was nauseated and teary-eyed. I heard Jack mumbling "Mary, Mary, quite contrary" in the low voice people use when they speak to you in dreams, and it was time to leave. But Lukas put his hands up to restrain me, and for a nanosecond I thought I was the young blonde from the other side of the bar and Lukas was escalating his pickup maneuver to include physical restraint. Then I saw he was just sweaty and pathetic, another man turned buffoon around women, begging me to stay and hear the end of the story. He signaled Chazz to pour me another bourbon, and I exhaled deeply.

"Virgil looks back to the grassy knoll when the limousine passes underneath him, and there's Train Man, disassembling the rifle, putting it into a suitcase, then running north and disappearing into the railroad yards. It sounds like a tall tale, but the journalist who related the story knows that Virgil's vision is extremely sharp. Virgil Pennebaker is a deaf-mute. He sees what others don't see—he just can't communicate it. And every attempt to inform the authorities becomes one more nightmare. He is dismissed, ignored, ridiculed by police and FBI. And when the truth-seekers of the Warren Commission come to town searching for witnesses at Dealey Plaza, Virgil Pennebaker's testimony proves of no interest to them."

"The words of a deaf man falling on deaf ears," I said.

My drink was finished, the blonde was gone. I felt that loneliness would be preferable to the pain of more

information, and I kissed Lukas lightly on the cheek—
the closest he would get that night to the sweetness of a
female body.

OCTOBER 7

How many definitions could we have redefined ourselves
into? How many shapes could we have twisted ourselves
into to obey the geometries of love? Cicely Angleton and I
once heard a poet read at the Jefferson Place gallery, and
I still remember a line: "The full recognition of the other
in their otherness." Maybe that's as close to love as you
can come. Jack and I came close.

OCTOBER 9

When Jack said he had to go to Dallas, against reason
and argument, I think he felt free somehow. I think he
knew.

They had already rehearsed it. They had already tried
out two assassinations on him. He told me about it, he
knew about it. One in Chicago and one in Tampa. Each
operation called for multiple shots from a high-powered
rifle, and a patsy who would be framed to take the blame,
someone to be set up as a lone nut, some disenchanted
soldier with a strange background. Each operation was
exposed before it could come to fruition. Which led to
Dallas. Dallas was where it would all come together, deep
in the phantasmagoria of Texas.

Dallas. Where John Birchers called desegregation
an attempt to transform the South into a black Soviet

Republic in order to mongrelize the white race. Where
the Reverend Billy James Hargis launched his Christian
Crusade to expose Satan at the heart of the United
Nations, world Communism, and President Kennedy.
Where H. L. Hunt, the richest man on earth, proclaimed
through his radio station that Medicare would make
President Kennedy a medical czar with potential life-
and-death power over every man, woman, and child
in the country. Where a man named Jimmy Robinson
received a ten-dollar fine for burning a cross on the lawn
of Jack Oran, a survivor of Auschwitz who had undergone
castration at the hands of Dr. Joseph Mengele. Where
Major General Edwin Walker flooded the city with
Wanted posters that bore a photograph of Jack Kennedy
and the ominous headline: WANTED FOR TREASON.

All this, Arthur Schlesinger had told me, and I passed
it on to Jack. I told him what everyone told him, that if
he went to Dallas, they couldn't guarantee they'd bring
him back alive. Bobby told Jack not to go at Bobby's
birthday party, just two days before the trip, and I heard
Jack's answer to his brother. He was so serene. He quoted
Winston Churchill's description of the heroic soldier
Raymond Asquith: "When the Grenadiers strode into the
crash and thunder of the Somme, he went to his fate cool,
poised, resolute, matter-of-fact, debonair."

It happens like that sometimes; the cloud that
condenses from the particles of ourselves lifts, and
underneath is freedom. Timothy Leary said we are
composed of trillions of cells, and in each of those cells

are trillions of something smaller, atoms, and in each
of those atoms, somehow, if you dig far enough, you
will find an empty space. We are empty space, me
and my short blond hair and my big mouth, and Cord,
humiliated on that dance floor, and that diagram of the
next assassination, and Jack smiling in the White House
the way he smiled at me at the Winter Festivity Dance at
Choate, and my ghost sister Rosamond on her quicksilver
stallion, we are, in the end, all empty space. Still, we
are charged to carry on. A billion-year sentence. Except.
Except. Except.

OCTOBER 11

I dreamed of Rosamond last night, ghost sister on her
moonlit horse, back at Grey Towers in the season of
jabbering crickets. She returns to me these days, growing
vaster in my thoughts as the vista of my life grows
smaller. Daddy Amos was on the piazza in this dream,
writing another of his diatribes against war, or perhaps
some manifesto about higher wages for miners—it all
occurred in the space of a milky blur. But hoofbeats
pounded Daddy's gravel paths and woke me up, and she
called to me as she passed. I didn't hear her, but I knew
she was saying my name: Mary, such a plain and obvious
name it seemed to me. The churning woke me up, and I
knew Rosamond was on her moonlit horse. Excalibur was
his name. It was midnight in my dream, the hour she
used to ride, and now she rode in the neurons of my brain
as I slept, her hair flying back like crystallized wind. I

watched from the casement of a bedroom full of rabbits, and thought: my sister is mercury, and I am lead. I will never fly like her. Then I woke up sweating—Rosamond, never to return, my older sister who took her own life—and I cried in my pillow. It is midnight. I am on the horse now. Will I be a ghost soon? Is she calling to me from where she sleeps?

———

That was where the diary ended. James Jesus Angleton closed the pages. His bone-thin fingers brushed a leather cover daubed with cloudbursts of paint. He lowered the book onto the coffee table in his den. It had been a slow read, the writing a slow-going left-leaning feminine hand. It appeared to have been written in bursts, some of the text seemingly plucked from memory against the ravages of human forgetfulness, some more reflective, as if intended for an audience it would never reach.

In a decade of counterintelligence and the voluminous scrutiny of documents, he had rarely lavished such fevered intensity on a piece of writing. It was a murder mystery tuned to the highest pitch, in which he himself was a main character.

He looked up. The fire still burned in the stone fireplace, and a phantom of fireglow danced in his black-framed glasses. The flames now rhymed with thoughts engulfing the mind behind the lenses, and he lit up a Virginia Slim.

Mary had told Anne Truitt of the diary, letting her know it was hidden in a mahogany box on a shelf in her studio. Should anything befall Mary, she should retrieve it at all costs. Mary had forebodings. She told Anne of her sense that forces were closing in. She would arrive home and find things moved. There were beeps on her phone, some mysterious electrical current intruding on her conversations. There was growing criticism from Agency wives, warning her to be cautious.

Angleton would never have known about the diary had he not been tapping Mary's phone. And he would never have retrieved it had he not picked the lock of Mary's studio just minutes ahead of her sister, Tony Bradlee, and her husband, Ben. This rapid descent on a diary in a painting studio had been ignited by the event now detailed on the front page of the *Washington Post* and spread before him on the coffee table:

WOMAN ARTIST SHOT AND KILLED ON
CANAL TOWPATH; MRS. MARY PINCHOT MEYER
WAS A FRIEND OF MRS. KENNEDY.

The story spoke of a forty-three-year-old blond socialite from Georgetown and her mysterious death on the Chesapeake and Ohio towpath by the Potomac, two bullets fired at close range, one in the heart and one in the head.

Angleton imagined the body lying there, inert. A churning arose from someplace invisible and invaded

his chest, something that felt much like longing. It was
so long since he had felt something. He still could not
fathom where life goes when it leaves the flesh, a mystery
that endured though he had earned his salary on death,
though he had witnessed and supervised and sighed
and turned his back on so many instances of life being
taken from so many bodies.

But she was different. She was Mary. He had kept a
memory locked inside him, and the memory had never
left through all the years and all the lies and all the
brutality confronted on a daily basis. It had survived all
the hard liquor and cigarettes he pounded into his body
to keep from feeling. It was a flash of flesh. A summer
morning in Pennsylvania when Cicely was still in
Vassar and had taken him to meet her roommate. They
had parked on the curving driveway of the estate and
walked around to the back. And there she was, on the
grass, on a blanket, on her stomach, nude, her buttocks
quietly offered to the sun and to any witness happening
by. The buttocks were neither too big and too fleshy
nor too flat and bony, but, for the glands and hormones
of the college-age James Angleton, a kind of perfection
of proportion. It was a transgression to see them, as he
stood holding Cicely's hand, staring at two white cheeks
and imagining the darkness that lay between them. And
then, when Cicely called out to her friend, the blonde
had simply looked up and smiled, smiled radiantly, he
had to admit, unembarrassed and oblivious to her state.
She sat up, exposing delicate small breasts with rather

large nipples, the transgression continuing to the front, and, reaching for a robe, exposing a small glimpse of moss between her legs. She kept smiling, unconcerned, and James Angleton never forgot the sight. He went on to marry Cicely, went on to become godfather to Mary's sons, went on to partner with Mary's ex-husband in the cesspool of counterintelligence, went on to feel continual jolts of pain as her assignations with the degenerate young president John Fitzgerald Kennedy were reported to him on a weekly basis. And now she was gone, and he held her diary, the final transgression: the white flesh of her buttocks, the triangle of hair between her legs, and now her diary.

He had tried to warn her. He had tried to stop her learning the secrets of her lover's death, what the mélange of anti-Castro Cubans, CIA operatives, foreign-born shooters, and mobsters all referred to in code as the Big Event. He had tried, in short, to save her life. But as powerful and adept as he was in controlling counterintelligence in the CIA, he was helpless to stop the forces from silencing a woman. Just as he had been helpless to stop them silencing a president a year earlier. It is a strange brand of tragedy to be aware of crimes of immense proportion but crimes you cannot stop because you care first for the survival of the Company, and second for the survival of the nation. He had done his best to riddle her with fear, to make her cease asking, to make her stop talking, to tame her, but as he knew from the day of the buttocks on that spring day in 1940, she lacked the gene of fear. She was a woman unsprung, and maybe someday all women would be like her, fearless against a world that for millennia had blocked them from the levers of power. He wondered what such a world would bring.

That she was one of a kind, he had no doubt. And working side by side with Cord Meyer, the man who had lost her, he knew the depths of the loss this man carried with him. Maybe that is why another man had risked his own presidency to be with her.

Angleton inhaled some cigarette smoke and glanced again at the newspaper headline. Then he picked up the leather-bound diary and the loose page that had fallen from it, a diagram of the operation to assassinate President John F. Kennedy entitled JM/RESET. He carried them to the fireplace and tossed them into the flames. The book of Mary seemed to turn liquid in the blaze, a story of a woman who no longer was, curling first into flame and then ash in the orange glow.

Author's Note

This is a work of fiction inspired by fact. With the exception of family members and public figures, all characters in this "diary" are fictional, and virtually all events, dialogue, conversation, and personal musings imaginary.

Mary Pinchot Meyer was a real woman who remains a cipher. Two books and numerous articles have scoured the mysteries of this private person who spent her life surrounded by famous ones. Each ran headlong into the veil of silence that went up among friends and family and colleagues following her unsolved murder. The most commonly recurring line in each book is: "Refused to be interviewed." And each devotes considerable time to the events after her death, such as the trial of a man charged with and then acquitted of her murder.

So Mary Pinchot Meyer remains a cipher. This is so

even visually. Less than a handful of crude snapshots exist of her as an adult, none looking at the camera, none posed, none offering a clear sense of what she actually looked like.

That she had an intimate relationship with John F. Kennedy is fairly well established, but no tapes or transcripts of their affair exist, and not a single word or interaction is recorded for history.

That she was a member of the Georgetown set in the early 1960s and attended parties, dinners, and cultural events with the likes of the Grahams, the Alsops, the Coopers, the Bruces, the Angletons, and her sister Tony and brother-in-law Ben Bradlee is also well established. But again, no tapes, no transcripts, not a single conversation, incident, or martini is recorded for posterity.

That she had a relationship with Timothy Leary seems probable but not confirmed, and certainly no conversation, let alone drug experience, is recorded for history.

That she was a painter in the Washington Color School is proven by paintings that exist in private collections and museums, thoroughly inaccessible to the public.

What we are left with is a cipher, but a fascinating cipher. So I took the liberty of reimagining her. Or perhaps just imagining her. I found an extraordinary woman who seemed to embody and anticipate every current of female liberation, political activism, and psychedelic exploration that would explode on the world just hours after her death in 1964.

This is a work of fiction, so even the "real people" in this novel speak and act in totally imaginary situations. But following her death, here is what really happened to them.

Antoinette "Tony" Pinchot Bradlee outlived her sister by nearly half a century. She and Ben Bradlee divorced in the 1970s, and Tony spent her final years quietly devoted to sculpture, ceramics, and the esoteric teachings of Russian-Armenian mystic George Gurdjieff.

Ben Bradlee went on to international fame as the *Washington Post* editor presiding over the Watergate scandal and the demise of Richard Nixon. He married society journalist Sally Quinn following his divorce from Mary's sister, and lived a life of ever-increasing awards and veneration. He died in 2014 at the age of ninety-three, denying his CIA affiliations to the end. All accounts of his ex-sister-in-law, Mary Pinchot Meyer—from the time and manner of his discovery of her death, to his withholding of facts at the trial of the acquitted murder suspect, to his memoir tale of collusion with James Jesus Angleton to destroy her diary—form a tortuous half-century of conflicting and contradictory narratives.

James Jesus Angleton continued as the head of counter-intelligence in the CIA until he was terminated in disgrace in 1975, following revelations of massive illegal surveillance and mail tampering of American citizens. He died of lung cancer in 1987, withered by decades of chain smoking, alcoholism, and secrets. His eccentricity and towering presence in the CIA, coupled with virtual invisibility, created a mystique that continues to inspire books and films to this day. Said one historian: "One could ask a hundred people about James Jesus Angleton and receive a hundred different replies, ranging from utter denunciation to unadulterated hero worship."

Timothy Leary carried on indefatigable, evolving from LSD guru to one-man cultural phantasmagoria: clown, seer, scientist, shaman, author, actor, international outlaw, then prophet and pioneer of the digital age. He died in Beverly Hills at the age of seventy-five, surrounded as always by friends, freaks, and followers mindful of his final pronouncement: "I'm going to give death a better name or die trying."

Joe Alsop continued writing his syndicated column until 1974 and remained a consummate connoisseur until the end. His private collection grew to include family portraits of illustrious ancestors, Japanese lacquer, Chinese porcelain, and ancient bronzes from Persia. His homosexuality pervaded gossip in Washington and files within the CIA and FBI, but he never publicly disclosed it. He died in Georgetown in 1989.

Frank Wisner continued a long slide into depression and mania and committed suicide in 1965.

Kenneth Noland painted on, a minimalist in terms of art but apparently a maximalist in terms of women. Mary Pinchot Meyer was but one of a long series of both married and unmarried liaisons. He died in 2010, his color field paintings celebrated in numerous exhibitions and museum collections.

Anne Truitt became an internationally renowned artist.

Her painted sculptures grace the collections of the National Gallery in Washington, the Metropolitan Museum of Art, the Museum of Modern Art, and the Whitney. She was awarded a Guggenheim fellowship and five honorary doctorates before her death in Washington, DC, in 2004.

Katharine Graham endured abuse, humiliation, and threats to the control of her family's *Washington Post* from a continuously unbalanced Phil Graham, which all ended with his suicide in 1963. She went on to legendary fame and veneration as the storied publisher of the *Post*, pioneering woman executive, and Pulitzer Prize–winning memoirist.

Cord Meyer moved into Mary's town house in Georgetown following her death. He continued overseeing the CIA infiltration of student and cultural institutions and the intimidation of media outlets into promoting the CIA line until his retirement in 1977. He died in 2001.

Mary's sons, Quentin and Mark, carried the burden of their mother's inexplicable murder into the tumult of the 1960s. They attended Yale and were "parented" by both their father, Cord Meyer, and their godfather, James Jesus Angleton. Quentin reportedly telephoned Timothy Leary impulsively and vainly at one point, demanding to know: "What happened to my mother?" Mark became a missionary. Neither ever agreed to speak to writers or journalists. Neither ever married.

Acknowledgments

My deepest gratitude to Sara Nelson, visionary editor who championed this work with a tenacity Mary would be proud of. Eternal thanks to my agent, Gail Hochmann, whose wisdom is matched only by her patience. And to the Mary in my own life who, since she's Cuban, is named Maria . . . grateful for Maria Rita Caso's unending friendship, coaching, and persistence.

My gratitude to Nina Burleigh and Peter Janney, who opened the door with their books *A Very Private Woman* and *Mary's Mosaic*.

For all those who supported and encouraged along the way, I have not forgotten: Jamie Ambler, Angela Ambrosia, Leanne Averbach, Suze Barst, Edith Dube, Michael Greifinger, Marcus Kemp, Moses Kravitz, Nicole Kubin, Ray Lawrence, Mitch Mondello, Niland Mortimer, Wendy Oxenhorn, Karin Parn, Darci Picoult, Lisa Ritter-Kahn, Scott Williams, Linda Yellin.

About the Author

PAUL WOLFE has been an architect, a songwriter, and a multiple-award-winning writer in advertising. He lives in New York City.